LAST CHANCE

LIBBY KIRSCH

Sunnyside Press

Sunnyside Press
PO Box 2476
Ann Arbor, MI. 48106
www.LibbyKirschBooks.com

Publisher's Note: This is a work of fiction. Names, characters, places, and incidents are a product of the author's imagination. Locales and public names are sometimes used for atmospheric purposes. Any resemblance to actual people, living or dead, or to businesses, companies, events, institutions, or locales is completely coincidental.

Cover art by DesignForWriters.com

Last Chance/ Libby Kirsch -- 1st ed.

ISBN 978-1-7337003-0-6

❀ Created with Vellum

PROLOGUE

His hands trembled and the first match dropped to the ground, unlit. Swearing, he plucked another stick from the orderly row and swiped it roughly across the strike plate once, twice, three times. Nothing. *Stupid cheap party favor.* He frowned and dropped the useless match to the ground.

The sharp smell of gasoline burned his nose and his head was growing fuzzy from the fumes. He tore another match from the book and pressed his finger near the head as he pulled it across the narrow friction strip.

An initial spark of heat forced his finger back as the fire caught the head of the match. He held it up at eye level and watched the pulsing, blazing flame dance in front of his eyes. Then he assessed the chaos around him in the dark room—the blood, the blond hair, the mess—and a smile spread across his face.

They'd see. They'd understand soon.

He dropped the match and the sudden force of heat pushed him out of the room. Swiping the red bandana off the floor as he stumbled across the tile to the door, he ignored the banging from the walk-in cooler and tripped out of the building into the dark alleyway.

The parking lot lamps next door spilled light across his path, and he crouched in the shadow of the dumpster. He wouldn't stay here long, but he had time to wait. All he had was time.

The quiet night was broken as the roaring fire built higher and hotter, right in front of his eyes. When the building burned orange at the edges, when the heat was intense enough to make his eyes water, only then did he pick up his cell phone.

"911, what is your emergency?"

"Fire at the abandoned restaurant down on Retreat Road," he croaked out, both trying to mask his voice and because the smoke had gotten deeper into his lungs than he'd anticipated.

"What is the address of the fire, sir?" The dispatcher's dispassionate voice was the opposite of his own mounting emotions.

"I don't know the address. It's in the building next to the Spot. I think there's a woman inside."

"Why do you think that?"

He didn't answer. Just launched the piece of plastic and glass, metal and microchips into the flames.

Before the phone completed its arc to destruction *he* came. Running, yelling, looking like the hero he longed to be, he came.

"Oh no—what—how did this—" Jason's eyes were glued to the red glow coming from inside. He skirted the sides of the building, disappearing for a minute on the far side, before he came back into view. He found a hose, and cranked the spigot around, only to yell in frustration when he realized the hose wasn't connected, and the water shot uselessly to the ground before turning to steam.

As if a garden hose could stop his handiwork.

As Jason's hands flew up to his head, clutching his hair in horror, he slowly walked around the perimeter, as if in shock.

That's when the man watching made his way back into the burning building, taking care to lock the door behind him. There'd be no room for heroes today.

He caught sight of Jason's face through the flames as the door closed. The last thing he saw was the red and white flashing lights of the fire trucks arriving.

It was too late, of course. Jason didn't know yet, but he would. It was only a matter of time.

He drummed his fingers against each other, still watching, always watching, from the relative safety of the kitchen; scanning the perimeter, watching the chaos that he'd unleashed.

Had he made any mistakes? He sighed. Yes, there were definite loose ends, but he had to hope things went according to plan. Would anyone notice the final piece of the plan as it came together? Surely not. Not with flames growling twenty feet into the air. Not with four fire trucks' lights flashing and spinning. Not with hoses connected and crowds gathering.

He waited until he was sure they knew. Until he could see the pain etched across Jason's face. Until he could see the terror in his trembling hands.

A team of firefighters gathered at the edge of the parking lot, coming up with their own plan. It was futile. You couldn't win against the initial surge of flames, the heavy, choking smoke. How long would it take to find them? Minutes? Hours?

He looked back at her limp, lifeless body. Her blond hair glowing red against the flames marching steadily toward her.

A blast shook the building, and the windows in the main dining room shattered.

"No, n-no. No!" Jason's cry echoed across the parking lot, sound trembling until it was sucked into the burned-out building along with Jason's hopes and dreams.

He shuddered against the heat, but felt a smile stretch across his face.

Jason deserved this.

Even Jason knew it.

CHAPTER ONE

One Month Earlier

The office was, predictably, a mess. The manila file folders stacked halfway up the wall listed precariously off center, and Janet Black carelessly rifled through one stack after another until she found what she was looking for and groaned.

"Really? Another identity theft case?"

Quizz Bexley adjusted her ball cap and grinned, her hair puffing out from the sides of her hat like purple wings. "Don't knock it. Those cases are our bread and butter." She adjusted the purple frames of her glasses. When Janet looked at her watch, Quizz said, "Oh no you don't. You owe me another hour today. Thirty minutes, at least!" she added hastily when Janet groaned again.

Janet threw herself down onto the couch and winced. The cushions might as well have been made of concrete for how much they gave when her body hit. She bounced more than sunk. She should be at her bar, the Spot, getting ready for a busy night. She *should* be preparing for her boyfriend's mother to arrive in Knoxville from Memphis for what was sure to be an exhaustingly revealing visit, crowding into the home they also shared with Jason's father—who they couldn't seem to shake after his parents had divorced and he'd moved in with them months ago for what was supposed to have been a week—maybe two—max.

Instead, she tucked her brown hair behind her ears and crossed one leg over the other, then flipped the file open across her lap and leaned back to scan the forms inside.

"Who investigates ID theft anyway? I mean, you just get your money back from the bank, close that credit card and move on with your life, right?"

"Sometimes. But what happens when the thief continues to use your social security number to get new credit cards?" Quizz asked.

"Jerks."

"Exactly. Jerks that we investigate and turn over to police."

"If we can stay awake long enough." Janet rubbed her neck and then grabbed a highlighter from the table and passed the bright yellow ink over the most salient information on the papers in front of her. When she'd gleaned all she could from the credit form, she headed to her own computer to type up some notes on the case.

Soon the only sounds inside the small, cramped office were keys tapping and Janet's stomach grumbling.

She jumped when the shrill ringing of the phone cut through the air. Quizz swiveled away from her extension, her laptop balancing on her knees, so Janet reached across the small space to pick up the receiver.

"Hello, Bexley and Associates."

Quizz snorted. The company name was actually Bexley Investigations, but Janet was in the early stages of her apprenticeship to become a PI, and the approval of her permanent license hung on her finishing the required hours with a qualified pro. If she was going to be here, working for free, she hated to feel like a secretary answering the phone, so she embellished the name when she answered.

She grinned at Quizz while the person on the other end of the line stumbled through their own greeting.

"Yes, hi. Uh—umm, hi. I'm looking for Janet?"

"This is Janet with Bexley and Associates. How can I help you?"

Quizz smirked and got up, then motioned to the door, and likely the bathroom at the end of the hall.

Janet settled into her uncomfortable seat. Whatever was waiting on the other end of the line had to be more compelling than a two-week-old identity theft case. After all, some of the most interesting things in life were difficult to explain succinctly. This could be good.

Quizz walked back into the office twenty minutes later to find the phone still pressed firmly to Janet's ear. She had three pages of notes scrawled on a yellow steno pad on the desk.

"Yes ma'am. I think we can really hit the ground running on this one and make a difference for you."

Quizz's brow furrowed and her eyes narrowed. Her nose wrinkled; in fact, her whole face shrunk by two inches in circumference as Janet watched, bemused.

"How many missing persons cases have we solved?" Janet repeated the client's question and looked at Quizz, her eyebrows raised.

Her mentor's eyes widened comically and she groaned. "None. We don't take missing persons cases."

Janet turned away. "Not many, ma'am, but we're a small firm and devoted to helping in cases like yours."

"Cases like whose?"

Janet peeked over her shoulder and saw Quizz advancing on her.

"We don't do missing persons cases. Period. We don't have the manpower."

Janet covered the mouthpiece, but it was too late. The woman on the other end of the line sniffled and said, "Who is that? Is that true? No—n-n-no missing persons cases?"

"It *was* true," Janet said. "But our firm recently doubled in size, and we're now more than happy to take on this kind of case."

"Oh, thank you." The woman blew her nose, and when she came back on the line her voice was steadier. "And you'd like which documents again?"

"We'll need anything you think might be relevant. Medical records, police reports, just bring copies of it all to me by close of business today, okay?" Janet glared back at Quizz when her boss popped a hand on her hip. She kept her voice soft, though, when she addressed the grieving mother. "I look forward to meeting you in person. Hopefully we can bring Lola back home."

"Lola?" Quizz said when Janet had hung up. "We don't do missing persons cases, especially not for girls named *Lola*." She shuddered visibly and dropped into her seat with a *thunk*. "You may be slowly taking over, but I do still get a say in some things."

"This case is special."

"Why? Because the mother sounds sad?" Quizz shook her head. "Well, I hate to burst your bubble, but they're all sad. The mothers, the fathers, the brothers. Even the dogs—you've never seen a sadder set of relatives than those of a missing girl."

"Yeah, but this is completely out of character for her! She's a star student, not some girl who'd up and take off with a boyfriend! I think she's in trouble."

Quizz's brow wrinkled again. "No one can sell a case like a mother, Janet. You don't know what's true yet and what the mother only *hopes* is true. So, I'm sorry, no dice. We're not taking the case."

Janet packed up her bag silently but turned back to Quizz before leaving the office. "I want to help."

"Missing persons cases are lose-lose," Quizz groaned. "Always have been. Most missing people don't want to be found. Also, there's no money in it! ID thefts—they pay the bills."

"But a solved missing persons case could put us on the map."

"But only if we find her!"

"And we will!

Quizz blew out a sigh as Janet twisted the knob and walked through the door. "I know you're not used to it, but I am the boss in this office. My word is the word. I know *that*, at least, is something you understand. And I'll tell the mother that myself when she comes in later today."

"No you won't!" Janet grinned. "I'm having her meet me at the bar. That's my domain."

The last sound Janet heard before the door slammed shut was Quizz laughing incredulously, and Janet thought, admiringly. Maybe.

CHAPTER TWO

Janet pulled up to the Spot and parked at the back of the smaller side lot. Walking over a grassy embankment, then across another parking lot, she gave the abandoned restaurant next door a dirty look. The buildings were 200 feet apart—and sometimes that felt like a long way; other times it felt stiflingly close. She turned her back on the eyesore, then made her way leisurely into the bar. They'd opened an hour ago, and sure enough, a few regulars were already parked inside.

Her eyes lingered on the frozen margarita machine whirling away on the main countertop in the middle of the room and she frowned. Jason's mother had bought the monstrosity when Janet had been home recovering from an injury, and though it was growing on her—helped in large part by the fact that margaritas had become one of their most lucrative drinks on the menu—she still didn't like how much space the machine took up.

"Hey, boss, how's it goin'?" Cindy Lou sipped sweet tea from a long straw. Her bleached hair was pulled half back that day, and long false eyelashes batted every time the assistant manager of the bar blinked. She wore short shorts and an ultra-tight V-neck T-shirt. The entire outfit left very little to the imagination, but Janet assumed it sparked plenty of dreams for Cindy Lou's target audience.

Past Cindy Lou, Mel came out of the bathroom, still rubbing her hands on a paper towel. She tossed the wadded-up paper into the air, banked it off the side of the Beerador—a seven-foot tall bottle-shaped refrigerator that sat behind the bar—and the towel landed in a trash can.

"Two points." Mel nodded and reached into one of the many pockets in her cargo shorts. She typed something into her phone and dropped it back into the pocket.

If Cindy Lou was dressed to impress, Mel was dressed to get stuff done. The bouncer's Doc Martens and shorts were work-horse pieces, and her loose, boxy T-shirt gave her plenty of room to move around without feeling restricted. She wore a ball cap on her head with the garishly bright University of Tennessee colors and logo.

"Just got off the phone with Nell," Cindy Lou said, propping her hip against the countertop. "She was sorry to miss you but wanted me to tell you two things. One, no one better be sitting in her seat."

All three looked over to Nell's regular barstool and Janet grinned to see it was empty. No surprise at that hour, but she loved that her most loyal customer considered it *her* chair.

"And, two, she's having a great time on the cruise with her grandkids and son-in-law."

Nell had gone through a difficult period last month, and she needed some time away to bond with her family. Janet's heart felt happy at the news, but she was distracted by the customer sitting near Nell's seat.

"Booker, what are you doing here?" The traffic cop perched on a seat just two away from Nell's regular spot. He was a regular but wasn't usually in so early.

He grinned and spread his arms wide. "I'm the official scout for the FOP dart tournament."

"Oh, yeah? And is the Fraternal Order of Police interested in having it here?"

He nodded and Cindy Lou squealed.

"I knew adding those dartboards was a good idea. Didn't I say that, Janet?"

"Well, hold up." Booker scratched his head. "We usually serve a buffet of sorts at the tournament. Bosses don't like when all we offer is alcohol, you know?"

"Oh." Cindy Lou's shoulders drooped, but only for a moment. "We'll order pizza. And wings! It'll be great!"

"Can you quote me a price, Janet? Looks like around twenty in the tournament and their dates." Booker drained his beer and tapped the bar with his palm. "By the end of the week would be great."

As he left, he held the door open for another customer. The woman who walked in was a stranger; her short, wiry yellow hair was frizzy at the ends and stuck out in every direction. A shawl draped over her bony shoulders, and even as she stepped inside the bar, she pulled the garment tighter around her thin frame as her eyes squinted to adjust to the low lighting inside.

"Pick any table." Mel walked forward with the laminated drink menu and a smile.

But the woman didn't move; instead her brow furrowed and she planted herself more firmly in her spot.

"I—I'm looking for Janet Black?"

"Well, you found her." Janet walked out from behind the bar. "What can I do for you?"

"I'm Misty Bridges. We—we spoke on the phone earlier today?"

"The missing girl's mother?" Misty nodded and Janet steered

her to the corner booth. Once they were seated Janet said, "I wasn't expecting to see you so soon."

"I thought, well, I had your attention...You know they say strike when the iron is hot and all that." The woman fidgeted with the end of her sleeve, and Janet noted that the yarn there had started to fray.

"You don't know what it's been like, these last few days. Police say she ran away, but I know that's not true. That's not my Lola, at least not—" She bit her lip as if she'd said too much and fell quiet.

"I was surprised I hadn't seen anything on the news about it. Or social media. These days someone's dog goes missing and the community finds it before nightfall."

Misty blew out a sigh and her lips pressed together in a thin line. "Dogs are lucky. People...not so much," she said under her breath.

Cindy Lou arrived. "I brought a sweet tea for you both. You need anything else, Janet?"

When the other woman shook her head, Janet sent Cindy Lou away. Once they were alone again, Janet leaned forward. "So, who are you working with at Knoxville Police Department?"

Misty took a worn, folded business card out of the pocket of her cardigan. She smoothed it out and slid it across the table. *Detective Kay Smith, Knoxville Police Department.* Janet knew a few cops over at the department downtown, but she didn't know this one.

"What does she say?"

"Well, not much, I'm afraid." Misty covered her mouth with one hand and Janet had the feeling she was trying not to scream. "She said they would start asking around, talk to Lola's friends, her teachers, see if anything stuck out. But right now they're not calling it a missing persons case so much as a runaway teen."

"That's a much different level of investigation."

"Not nearly the manpower we want—we need! It's just this one cop asking Lola's math teacher a question. It—it's just not—"

The door opened and a beam of sunlight cut into the dark space, landing directly in Misty's eyes. She squinted, and her words cut off as she shielded her eyes with one hand. She clearly recognized the man entering the bar. Her shoulders drooped ever so slightly. She forced her eyes wide. "Paul, come meet Janet. She's the woman I told you would find Lola."

CHAPTER THREE

"I'll do what I can," Janet said, twenty minutes later, "but it sounds like a difficult case."

Misty stared, unblinking at Janet, but Paul was already up and out of his seat.

"Let's go, Misty. We're late." He walked through the door without a backward glance. The chimes that jangled when the door closed felt inappropriately cheerful.

Misty slowly pushed herself up from the bench seat, and took her time closing her cardigan sweater over her chest. She crossed her arms over the fabric to keep it in place, then turned her eyes back to Janet. "You'll call Detective Smith?"

Janet nodded. "Right away. How'd you hear about Bexley and Associates?"

"A flyer came in the mail a while ago. The name stuck in my brain, I guess." Misty's lips once again pressed into a thin line and the corners tugged down before she turned and left the bar.

Janet stared at the doorway until Cindy Lou tapped her on the shoulder.

"I don't like that Paul fellow. What a drag." She shook her

head and stirred her tall sweating glass of sweet tea with a black straw.

Janet cocked her head to the side. "You do know their daughter is missing. Was he supposed to tap dance here and do a show for you?"

Cindy Lou's hands fluttered in the air, brushing off Janet's sarcasm. "You know what I mean. He looked irritated to have to deal with this, instead of worried about his daughter." She frowned. "I don't like him."

Janet turned to the bar and deposited the still-full glasses of sweet tea and cardboard coasters onto the counter. She had to agree with Cindy Lou. Misty was exactly what you'd expect the worried mother of a missing teen to look like. Paul, on the other hand, appeared to have more important things on his to-do list than hunting down a wayward teen. But before she could say as much to Cindy Lou, the chimes rang again, indicating a new customer had walked in. Janet frowned; it was too early for so many people to be coming into her bar. This was supposed to be a quiet time—time to get organized for the night ahead.

Cindy Lou greeted the customer, but whatever the woman said in response left her assistant manager saying, "Oh," as if she'd just found out she read the wrong book for a class report.

Janet turned to see who had entered. A nondescript woman with dark hair wearing a lumpy business suit and holding a white plastic clipboard in her hands walked past Cindy Lou and stopped two feet away from the bar.

"Are you Janet Black?" Her eyebrows disappeared under her bangs as she waited for Janet's response.

"Who's asking?"

The woman frowned. "He said you're a piece of work." Before Janet could ask who "he" was, she continued. "I am Amelia Turner with the state's Alcoholic Beverage Commission.

It has recently come to our attention that you do not serve food at this establishment. Is that correct?"

Janet already didn't like Amelia Turner, her pointy nose, or her disapproving expression. But there was no sense hiding the fact that they didn't have a kitchen.

"We certainly do serve food." Cindy Lou's voice came from behind the visitor, and surprised Janet enough that she had to hide her smile behind a cough.

Cindy Lou crossed her arms under her ample chest and raised one eyebrow as she assessed Amelia Turner with a frown.

Amelia reached forward and gingerly slipped a sticky menu from the slot on the counter. Her eyes scanned the front, then flipped it over. "Blank on the back. I see five beers listed, and that's it." She glanced over at Cindy Lou. "Where exactly is the food menu?"

Cindy Lou smirked as if she was winning the argument. "We serve trail mix. And refill the bowls all the dang time."

Amelia grinned lightly and made a note on a clipboard. "According to section 554 – 215a, any establishment that serves beer, wine, or spirits is required to also have a full-service food menu."

Cindy Lou sidled up next to Amelia, who in turn took a step away. Undeterred, Janet's assistant manager leaned forward. "Well, Amelia Turner from the Alcoholic Beverage Commission, I am happy to tell you that the Spot has been grandfathered in for the last twelve and half years to that new state requirement. I remember when our old owner, Bernie, read the article that he didn't have to build the kitchen." She glanced over at Janet. "Was pissed as hell that he'd spent money on architecture plans for the addition, but ultimately saw it as saving a fortune on the project."

Janet's jaw almost hit the countertop. She'd never heard Cindy Lou sound so knowledgeable. But Amelia Turner didn't share her wonder.

The state flunky looked down at her notebook before turning to address Janet. "Was there, or was there not, recently a sale of this establishment?"

A shot of unease slid down Janet's throat and lodged into the base of her neck, making it difficult to swallow. She noted that Cindy Lou's smile disappeared as well.

"That is true." Janet and her boyfriend, Jason Brooks, had purchased the bar together several years ago, but Jason had recently sold his half of the bar to her at her urging. She wanted to own her own business, be her own boss, report only to herself. And she'd been absolutely certain it was the right choice up until twenty seconds ago.

"The state of Tennessee passed a resolution three months ago stating that any transfer of liquor license—even between existing owners—would nullify the clause that had grandfathered your businesses in up to this point."

Cindy Lou's jaw hung slack. She wrinkled her nose. "What are you saying?"

"I'm saying the Spot has thirty days to come into compliance with the laws of the state of Tennessee that govern alcohol sales and distribution, or your license will be revoked and the business will need to close." Amelia Turner tore a few sheets out of her notebook and slapped them onto the counter between herself and Janet. "Here is the relevant information and my contact number should you have any further questions." She looked around the bar and her eyes softened. "It looks like a nice place, but my boss is adamant that I address this issue immediately."

She turned to leave the bar when Mel stepped in her path.

"Who exactly is your boss?" Though Mel's smile was friendly, Amelia shuffled back a few steps before answering.

"As it turns out, I have a new boss. He just moved over from another department. His name is Gary Donaldson."

Mel pushed the door open and held it for Amelia. "You have a nice day."

"And you, as well."

When the bearer of bad news was gone, the three women gathered at the bar.

"Gary Donaldson?" Cindy Lou moaned. "Why can't that man just leave you alone?"

Mel crossed her arms. "You need to call O'Dell."

"I know." Janet frowned. "And I will...soon."

Detective Patrick O'Dell was a homicide detective with the Knoxville Police Department, and he and Janet had a semi-complicated relationship that he wanted to expand, and she was happy to keep exactly where it was. It turned out O'Dell and Gary Donaldson had a colorful history—that started when O'Dell went on a few dates with Donaldson's ex-wife. Now the state employee had been making it his business to try and put Janet out of business as a strange way of getting back at O'Dell.

However, just then the last thing she wanted to do was engage with the most engaging cop she'd ever met. Recent history had shown her that having O'Dell nearby didn't help her relationship with Jason, so for now, she'd trust her gut and try and figure things out on her own.

CHAPTER FOUR

Janet handed the papers to Jason, then leaned back against the couch cushion in the family room and crossed her arms over her chest. Her lips pursed, and she made a herculean effort to smooth them out. She'd gotten home a few minutes earlier but hadn't been able to relax since Amelia Turner's visit to the Spot.

Jason scanned the sheet. The *whirr* of William's power drill droned in the background. Three seconds on, then five seconds to reload a new screw, then three seconds on again. It was surprisingly relaxing compared to some of the hammering that had been issuing from the kitchen in the last weeks of the renovation project.

When Jason looked up, his eyes searched Janet's. "How long do we have to come into compliance?"

Some of the tension leached out of her shoulders as she leaned forward to rest her elbows on her knees. The simple fact that he'd said "we" was enough to remind her how much she loved the man sitting in front of her. "Thirty days." She reached up and rubbed her neck. They should have used a lawyer to handle the business sale, instead of printing forms off the Internet. Cutting corners always ended up costing you more in the long run. She should know that by now.

But Jason only shook his head. "That can't be. It must be thirty days to show them you're planning to come into compliance. They can't expect a full addition and renovation of the space in thirty days. It'll take that long to get a contractor in there to give us a quote."

Whirr. Pause. *Whirr.*

She relaxed even more, and the knot at the base of her skull eased up. She hoped he was right. Janet looked over Jason's shoulder through the open kitchen door. "Is that the last set of upper cabinets?"

Jason turned to glance at the space. "Can you believe it? Eighteen months without a kitchen, and Dad said he should be ready to install the oven by the weekend."

Janet smiled in spite of her sour mood. As much as Jason's father tended to grate on her nerves, she couldn't complain about his work ethic. In the six months since he'd moved in with them, he'd managed to lay a cork floor, install all the base cabinets, and was now almost done with the upper cabinets. They'd probably call in a specialist for the countertops and sink, though they hadn't broken the news to William yet.

If only he could find his own place to live after the divorce so easily.

Before Janet could comment, there was a light tap at the door followed by the doorknob turning with a squeak. A cheerful voice sang-spoke, "Knock, knock!"

Janet stared wide-eyed at her boyfriend and he winced back apologetically before jumping up to greet his mother.

"Come on in, Mom."

"She just did," Janet muttered under her breath as she stood.

Jason and Faith hugged in the entryway. A headband pushed her graying blond hair away from her face, but a few disobedient strands stuck up, and she reached up to smooth them back into place after the hug.

Her full lips, so similar to Jason's, were currently pulled down into one of those happy frowns some people managed to do, and her brown eyes looked adoringly up at her only son.

"How's my favorite Jason?" Her gaze drifted over to Janet's and her smile-frown deepened. "And the lovely Janet Black. How are you, dear?" She crossed the room and pulled Janet into a hug, then settled onto the couch across from her and patted the seat next to her for Jason. Her son obliged, resting an arm across his mom's shoulders and giving her a squeeze.

"It is so lovely to see you both. I sure won't let so much time slip by between visits again." She shot a dark look over her shoulder when the *whirr* of the drill punctured the air. She and William had gone through a bitter divorce recently, and Faith had purposefully kept her distance with her ex living in her son's house. Even though Faith was quick to tell anyone with an ear that she couldn't stand William, in the past, she'd taken special care with her appearance when they'd all gotten together. Janet was surprised to find her looking wind-swept and scattered. The details of why were quickly explained.

"I am so irritated with my hotel. I booked an open-ended reservation—" Janet cringed, "—and when I went to check in today, they said they can't actually do that! If I'd have known, I would have booked somewhere else. What with that big Comic-Con starting next week, there won't be any rooms available if I need to extend my stay!"

"Lots to do with the restaurant, then?" Janet asked in what she thought was a diplomatic voice, but she must have missed the mark based on the look Jason shot her.

"Oh, honey, you just have no idea! When I bought that place at auction, I thought there'd be a little bit of paperwork and that'd be it. Boy, was I wrong." Faith shook her head.

"Well, you're not alone in your troubles," Jason said. "Janet was just telling me that the state is trying to screw her over. Again."

Faith's expression darkened. "Language, dear," she admonished, but still turned to Janet with concern. "What do you mean? What's going on?"

Before Janet could explain, William came out of the kitchen rubbing a bandanna roughly across his forehead. "Well, that's done." He stopped short when he saw Faith. "Oh, I didn't know you were here."

The skin around Faith's eyes tightened and she smiled stiffly. "William. I see you're hard at work. Don't let me stop you."

"Never have. Never will." William's expression turned triumphant as Faith's lips pulled down into a genuine frown.

Jason hopped up and started backing out of the room.

Unbelievable.

They'd discussed just the night before how his penchant to leave before his parents could dig into an argument often left Janet in an awkward position. He'd agreed not to do it again, but now that he was backing out of the room, he refused to make eye contact.

"Sorry to leave you guys so quickly, but my break is over." Janet glared across the room. He owned his own computer security business, his break was as long as he wanted to make it. He caught her eye and glanced down at his watch belatedly, then looked up with a grin. "Big job just came in from Memphis. Might have to travel that way at the end of the week. Okay if I stay at the house, Mom?"

"I was just in Memphis," William said, a smug smile on his face.

"Why's that?" Faith cocked an eyebrow.

"Visiting Connie. She's got a beautiful place there. I've always thought that Memphis is a great city, haven't you, Faith?"

Faith turned her back on her ex-husband, clearly not interested in hearing about his new girlfriend. She smiled at her only son indulgently. "Of course, dear. Spare key is where it always is."

Jason nodded and then disappeared.

William and Faith, avoiding each other's eyes, instead stared at Janet.

She cleared her throat. "So, Faith, what's the word on the business license?"

Jason's mother had bought the abandoned restaurant next door to the Spot at a public auction several weeks earlier. Or as William liked to say, she'd bought it right out from under him. Now she was waiting on the business license to come through before moving forward with her plans to re-open the long-closed restaurant. It had been known as Old Ben's place for as long as Janet had lived in Knoxville, but the former owner had moved to Florida several years ago and had stopped paying property taxes. Now it was strange to think about someone else owning and operating the business under a new name.

"Nothing yet, and I'll tell you what, it's driving me crazy." A life-long southerner, Faith would never let her frustration spill over the surface. Her face was as sunny and cheerful as if she'd just learned she was going on vacation. "But enough about me—"

"No kidding," William said.

"What's all this?" Faith motioned to Janet's paperwork lying on the coffee table as if William hadn't spoken.

Janet went over the highlights—or lowlights—of the new situation with the liquor license at the Spot.

"And all this happened because Jason sold you his share of the business?" Faith narrowed her eyes and Janet frowned. It was all her fault, really. It had been her idea to own the business outright. Her idea to have Jason turn his shares over to her. Her idea, all of it. Her fault.

William headed toward the pair but couldn't bring himself to sit in the open spot next to his ex-wife. Instead he hovered in between them so that Janet had to crane her neck uncomfortably to look up at him. "So what are you going to do?"

"We did some digging in the office and found the old architectural plans for a kitchen addition. I guess we'll move forward with that. I mean, what's another fifty-thousand-dollar loan when you already owe so much?"

"Darlin', sounds like you need an interior designer." Faith straightened her skirt and crossed her legs primly at the ankle.

William guffawed. "Janet does not need your help with this, Faith. She's probably already got it all planned out."

Faith's expression darkened and she leaned back against the cushion to get a better look at her ex. "You have no idea what Janet needs. She probably needs *you* to finish the kitchen, that's what she needs."

William crossed his arms. "She needs a little space in her own house. That's what she needs."

A laugh exploded from his ex-wife, short and choppy. "That's rich, coming from you. How long have you lived here now?"

Janet stood up, but Jason's parents didn't even notice. By now they were deep into their regular argument, each trying to one up the other while also trying to prove how invaluable they were to their son's life. She backed out of the room and gently closed her bedroom door.

She kicked her shoes off and laid back against the pillows on her bed. As much as she hated to admit it, she hadn't thought much beyond getting the actual kitchen built. But Faith was right. She would need someone to design the space, help her figure out what kind of plates to buy, silverware, heck, even pots and pans. She sat bolt upright. She was going to need to hire a chef, maybe waitresses, too.

The cost for this project kept doubling every time she considered it.

The dates on the mini-calendar on her nightstand from a local realtor pulsed with each second. Thirty days wasn't long to figure out all of this while running a business and looking for a missing teen.

She texted Cindy Lou to put an ad up for the chef position, but the unsettled feeling in her stomach didn't abate.

It felt like the beginning of a bad joke—a business owner sets out to hire an architect, a builder, and a chef...

She had no doubt that in the end, *she'd* be the punchline.

In reality, she needed even more than those contractors and employees. She sure as hell wasn't going to bring Faith into that hot mess, though. Never in a million years did she need the chaos at home to enter her work life, too.

CHAPTER FIVE

"So what's this girl's name again?" Quizz tucked her car keys into a purple fanny pack, then twisted the pouch around so it rested on her butt. She looked up, and upon seeing Janet's scrutiny, said, "What?"

Janet hadn't seen a fanny pack in use since she'd left her small hometown in Montana many years ago. She shook herself and focused on the question. "Her name is Lola, and she's a senior here at Boulder Ridge High School."

"You have a good picture of her?"

"Mm-hmm. Lola's mom gave me one." It had been six days since Misty hired Janet—and Quizz—and she'd spent the bulk of her investigation so far doing online research. Lola didn't leave much of a footprint—which was unusual for a teenager these days. Facebook was a dead end, and Lola didn't have an Instagram or Twitter account.

But now that school was back in session after an oddly placed early winter break, Janet was ready to talk to the people who might have known Lola best: her classmates.

Janet held out a five-by-seven school photo of the girl. Her blond hair was loose around her shoulders and a small grin revealed a mouth full of metal. "It's from two years ago, but her mom swears she's hardly changed. Just got her braces off."

"What do the police say?"

Janet shook her head. "I don't know. I put a call into the detective who was assigned to the case but haven't heard back."

"What about your contacts? You put in any *other* calls?" Quizz drilled her with an unblinking stare, but again Janet batted the question away.

"Just waiting on the detective in charge of this one." They stared at the school building, quiet at this time of day. "This feels weird." Janet motioned to the parking lot then turned to face her mentor. "You sure we can't just go in and ask for help at the office?"

The lines of disbelief that formed on Quizz's face were all the answer Janet needed, and she held up her hands in defeat, but the other woman spoke anyway. "The rules at a school are unlike those you'll find anywhere else. Getting into the building is a pain in the ass. But asking an admin to talk to a student?" Quizz ran a hand through her hair and shuddered visibly. "Might as well ask the principal to chop off an arm. Too many hoops to jump through." Quizz looked down at the picture one more time. "She kind of looks like you."

"She's blond and seventeen. Are we looking at the same picture?"

"I mean the eyes. And her nose, maybe. Ahh. Here they come."

Janet leaned back against the front panel of the car. She didn't have any experience with kids or schools, so she wanted to let Quizz take the lead on this one. But after the first two students headed out of the building toward their cars, then a few more, a virtual flood of people exited the building. The women split up, heading in opposite directions, each with a picture of Lola.

A blond girl—preppy—stared at Janet with a question in her eyes as she approached.

Janet held the picture out as her greeting. "Do you know Lola?"

The girl shrugged. "Sure. I mean, the school's not *that* big."

"Her mom reported her missing. I'm trying to figure out where she might have gone."

"Yeah, police were here asking the other day." The girl crossed her arms over her chest and looked around again, clearly nervous.

"Anything new come to mind that you forgot to tell them?

The girl glanced behind her and lowered her voice. "I don't know anything, but that girl back there? The one with brown hair and, like, way too much eye makeup? They're pretty close."

Before Janet could say "thank you" the blond was in her car, firing up the engine, cell phone pressed to her ear. Janet stepped out of the way and then headed toward the brunette with a friendly smile.

"I hear you were friends with Lola." The first girl was right, this one wore way too much makeup, each eye ringed with enough black pencil and smudged shadow on the upper lids to make a panda jealous.

The girl's dark lids narrowed. "Am."

"Excuse me?"

"I *am* friends with Lola. You said '*were*' like it's past tense."

Janet cringed inwardly at her slip. "You're right, of course. I'm Janet Black with Bexley and Associates Investigations. Lola's parents asked me to look into her disappearance."

The girl snorted. "Oh, her parents did, huh?"

"Well...her mother did most of the talking," Janet clarified. "Did Lola and her dad not have a great relationship?"

The girl looked to her side and when she saw they were alone she stepped closer. "Did you meet him?" Janet nodded and she scoffed. "He's not her father. Paul's been dating her mom for a few months now. What kind of PI are you that you didn't even know that?"

Janet made a mental note of that bit of information and asked another question. "Do you think she ran away?"

The girl closed her eyes and ran a hand through her hair. By the time she opened her eyes, liquid had pooled at the corners and she stared at a spot just above Janet's head. "Honestly, I don't know. This isn't like her, but she hasn't been herself lately..." She clamped her lips and shook her head slightly.

"Ever since when? Did something happen?" The girl had something to hide, but Janet couldn't quite read her body language. She was holding something back. Was she worried she might get Lola in trouble? Was she worried *she* would get in trouble? Janet decided to press the issue. "What's your name?"

"I'm Amanda Rhodes."

"Listen Amanda, Lola's parents—I mean, her mom—is worried, and with good reason. Good things don't happen to teenage girls that go missing. If you know anything, now's the time to say something. No one's looking to get anyone in trouble. We just want to bring Lola home, you understand?"

Amanda's shoulders sagged as if the weight of the world had suddenly become too much. She sucked in her bottom lip and looked down at her toes. A new batch of students poured out of the building, their voices carrying across the asphalt parking lot. Amanda tensed, glanced behind her, and started moving away from Janet.

"I've gotta go. But if I were to pinpoint when things started going weird for Lola, it would be when she started dating Matt."

"Matt? I haven't heard anything about a boyfriend. Is he a student here? What's his last name?"

Amanda shrank farther away, and Janet tried to soften her

voice. "Just a last name, Amanda. That's all I need. I don't have to tell anyone we've even spoken."

"I can't. I wish I could, but I don't know."

"So—not a student here, then?"

Amanda shook her head. "She met him online. That's all I know. Well, that and I didn't like the guy. Overbearing asshole if you ask me."

"Hold up, did you meet him?"

"No—just...just based on what Amanda told me about him. He didn't want her going to parties. I mean, she missed Larissa Jenkins' birthday party, and her parents hired an actual band to play!" Her cheeks turned pink and she took a step back. "What do I know, though, right? She said it was love. Listen, I've got to go." Whatever Amanda's plans had been for lunch, she had obviously changed them. She pivoted on the spot and hurried back into the building without a backward glance.

Janet followed and shoved a business card into Amanda's hand. "Call if you think of anything. Sometimes even small details can make a big difference."

"Please step away from the student." An official voice rang out across the parking lot and even though Janet was many years removed from high school, she still froze, her shoulders tense, as a bowling ball settled into the base of her stomach. She turned and found a thin stooped man with an impressively authoritative expression facing her. "This is private property and you are not allowed to even *be* here without prior authorization, and you certainly may not speak to my students. Follow me into the office. The police are on their way. They'd like a few words."

CHAPTER SIX

What was it about sitting in a principal's office that made you want to shrivel up and die? Janet sat slumped in an uncomfortable chair in front of the principal's desk. Quizz seemed to find the whole situation amusing, and she'd somehow made friends with the receptionist. While Janet sulked, the other two women chatted amiably about hair dye and the usefulness of Kool-Aid as an accelerant in the process.

But Janet felt the injustice of the situation and sat glowering across the desk at the principal. He was completely unaffected, and in fact, the worse Janet's mood shined through, the happier he became. He'd started humming five minutes ago.

"I just want to point out—again—that Lola's mother hired me to look into her disappearance."

"So you've said." The principal clearly didn't believe her, and he eyed her like she might steal his paperweight if he looked away for even a moment.

"While we're waiting, why don't you tell me a little about Lola? Do you have any guesses where she might have gone? What might have driven her to want to leave?"

"Ms. Black, I'm not going to answer questions from anyone except the police detective who's charged with investigating this case."

She threw herself back against her chair, disgusted. Curious students slowed as they passed the office window, but Janet hardly saw them, her vision clouded by anger. It took a moment for her to realize that the buzzing in her head was actually the front door buzzer, indicating someone wanted access to the building. Janet glanced over to the black-and-white security camera monitor and nearly gasped aloud when she recognized Detective O'Dell. Surely they wouldn't send someone so senior for a small case of school trespassing? His grinning mug, though, said just the opposite.

The receptionist buzzed him in and within seconds he crossed the threshold into the office. Janet hadn't laid eyes on him in weeks, and she unconsciously licked her lips as she drank in all six foot two of him. Nothing had changed, from his strong, muscular shoulders, to his close-cropped sandy blond hair, and those sparkling, mischievous green eyes which currently twinkled down at her.

"Principal Adler, nice to see you, sir. I heard we've got a problem here. Ladies? What's going on?"

Principal Adler stood up with a welcoming smile. "Detective O'Dell, didn't think we'd see someone so high-ranking here, but delighted to hear the department is taking things seriously."

O'Dell smiled good-naturedly at the principal's slightly condescending tone and widened his stance. "I heard the call-out come over my radio. Since I was in the area, I told the dispatchers I'd handle it personally." His eyes twinkled again and Quizz clicked her fanny pack back into place as she stood from the chair by the receptionist's desk.

"Thought we were on okay ground in the parking lot, but

now that I know the rules, we'll know what to do next time. Detective, let's roll."

Despite Janet's grumpy mood, she had to hide a laugh at Quizz's ability to stay cool under pressure. Playing dumb was a great excuse to get out of almost anything—at least, the first time.

"Ladies, follow me. We'll head downtown to sort things out."

Quizz turned away, but not before her irritated expression belied her calm demeanor.

The two women waited by the front doors while O'Dell and Adler discussed a school resource officer who wasn't up to snuff, according to the principal. O'Dell finally led the way outside. Quizz and Janet peeled off toward Quizz's car when O'Dell turned, a hand out toward his car.

"Oh no. Someone's got to come with me downtown to make this look good, otherwise old Adler will raise hell at the next City Council meeting."

"I drove here, so I'm out." Quizz jangled her keys in the air and sidestepped away from the other two.

Janet scowled, and a grin stretched across O'Dell's face. "Looks like it's you and me, Janet. I'll even let you sit in the front seat, how's that?"

Janet marched in front of O'Dell, secretly glad he wasn't going to make her sit in the back. She waved goodbye to Quizz, then climbed in next to O'Dell.

They both stared forward until the silence between them stretched too long. When she turned to face him, she found he was still grinning at her.

"Oh, shut up."

He chuckled. "Admit it, you were happy to see me when I walked in that office."

Janet grinned despite her best effort to keep her face smooth. He chuckled again, and she finally relented. "Okay, fine. I was glad to see you."

He started up the engine with a celebratory laugh. "Hot damn, I'd say that's progress."

Janet buckled her seatbelt. "You're not really taking me downtown, are you?"

"Might as well come with me. Heard you been asking around about that missing girl. Why don't you talk straight to the source?"

"You mean Detective Smith?"

O'Dell nodded.

"She hasn't been returning my calls. She in today?"

"You bet. She's in and she's expecting you. I radioed earlier to let her know I'd be bringing you downtown. She's nice, you'll like her."

Janet tried not to feel the flutters in her belly when he took one hand off the steering wheel and rested it just inches from hers. *I have a boyfriend, I have a boyfriend*, she repeated to herself, but she didn't pull her hand away.

She'd gotten to know O'Dell well over the last few months, though not as well as he'd have liked. Despite his interest, Janet was committed to Jason, so she batted down her every inclination to flirt with the attractive man next to her.

"How's business?" he asked, keeping his eyes on the road.

"Which one?"

"You pick."

She grinned. "Well, as you can see, I'm hitting it out of the park with my PI apprenticeship."

He chuckled and chanced a quick sidelong look at her as they approached a red light.

"Cops called on you at a school? If we're putting that in the success column, then I have to wonder, what constitutes a failure?"

Her face heated under his scrutiny, and when she turned, their eyes locked. "I guess an actual arrest." The silence stretched between them, sparked; electricity zinged out from their connection.

"Green light." She motioned with the hand not resting close to O'Dell's out the windshield.

"I wish." He sighed and eased his foot off the brake.

Janet cleared her throat, cleared her mind. "In other news, we'll be making big changes at the Spot."

"Oh yeah, why is that?" O'Dell pulled his hand away and shifted his body so that he was closer to the door.

"Well, our old friend has changed jobs." She said Donaldson's name and O'Dell's eyebrows raised.

"I heard he got kicked out of the Commerce Department after *someone* lodged an anonymous complaint against his conduct," he said, his expression leaving no doubt that he was the one who'd filed the complaint.

Janet sighed. Funny how things like that could backfire. Everything had unintended consequences. Her need for independence was going to cost her tens of thousands of dollars in a new kitchen. O'Dell trying to right the score between him and Donaldson meant a new threat from the ABC.

"Turns out he got hired with the Tennessee Alcohol Beverage Commission. And guess who is suddenly not in compliance?"

O'Dell cringed. "Oh no, I feel very responsible for this all of a sudden."

"As you should." Janet bit her lip. "But mostly I blame Donaldson."

"Asshole." They said the word in unison, then both laughed.

O'Dell reached over and squeezed her arm, then moved the gear to park. His touch zinged across her arm and settled into the base of her stomach. She sucked in a quick breath of air that was louder than she'd intended.

O'Dell's lips tipped up at the corners. "We're here."

Janet had never been so relieved to get out of a cop car.

CHAPTER SEVEN

O'Dell led the way past the receptionist down an ugly long narrow corridor of the police headquarters building in downtown Knoxville. Janet nodded to a surprising number of officers she'd gotten to know over the last several months, ever since O'Dell had turned the Spot into the de facto hangout for off-duty cops.

There was Riviera, the homicide detective, along with Booker, and another traffic cop named Mary Stafford.

But O'Dell's steps didn't slow as he weaved his way past all those desks into a section of the department she'd never entered before. Bulletin boards lined the hallways and the haunted, hollow eyes of dozens of missing children followed their every step. Were the empty rectangles hopeful—a found child—or sinister—a dead child? Before she could ask, O'Dell slowed and tapped with his knuckles at an open door.

"Kay, I told you I'd bring Janet by? Well, here she is." He held his hand out into the office and Janet squeezed past him to enter. The flush that colored her cheeks wasn't lost on Detective Smith. Her eyes narrowed briefly before she stood. "Thanks, O'Dell. I'll bring her to you when we're done."

O'Dell's lips pursed and he studied Janet one last time before he turned and left the small space.

Smith's eyes traveled to Janet and she smiled faintly. "Heard a lot about you. Have a seat." She motioned to a cold, hard, uncomfortable-looking seat.

The chair met all of Janet's expectations and then some. She shifted so that her right butt cheek took most of the pressure.

"So, you want to know about the Bridges case." She looked up and Janet nodded. "There's not much to share, unfortunately. This is actually the worst kind of case to come in. Mom thinks she's been snatched, school thinks she's a runaway. And we have no evidence to support either theory. It's hard to know where to go from here." She folded her hands across an open case file. "I got some three dozen runaways, and at least half the families are convinced their child would never leave. It takes some digging, but we usually find out that yes, they would."

Janet rubbed her hand across her chin. "So what happens? The case is over before it's even started?"

"Not technically. We do what we can, which unfortunately is very little."

"What about TV? Can't you call the news? Have them feature this case on the evening newscast?"

"Unless it's a missing white mother or a child under ten, they're not very responsive. We talk to the family, talk to the neighbors, talk to the friends at school." She leaned back in her chair and tilted her head to the side. "O'Dell said you were out at the school today. Not a chatty bunch, at least that's what I found."

Janet sighed and leaned back in her seat too, then jolted forward when her back protested the lack of support. Her eyes traveled the walls of the office, the dozens of kids staring at her from their posters on the wall. She glanced at Detective Smith, took in the small crow's feet around her kind but intense eyes, and wondered how anyone could do a job like this around the clock.

"I talked to one girl, a friend of Lola's."

Smith hinged forward and ran a finger down the open case file until she found the information she was looking for. "Amanda?" Janet nodded. "She tell you about this boyfriend? This Matt fellow?" Janet nodded again and Smith ran both hands through her hair. "It's been a dead end for us. Can't get a line on any of her social media habits, her Facebook account was practically empty, and no emails to anyone other than teachers and her mother. We haven't found any connection to anyone named Matt, except some poor kid in the chess club who vaguely knows Lola, but had never talked to her." Her eyes narrowed and that intense gaze sharpened. "Did Amanda have any new information? Or just the theory?"

"No, nothing new. Just got the impression she didn't like *Misty's* boyfriend any more than she liked Lola's new boyfriend."

Smith shrugged. "Show me a teenage girl who doesn't complain about the predominant father figure in her life, and I'll show you a winning lottery ticket."

Janet bit her lip, but a chuckle slipped out anyway. She certainly had experience in not liking her dad when she was in high school. They'd come a long way since then, but back then she likely would've sounded like any other teenage girl complaining about a father.

"There's not enough time in the day for my caseload, so I'm happy for the extra set of eyes on this. Stay away from the school, or you'll end up back here without O'Dell as your escort. Lots of kids from Boulder Ridge High hang out at a place called 'the Annex.' It's over behind the horse farm off Liberty. I hear Friday nights are pretty hot there. You might get more information out and about than when they're buttoned up at school." Smith stood. Her time with Janet was up. "I'll walk you back to O'Dell. I'm sure he'll want to say goodbye."

O'Dell's crush on Janet might have been the worst-kept secret in the entire Police Department. Janet slunk along behind Smith to O'Dell's desk.

He escorted Janet out of the office.

"I got a few minutes. I can drive you home, or to work?"

"The Spot, thanks." He smirked, and she knew *he* knew she didn't want Jason to know they had been together. They drove in comfortable silence to the bar and when he stopped the car, he turned to face her. "Would it be okay if I come in later today, or will that cause trouble?"

The flutters in her chest were back, but she tried to ignore them. "We'd love to have you, O'Dell." He searched her face for a long moment before nodding, almost to himself. She let out a breath and recognized the truth in her words. She wondered if O'Dell did as well. He was like a magnet to her, and even though she was committed to her relationship with Jason, she couldn't seem to shake the feeling that she wanted to keep O'Dell close.

"All right. Then I'll see you soon."

The words held a promise that Janet hated to investigate. So she didn't, choosing instead to pretend like it was no big deal.

She watched O'Dell drive away and jumped when someone laid a hand on her shoulder.

"Who was that?" Faith must have come from the shadows of the building, and Janet wondered what she'd been doing lurking outside the bar.

"Oh, Faith. I didn't see you there."

The other woman's eyes narrowed, and she looked from Janet to the disappearing taillights of the detective's car. "Are you in trouble?"

"Probably." Janet smiled and stepped lightly toward the main door to the Spot. "In fact, Faith, I almost always am."

CHAPTER EIGHT

Inside, Faith linked her arm though Janet's and steered her toward a stranger sitting at the corner booth.

"Janet, after our conversation last week, I took the liberty of calling an old friend in the construction business. This is Bruce Hobak of Hobak Designs."

Bruce unfolded his lanky six-foot-plus frame from the bench seat and shook Janet's hand. His grip was firm and warm. He motioned that the ladies should sit across from him, and Janet tamped down irritation at being invited to sit at a table in the bar she owned.

"We might have a great fit here, Miss Black." He ripped the tops off two sugar packets and poured them into a glass of tea. He didn't speak again until he'd stirred it, set the spoon down on the empty wrappers, and took a sip. "I had a big cancellation this week, and Faith tells me you already have some plans drawn up for a kitchen expansion. We might could help each other out. Your small expansion here would keep my crew busy and stay mostly on schedule with our next job, and you'll get your kitchen built and ready to use by the city's deadline."

Well, you couldn't say it any better than that, Janet thought with a smile. If he'd added a bless-your-heart somewhere in there, it'd be all the southern lingo she could handle.

"That will give us a chance to get the rest of the building up to code."

"The rest of the building? What do you mean?"

"You need fire extinguishers and fire doors at all points of entry." He looked around the space and wrinkled his nose. "I don't see either?"

"Well, of course we're up to code!" She shot Cindy Lou a look. The other woman surreptitiously wrote a note on the pad by the cash register. Janet could only imagine what it said. "Buy fire extinguishers and fire doors." She tallied the additional cost and felt her chest tighten before she pushed down her frustration and dug around in her purse. "What about the necessary permits?" Janet smoothed out the wrinkled paperwork from the city on the edge of the table, then scanned the official language in the complaint, looking for the required permits. "How long do they take to get?"

"I've got contacts in all the relevant departments. Shouldn't take but a day, and we can start work without them."

"You can?" Janet looked up doubtfully at the contractor, and thought about Gary Donaldson, likely doing his best behind the scenes to derail any of her plans coming into compliance. "I don't know, I've got a guy with the city who's not a big fan—"

"Well then, this really is your lucky day," Bruce interrupted. "I've got big fans everywhere. We'll be fine. Can I take a look at the drawings? That'll help me come up with a more accurate quote for the project."

Janet excused herself to find the architectural plans in the office. Bruce spoke like he was an hour away from digging up the parking lot for the foundation. Janet hadn't even contacted a bank yet to see if they'd entertain the idea of loaning her money for the project! But she supposed it didn't hurt to have a plan in place, in case things went well. She found the roll of papers in the closet, tucked them under her arm, and headed back out to the main room, slowing as she approached the corner booth again to listen to Bruce and Faith's conversation.

"Candy'll be so sorry to hear that, Faith. We always did love working with you two. So William's still back home in Memphis?"

Faith covered her mouth when she saw Janet approach.

When she didn't answer, Janet spoke up. "No, Jason's father is here in Knoxville, too."

Bruce looked confused, but Faith smiled. "I'm sure he'll want to help out, Bruce. You know Jason's dad loves construction projects."

Bruce's eyebrows shot up and his mouth opened, but Faith beat him to the punch.

"He'll do the outside and I'll do the inside." She patted the spot next to her on the seat. "Did you find the plans, Janet?"

Janet tried to keep her eyebrows from meeting in the middle. She felt like *the plans* were being made right there in the booth without her, and she didn't like it one bit.

"I'm not sure if they make sense. Like I told you last week, Faith, the former owner of the Spot had them drawn up. I have no idea what something like this will cost, and if it's even an option for me right now. I'm a little cash poor after taking over the business completely."

Faith nodded dismissively. "Well dear, there's opportunity cost with every chance for growth, and that's exactly what this is. Now, Jason might not have told you, but his father and I have done many projects together. William is great at the construction side, and I, of course, excel at bringing out the—the hidden beauty of a space." Her gaze swept the Spot uncertainly before she focused on the main bar area like she was accepting an unspoken challenge to her abilities as an interior designer. "No matter how buried it might be."

"Why you lookin' at me, Faith?" Cindy Lou called from behind the counter.

Janet coughed out a laugh, then nearly choked when Bruce slipped a sheet of paper in front of her.

"Based on the drawings, the total job will be about $150K, from start to finish. That includes digging out a basement under the kitchen, which will not only be great for storage, like in this drawing, but it'll also give us the room to run utilities out to the new space. Talk to Jason, and his dad—but get back to me at this number by tomorrow, and I'll do a walk-through with actual measurements to get you a proper quote." He slipped a business card on top of the construction estimate and stood. "Faith, nice to see you. Give William my best. Candy and I are pulling for him."

Faith hid a cringe behind a cough and walked Bruce out. Janet studied them as they walked away. Had Bruce just boldly told Jason's mother that he and his wife were taking William's side in the divorce? She got up from the table and walked toward Cindy Lou with Bruce's dirty glass and trash. People in the south could be so strange.

"So, what do you think?" Faith walked lightly back into the bar several minutes later and took a seat across from Janet, who was restocking the Beerador.

"I think it's more money than I have to spend."

"But you have to do it, Janet! The state can close you down without a kitchen. Is that what you're going to let happen?"

Janet rolled the tension out of her neck before turning to face Jason's mother. "I can't spend money I don't have, Faith! And I also can't take the first offer that comes my way."

"Truth." Cindy Lou picked up where Janet had stopped with the Beerador, and Janet grinned, glad that someone had her back.

"I mean, there's got to be a better way. I'm going to have to hire a chef, and probably a waitress or two—"

"Plus buy tableware, silverware, serving trays—all the same things I'll be getting for my restaurant." Faith ticked more items off on her fingers. "You'll also need to come up with a menu, set up an account with vendors to buy the food on a regular basis, and then print new menus." Jason's mother gazed out the east windows, her eyes connecting with the roofline of the abandoned building she'd bought at public auction. "But you've got to do it, Janet. It's like I told William last night: if you want to attract a limo crowd, you buy a limo, not a used RV."

Cindy Lou and Janet exchanged a look. Janet grinned and Cindy Lou swatted her with a dishtowel. "How long are your permits supposed to take, Faith?" the assistant manager asked. "Shame your pal Bruce can't rush *your* applications through."

"It's a completely different department." Faith heard the defensiveness in her own voice and hurried to smile. "He works with building and zoning, not business and permits."

"Still, seems like there'd be some overlap." Cindy Lou clunked the final bottles into the massive refrigerator and pushed the door closed. "Wonder if he'd try for you, anyway?"

"I asked him to do just that before he left," Faith confessed. "Fingers crossed. I had no idea this would take so long. Then again, it wasn't clear at auction just how many liens there were against the property, either. It's been a paperwork nightmare, that's the truth."

"Do you trust Bruce?" Janet asked, thinking about how he'd openly declared himself Team William just moments earlier.

"More than I trust myself." Faith stood and walked to the windows, looking out across the parking lot toward her restaurant again, and repeated quietly, "More than I trust myself."

CHAPTER NINE

"Where are you going?" Cindy Lou was elbow deep in the refrigerator chest behind the bar, trying to rescue an earring that had dropped inside.

"I'm going to check out used RVs."

Cindy Lou snatched her hand out and shook it vigorously from the cold but didn't look up from the cooler. "Dagnabit. I knew the earring back was bad this morning, why I didn't..."

Janet grinned and headed out of the building, checking her phone for an address as she walked to her car. Faith had left to inspect her building again, and now her blond head was barely visible through the windows of the abandoned restaurant.

The search results page finally loaded on her phone and she scanned the list. Another few taps loaded directions onto her device. She climbed into her car and fired up the engine, then twisted the heater dial down to low, because a tiny spark of excitement warmed her from within. If this worked out, this could be a cheap, easy solution to her kitchen problem, and as a bonus, would irritate Faith enough that she might wash her hands of the Spot and focus on her own restaurant instead.

The used car dealership was only a few miles away from her, off MLK Boulevard. She eased into the lot and scanned the offerings. She was looking—not for a used RV as Faith had mentioned —but for a used food truck. Surely there was an affordable option somewhere in Knoxville that no one wanted anymore.

A young man wearing a brightly colored Polo shirt and a blue sports coat strode toward her with a grin, the winter sunshine glinting off his slicked-back hair. Was it wet, or had he just used lots of gel? She'd know in just a few more steps.

"Hi-welcome-to-Krazy-Kam's-Kar-Lot-I'm-Dean-what-are-you-looking-for-today-I've-got—"

It was clear he wasn't going to take a breath anytime soon, so Janet cut him off. "You got any food trucks?"

"F-food trucks?"

She felt a slight uptick of satisfaction that she'd managed to silence Dean, at least for a moment. She tilted her head to the side and waited.

He looked back to where an older version of himself stared through the open doorway of the business office. The older man gave him a quick thumbs up and smiled encouragingly. Dean's head swiveled back and he took a loud, deep breath.

"Ma'am-we-don't-have-any-food-trucks-but-we-do-have-trucks-in-which-you-can-eat-food-and-sometimes-that's-all-you-really-need—"

"Is that your dad in there?"

Dean sucked in his cheeks. "Yup."

"First day on the job?"

"How'd you know?"

"You left the tags on the suit jacket." She pointed to his right armpit, and he swiped the paper sales ticket with his left hand.

"Bah. I thought the Polo shirt was enough, but Dad said if I look like a pro, I'll be a pro." He shrugged. "What can I say?"

"You know of any places that might specialize in used food

trucks?"

He shook his head. "Nah. Let's go ask my dad." He turned and his shoulders drooped as he led the way to the small shack in the middle of the parking lot.

"Dean Kamstetter, nice to meet you." The wrinkled version of his son pumped Janet's hand firmly up and down several times before pulling her closer. "How'd he do out there?"

She smiled. "Legendary. He's going to be great."

Dean Senior smiled. "What can I do you for?"

"She's looking for a food truck." Young Dean was busy trying to cut the tag off his jacket without cutting the fabric, and his tongue pushed out between his lips as he focused. "I said we don't have one, but you'd know where she can go."

"Don't have one? Don't have one?" Dean Senior's voice rose an octave and his son dropped the scissors and looked up at his dad, his nose wrinkled.

"I think I'd notice a food truck parked around here!" He tipped the tag into the trash can and crossed his arms, but his face was oddly engaged, as if waiting for something exciting to happen.

"You must have missed it because it's so gorgeous, so clean, so amazing, that you probably couldn't look at it long enough for your eyes to register what it was." Old Dean wiped at a sheen of sweat on his forehead, then prompted his son with a quick head jerk.

"Well, where is this thing of beauty, then?" the young one asked.

Old Dean's mouth moved right along with his son's as he asked the last question. They were trying to play Janet, but why?

"Let's see this magnificent beast." Janet walked out of the small office first and scanned the lot. Plenty of beat-up Buicks and Fords, but nothing that resembled a food truck that she could see.

The Deans were close behind and the elder breathed out, "There."

She turned to where he was pointing, and across the street, parked in the shadows of a mechanic shop, an ancient-looking food truck clung to life.

She took an involuntary step back. "Does it—I don't know, does it work?"

"Does it work? Son, tell her about it."

Still trying to fish the other half of the plastic fastener out from the inside of his jacket, Young Dean jumped and shrugged the suit back up over his shoulders. "Dad, don't sell her that piece of crap. I'm sure there's a nicer one somewhere—"

"Son! First rule of business, give the customer all the information and let *them* decide what to do!"

Dean Junior sighed and crossed his arms. "What's your name?" His father nodded approvingly.

"Janet."

"Well, Janet, the engine of that there truck has been partially rebuilt, but when the mechanic went out of business, the work on the engine stopped completely. It might coast downhill a bit before completely stopping, but the engine won't do a thing."

Janet squinted at the beast. It was bright red, with *Timmy's Tacos* painted in mustard yellow across the front, under windows that were closed tight. The boxy vehicle was the same size as a UPS truck, and she mentally tallied the distance between here and her bar. Less than two miles. According to Dean, the truck would never make it.

"Bring her over, Dean, show her the amazing inside of that gorgeous giant!" Senior practically shoved his son toward the abandoned mechanic shop, throwing a set of keys toward him before he turned back toward the small office, muttering, "All you gotta do is *try* for the sale, and my kid wants to try to *lose* the sale, jeez."

"Well, come on." Young Dean led the way across the street. Janet slowly lapped the truck, while the salesman wrestled with the lock on the door.

When he pried it open, he motioned grandly that she should go in first.

She tentatively poked her head in. Dusty, grease-splattered aluminum, streaks of black grime, and a questionable odor met her when she was fully inside the vehicle.

But.

But the set up would easily allow for one chef plus another employee—a cash register operator—to move around each other and work. Under the patina of neglect, she could see good bones inside the cooking equipment. The fry baskets could easily be replaced, but the stove and cooktop had been lovingly maintained.

She climbed back out. The tires were nearly flat. The passenger side rear tire might have a rotten spot that would need to be addressed before she could even attempt to get it towed.

Dean clucked his tongue but waved encouragingly at his father, who'd taken out binoculars to keep tabs on the sales pitch.

He turned his back on his old man. "It's in rough shape. That rear tire is shot. I don't know if you saw the rusted-out fry baskets, but those would be easy enough to replace. I don't know. It's a risk. What do you think?"

"Does the generator work?"

"Let's check." He walked around to the back and pulled the doors open. They both studied the generator for a long moment, then Dean flipped a switch and turned a key. Nothing happened. "Could be out of gas?"

She frowned. She didn't need the generator; after all, she could just run some kind of extension cord from the bar out to the truck, but Dean didn't need to know that.

"How much?"

His eyebrows shot up and he stuttered for a moment before regaining his composure. "Sticker there says ten thousand."

"How much, Dean?"

He rubbed the back of his neck and his lips moved soundlessly.

"The engine doesn't work, the tires need to be replaced. Insides are in a bad way. Generator might be busted...I'll give it to you for five."

"Five thousand?"

She crossed her arms. She'd gladly tow the truck to the Spot for another 250 bucks, and not lose a minute of sleep over saving herself $145,000 and a year-long renovation headache. She also couldn't wait to see Donaldson's face when he heard the news.

Dean looked over at his old man, who even from across the street was vibrating with excitement. "I've got a friend who does custom paint jobs. You mention my name, he'll give you a discount."

"Eat at the Spot."

"Excuse me?"

"Oh, that's what I would have your friend paint on the truck. Eat at the Spot."

"Nice."

Janet patted the side of the truck, and a bolt that kept two panels of siding together popped loose. She snatched her hand back, and Dean rubbed the back of his neck again. "Four thousand," he blurted out, his expression hopeful. "And how about this, we'll tow it anywhere you want for free." He stuck his hand out and waited.

A slow grin spread across her face. She was coming into compliance with the law for less than five thousand dollars, Faith would be appalled, and she couldn't be happier. She reached out and grabbed his hand.

"You've got yourself a deal, Dean."

CHAPTER TEN

The next day, Faith sat in the corner booth with Jason, occasionally shooting disgruntled looks across the room toward Janet.

"Whoo boy. She ain't gonna get over it, is she?" Cindy Lou pushed a flyaway hair off her forehead with the back of her hand and then finished slicing a lemon. "It's like she'd already planned how she was gonna to change this place and can't believe it ain't gonna happen."

Faith's brow furrowed and she leaned toward her son. Whatever Jason said coaxed a smile from the older woman, and Janet turned back to her job behind the bar.

The Spot had just opened for business. Thanks to a rush job, the food truck was at the paint shop getting a fresh coat, and with that situation settled, Jason was supposed to be helping her break into a cell phone she'd just acquired. Misty had breathlessly brought it in the day before after finding it stuffed between Lola's mattress and the wall in her room. While she waited for Jason to wrap up with his mother, she turned to her assistant manager.

"Did you post the ad?"

Cindy Lou rinsed the cutting board off and slid the knife into a small wooden block on a shelf under the counter. "Not yet. I thought I'd wait until the truck came back—make sure it all works, you know? But then I'll post it online—say we're looking for a full-time cook, familiar with fry baskets and flan."

"Flan?" Janet chuckled. "We won't be serving flan here, I can promise you that."

"I figured that would help weed out the losers." Cindy Lou added, "Plus I was going for alliteration."

Janet finished pouring vodka into a new bottle. "Hmm, then maybe fry baskets and fettuccine? Nah, even that's probably not likely. Oooh, I know, fry baskets and frozen burgers." It was Cindy Lou's turn to chuckle.

Janet tossed the empty bottle into the recycling bin and screwed the cap on the now-full bottle and set it back on the shelf before turning to study her assistant manager. "What's wrong with you?"

Cindy Lou massaged her lower back and pushed her hips out with a grimace. "I threw my back out yesterday and feel like I'm going to break clean in half."

"What were you—wait, don't answer that."

Cindy Lou's wicked smile was all the confirmation Janet needed that the injury wasn't sustained on her own.

"I'm gonna do some stretches in the office. Be right back." Her blond head bobbed—slightly off-kilter—around the bar and disappeared into the back office. Janet wiped down the prep area, then tossed the dishrag into the sink and called to her boyfriend.

"Jason?"

He half-stood, then leaned across the table to kiss Faith on the cheek before heading her way.

"Just trying to smooth over the disappointment." His low voice suggested a funeral, but he winked to show he didn't agree with his mother's grave assessment of the situation. He held his hand out for the phone. "Sorry this took so long. Let's take a look."

"Work's been really busy for you lately, huh?" She headed around the counter and took a seat next to him while he set up his laptop. Lately, he spent more time in his basement office than out of it.

"Yeah, it's that big job from Quali-Corps. I knew it would be a beast, but I didn't know it would be *this* busy."

Quali-Corps had offices in all the major cities in Tennessee, and snagging them as a client had been a major coup for Brooks Security.

"What can I do?"

"Just keep being patient with me." He caught her hand in his when she held out the phone, and he stroked her palm lightly with his thumb. "I'm looking to hire help—it's too much for me to do on my own, and then hopefully we'll be able to see each other during daylight hours again."

"Help? Like an employee?"

"Exactly. Since I'm not at the Spot as much, I thought I could handle everything, but it's intense. I probably have enough work for two or three full-time employees, but I figured I'd start with one and see how it goes. I mean, the job's not for everyone, you know? Working out of a home basement."

"Well, maybe it's time to upgrade office space, too?" Janet swiveled her seat around to face her boyfriend.

His lips tilted up at the corners. "Yup. Time to upgrade, time to expand—and no time to do either." He dug through his bag and pulled out a small clear tackle box of coiled cords, then ran his finger across the lid until he found the right one. "This should do it."

"You think you can hack into the phone?" Janet studied the cell phone. "Misty said it's not Lola's normal cell phone, so she's not sure what to make of it."

Jason plugged the phone into his computer and tapped a few keys. "I've got a great code-breaking program here. It'll be pretty easy on this old phone. Looks like a four-digit password—no fingerprint or face recognition ID, no problem." After a few more keystrokes, he sat back. "Should only take a few minutes. Where'd she get this thing, anyway? Her mom said it's not the one they bought her?"

Janet's nose wrinkled. "Right. Misty asked the police to trace Lola's iPhone, and they tried immediately, but they said it must be turned off. It's not pinging off any cell phone towers anywhere. Then she found this one tucked between the mattress and the wall—and I think she's trying to convince herself it belongs to the cleaning lady or something."

The computer beeped, and Jason looked down. "We're in. Password is fourteen eighty-seven...shall we?" He held the phone up and Janet leaned across the space to get a better view. "Okay, let's see...the messaging app is completely empty." He tapped a few more icons and shook his head. "If she used this phone, she sure didn't use it very often."

Janet reached forward and tapped the photo icon. "Let's see what kind of—Oh God! What the—" She flinched away from the picture and simultaneously snorted out a laugh.

"What?" Cindy Lou materialized in front of them.

Janet grabbed the phone from Jason and twisted it around so her assistant manager could see.

She whistled low. "A dick pic? In all my years, I will kill my son if he ever sends one of these to a girlfriend."

Cindy Lou leaned in closer, making Janet chortle anew. "Just can't get enough, can you?"

Her nose wrinkled. "No, believe me, while this is an impressive representation, it's not the best I've seen. But I'll tell you what, I've never seen a birthmark like that. On his stomach? It looks like the Hawaiian Islands! With his belly button in the place of the one island, what's it called?" Cindy Lou sucked on her teeth while she thought. "Kauai? Why are you looking at me like that?"

Flustered, Janet tried to come up with something that wasn't as offensive as saying she didn't think Cindy Lou would have known the names of the islands.

"I'm smarter than I look," she said, flipping a grin before she turned away.

Faith appeared on the other side of the bar. "And why is that, Cindy Lou? You don't need to impress men with your chest when your mind is so sharp. That's sexy, too."

Janet turned to share a secret laugh with Jason, but he was already packed up. He shot an apologetic look at Janet as he shrugged into his coat.

"Sorry, I've got to go. I'm so behind—gotta meet with a potential hire, and then get back to work." He squeezed her shoulder, grabbed his tackle box of cords, and headed to the door.

"Jason!"

She didn't think he was going to stop, but after a few faltering steps he turned back, his face oddly blank.

"The phone?"

"Oh." He set his bag down on the closest table and forced a chuckle. He dug into the bag and gently set the phone down with a frown before hiking the bag over his shoulder again.

Janet watched him leave, an unsettled feeling in her stomach. Had she offended him by laughing at the sexting photo?

She collected the phone, noting absently that Mel looked similarly concerned by the turn of events, then she ducked into the office, determined not to get sucked into another long conversation with Jason's mother. The last thing she heard before she closed the office door was Faith chattering on about Cindy Lou's many assets.

CHAPTER ELEVEN

The shriek of the tow truck's backup alarm split the air in two-second bursts, and though Janet pointed toward the building the driver didn't adjust the wheel.

"Over—no—closer to the wall." She cupped her hands around her mouth and shouted, "Closer!"

The driver rolled his window down and squinted at Janet. "What?"

"Closer to the building! I want just enough room to walk behind the truck to plug it in—that's all!"

"Why didn't you say so?" The driver grumbled, but pulled forward and cranked the wheel around. With some kind of reverse-engineering magic, he positioned the food truck into place. By the time he disconnected Janet's new rolling kitchen from his tow dolly, the front bumper was exactly three feet to the right of the main entrance, and twelve to eighteen inches of daylight shone between the top of the truck and the roofline. The truck's rear bumper lined up with the end of the building, and if she stood between the exterior wall of the Spot and looked toward her new food truck, she could just make out Faith's sad empty building across her parking lot, up the grassy embankment, then at the end of Faith's parking lot. Several hundred feet separated the buildings, but Janet had to wonder what would happen when they were both serving food. Competing with Jason's mother for business? She shuddered at the thought.

After the tow truck drove away, she stood alone in the parking lot, studying her new acquisition.

"How's your missing girl case coming?" Faith stood at the back of the building. She must have come out the back door and walked around to see the food truck with her own eyes.

"Oh... it's..." Janet hesitated, not sure what she should share with Jason's mother.

"I overheard Cindy Lou say something about Hawaii. You don't think she's gone on vacation, do you?"

Janet shook her head. "No, nothing like that. We—well, we don't know much, to be honest. I haven't been able to figure out much more than the police."

"The phone?"

"Dead end." Janet looked away, not wanting Faith to pry into every single facet of her life. Faith didn't need to know about the sexting picture—especially when Janet hadn't even decided whether to tell Misty about it. Lola's mother needed to know that there was a good chance Lola had voluntarily gone off with a boy. But the fact was, they must be close. Kids in high school didn't have many resources to stay hidden for long. She hoped it was just a matter of waiting them out, and then being able to deliver Lola back to her family.

Faith rounded the food truck without looking at the offensive vehicle, then came to a stop next to Janet. "You know, some outdoor seats would be nice here." Faith smiled tentatively from where she stood in the open doorway to the Spot. "I know you don't want—or need—my help with anything, Janet, but I'd say some nice tables, even just one or two, would be a really lovely thing for your customers."

Janet grimaced, but smoothed her expression before turning to face Jason's mother. "I—I think that's a great idea, I just—I don't have time to get that organized." She made a mental note to order several new trash cans to set outside.

Faith's eyes lit up, but she looked away. "I might have some time while I'm waiting for my permits to come in." She walked in front of the truck and assessed the space. "It looks like we could take a ten-foot square area here, and mark it off with a simple pergola—Erm..." She bit her lip when Janet frowned. "I just mean some nice, ahh, smallish off-set umbrellas for shade, you know, so it's comfortable to sit here and eat, even in the summer months." She turned to Janet, her expression hopeful. "Don't you think?"

Janet took in Faith's expression, her lively eyes, her upturned lips, and realized—however crazy it was to think—that Faith would take joy from helping Janet with this small job. And if she could allow herself to give up control—just a little bit—for Jason, that it seemed the least she could do.

She blew out a long, quiet breath, and then turned to Faith with a smile. "Okay, Faith. Go for it."

"Really?" Faith's eyes sparkled, and Janet gulped.

"But just a small budget, Faith. I mean, less than a thousand bucks. See what you can do, okay?"

"Oh, you're going to love it, Janet! I think we can do some really exciting things out here, and yes—I do surely love a good budget as a place to start."

Start? Before Janet could get Faith to clarify, she was off and running, talking about materials and suppliers and spacing. Janet backed slowly into her bar, only chuckling when Faith didn't notice that she'd left. She had a feeling she was going to regret allowing Faith to "help." Then again, how much trouble could the woman get into with only a thousand-dollar budget?

She'd soon find out.

CHAPTER TWELVE

When Janet got into work the next morning, she was fighting off a funk that threatened to take over her attitude for the day. They'd been out of coffee grounds at home, so she'd had to stop by a coffee shop and pay five dollars for an extra-large brew that was bitter and too hot to drink, anyway.

By the time she pulled into the parking lot of the Spot, her attitude took a turn for the worse. An excavator blocked the back half of the lot along with a dozen construction workers. She squeezed her eyes shut, but their orange vests pulsed brightly against the back of her eyelids; the endless drone of a jackhammer drilled right down into her brain.

She looked at her door handle—did she want to risk it? Of course not; she was going to call this day what it was—a total loss. Janet eased the gear shift into reverse, but before she lifted her foot up from the brake, she spotted Faith, weaving between the workers, no doubt offering helpful tips and tricks. Unbelievable!

Janet shifted into park and smacked Jason's name on her cell phone with unnecessary force. The call went straight to voice-mail. She disconnected without leaving a message and then climbed out of her car so fast that coffee slopped out of the small sip hole in the flimsy paper cup and landed on her thigh. She swore when it sunk immediately through the denim and burned her skin.

Tut-tut-tut-tut-tut. The jackhammer was relentless.

"Faith!" she shouted, but it wasn't loud enough to compete with the construction equipment. She walked forward and raised her voice. "Faith! What the hell is going on?"

A smile stretched across the older woman's face as she raised her hand in greeting. "Isn't this fabulous, Janet? Come see what we're doing!"

Janet squared her shoulders and stalked toward the construction zone. She zigzagged past several orange barrels and came to a stop inches from Faith and her friend Bruce Hobak.

"What is happening?"

Bruce motioned to his crew to stop, and blessedly, the area plunged into silence.

Janet stared at Faith as she motioned to the small crew of workers. "I greenlighted a one-time one-thousand-dollar expenditure for picnic tables, don't you remember?" At Faith's innocent expression, she turned to point at the food truck—now covered in a thin layer of dust. "No kitchen addition. Food truck." Her words were rudimentary at best, but Janet worried if she added any adjectives, she'd start swearing at her boyfriend's mother, and she might not be able to stop.

Faith smiled as if she were about to deliver a winning lottery ticket. "This one's on me, hon."

"*On you?*" Janet repeated. "What are you talking about? What are you doing?"

Bruce Hobak turned toward Faith. "What's this? You said everyone was on the same page."

Faith's back stiffened, but she gamely kept the smile on her face. "Bruce, you keep right on doing what you're doing. Janet

and I just need to have a little girl talk. We'll figure this right out."
She winked at Bruce and then motioned that Janet should head
into the Spot.

Janet looked incredulously between Faith and Bruce and
back to Faith again. *Girl talk?* The last thing that would settle this
—this usurping of power over Janet's business plan by Faith—was
girl talk. But Janet stalked ahead of her boyfriend's mother into
her own bar. As the door closed, the jackhammer came back to
life and Janet pivoted, ready to launch into Faith, but the other
woman spoke first.

"You don't have to thank me, Janet. I wanted to do this. For
you."

"Thank you?" Janet had never heard her voice get so high,
and she took a deep breath to calm herself. Once again Faith was
faster.

"That food truck is a stopgap solution, hon, but I respect your
decision to save money now with a cheap, temporary thing. And
though I want you set up for long-term success, Jason's father
convinced me that this is your call." She sighed, then brightened
perceptibly. "So I decided to really throw myself into the patio
plan."

"What *patio plan?* You mean the picnic tables?"

"Well, that would have worked, sure, but to really own the
outdoor eating space, I thought we could do so much better.
That's why I called Bruce in for the project. You're going to really
love what he's come up with. And like I said, it's my gift to you."

Janet cleared her throat. "I cannot accept this gift, Faith." She
worked hard to keep her voice level and calm. "This is not something for which I can pay you back. And not only is this too
much, but I don't want it!"

Faith's eyes shifted from bright to crafty. "You can't not like
the plan, Janet, you don't even know what it is!" She laughed
lightly. "Come on out and Bruce can show you the plan he drew

up for me—er, us—last night!" Faith's expression hardened. "This is clearly the way forward, Janet. If you don't see that now, surely you will by the time the project is complete."

Janet's hands flew to her hips and she opened her mouth, but before words could come out, William walked into the Spot.

"What's going on out there?"

Faith smiled brightly at her ex. "I'm helping Janet to really own the outdoor eating scene in Knoxville. By the time Bruce is done..." She turned back toward Janet and said, nonchalantly, "... which, by the way, hon, today is demo day, but then his crew can't come back for a few weeks for the building part. I told him that would be just fine, and ultimately, this schedule will get us across the finish line just a bit earlier." She smiled and looked up through her lashes at William. "And you should see what Bruce came up with, William. Really gorgeous stuff out there."

As Janet fought off the temper tantrum that was building in the base of her stomach, Faith asked William, "What are you doing here, anyway? I thought you had plans with Connie."

"I was supposed to, but..." He fiddled with the top button of his shirt, then blew out a sigh. "Well, she's stopped returning my calls."

"Oh." Faith turned away, so only Janet could see her smile. "Well, I'm awful sorry to hear that, William."

He grimaced. "I'm sure you are."

"What were you supposed to do, anyway?" She'd recovered control of her expression and faced her ex-husband, looking appropriately disappointed for him.

"She's been wanting to try a hike down at High Ground Park."

Faith couldn't stop herself from asking, "Since when do you hike?"

William flinched, and the ensuing pause was so long that Janet looked up, distracted from her bad mood.

"Janet, will you excuse us?"

Faith scoffed. "We do not need to discuss my reaction to your girlfriend, William. If you don't want to see me smirk, then don't bring that woman's name up in front of me."

William stepped closer. "It's not that. I–I got a phone call, and I thought you and I should discuss it."

Faith sucked in a quick breath. "Is everything okay?"

"I'm not sure. That's why I thought we should talk."

Faith froze, only her eyelids blinking repeatedly. After a long moment, she wiped her palms on the seat of her pants and led the way to the corner booth without a word.

When they were both seated, they turned to stare at Janet. Suddenly she felt like an intruder in her own bar.

"I...I guess I'll go talk to Bruce."

"Ask him to show you the finished plans. It's going to be gorgeous, Janet!" Faith did her best to recapture her earlier haughtiness, but Janet thought her voice sounded thin and worried.

As she walked to the door, and before the rising construction noise hammered too far into her brain, she turned back to look at Jason's parents, now huddled in the corner booth, heads together. What were they up to? And where was Jason when she needed him? These were *his* parents causing her trouble, and he was missing in action again.

She looked down when her phone chirped. It was a text from Quizz.

Where are you? You need hours this week.

She brightened marginally. She'd much rather go to Quizz's office than go over construction plans. She waved off Bruce's attempt to call her over and instead headed for her car. What better way to take out her angst over her boyfriend's mother than doing some legitimate investigative work?

CHAPTER THIRTEEN

"Okay, so now the question becomes, what are you going to do about it?" Quizz's heels plunked down on her desk and she assessed her apprentice over the rim of her glasses.

Janet tilted her head to the side and squinted at the printout in her hand. "I guess I need to go to the cafe where the bogus charge was made?"

Quizz nodded. "Exactly. Ask the clerk there if they'd recognize the person who used the stolen card. Thankfully the perp was dumb. They made a huge order from a small shop. They'll be more likely to remember who made the charge than if they'd just bought a coffee and a muffin."

Janet tucked the papers into her bag and headed to the door when Quizz spoke again. "I wasn't expecting you to come right in —I thought you were working today at the Spot?"

"I needed to escape." Quizz pushed her glasses up her nose and stared. Janet sighed and added, "Jason's mother is trying to take over my business."

Quizz's rueful smile turned mischievous. "I know the feeling. What's the latest on the missing girl?"

Janet filled her boss in on the cell phone and the picture. Quizz whistled low. "What did the mom say?"

"Nothing yet. I'm going to wait to tell her until after I head to that hangout spot Friday night. I'm hoping I can get some information from the kids on the boyfriend."

Quizz nodded. "All right. Well, good luck at the coffee shop. Don't forget, identity theft cases pay the bills! Call if you run into any problems."

Janet left the office with a promise to do just that.

The coffee shop was small, tucked away in an alley between store fronts, but Janet found it easily enough. Inside, several dozen potted plants softened the exposed brickwork. Some crept up from the floor and countertops, others twined down in spirals from hanging pots.

The clerk on duty, Amber, had a short, perky pixie haircut, and she was cheerfully unhelpful; over-large brown eyes exuded disappointment through her cat-eye glasses at not having the right answers to Janet's questions.

"I really am sorry, but like I said, I just started working here last week. I can call Brenda? To see if she remembers that order? But I don't know if she would, all these weeks later. You know what I mean? We take a lot of orders every day. Lattes and americanos, flat whites and everything in between."

Janet grimaced. "Well, I'd assume this order might jog her memory. I mean," she looked down at the fraudulent charge on her client's credit card statement, "how many times does someone order ten gallons of coffee and ten dozen muffins? Do you even have a bakery on site?" She glanced around the small space doubtfully.

"Oh, no!" Amber trilled at the thought. "We get them from

our supplier, Jenny's Bakery. I can't imagine why someone would order that many muffins from us! The markup alone would have bought an extra dozen if they'd gone straight to Jenny's!" She looked up guiltily. "Although of course you can't beat the convenience of having everything you need all in one place."

"Okay. Let's call Brenda." She was done with Amber, and maybe the other employee could shed some light on the case.

Amber shot an apologetic look at Janet when an actual paying customer came in, and Janet stood off to the side, staring broodingly at her phone. Jason was out of town working on his new client's enormous caseload but had assured Janet that he'd hired someone to help him out. It was a local computer security expert, Mike, who'd luckily been able to start immediately.

Jason said he'd be swamped for a few more days while he got Mike up to speed on the project, but after that, he promised to help out at home more—and keep his parents in line.

Janet wasn't sure that would happen, but she'd be glad to have the chance to actually see him on a regular basis. She dismissed a text from Cindy Lou (*Crisis at the Spot. Need you here now*) and dialed his phone. The call went straight to voicemail again, in a way that meant he'd either declined the call or had his phone turned off.

She sighed, thinking about yet another crisis at her bar, and turned to look around the coffee shop while Amber's customer made the apparently agonizing decision of whether to get an iced coffee or a hot one.

"Are you muttering?" A woman stood at her elbow, one eyebrow raised.

Janet cleared her throat. "I might have been." She stepped farther aside. "You go ahead—I'm not waiting to order."

"I work here—so if you're not waiting to order, what are you doing?"

Janet stepped back and assessed the newcomer. "Are you Brenda?"

She nodded.

"Super. I'm with Bexley and Associates," she handed over a business card, "and we're looking into a credit card theft case for a client."

"Are you a PI?" Brenda asked.

Janet nodded. "Mostly. I'm hoping you might remember the person who charged a large order just last week. Several dozen muffins and gallons of coffee."

Brenda assessed her through narrowed eyes. "What do you mean, 'mostly'?"

Janet snuck a look at Amber, thoughtfully answering a question about the different kinds of nut milks available, and realized she missed her blankness. "It means my associate just handed me this case this morning, and now I'm trying to get to the bottom of who stole money from my client's account. Does the order ring any bells for you?"

Brenda's narrowed eyes relaxed and she nodded. "Sure. He's actually become quite a regular. He usually sits right at that table by the window."

Janet looked over, but the seat was empty. "When did you last see him?"

The new barista's lips scrunched together and she looked down at the floor. "Hmm...maybe last week? I know he hasn't been in this week yet, because I started upping our muffin order with him as a regular customer, and I just had to throw a bunch away yesterday." She bit her lip and looked up. "I feel terrible about this, but I knew he wasn't Karla. He said Karla was his wife, and the card never got declined, so I honestly didn't think anything of it."

Janet stepped closer, ready to take advantage of Brenda's

chatty, informative nature. "So who was he? Did you ever get a name?"

"Sure..." She grimaced. "Why are the handsome guys always thieves or cheaters? Ugh." She shook her head and squared her shoulders. "His wallet fell out of his back pocket right after he started coming in and I saw his driver's license. Not Karla. That's when he told me about his sick wife." She shook her head again angrily. "The ID said William Brooks. Do you need me to file a police report or anything?"

Janet stared at the other woman like she'd just started speaking a new language. "Did you say William Brooks?"

"Uh-huh. Real handsome, tall. I could probably help a forensics sketch artist come up with a pretty good mug shot—"

"That won't be necessary, thank you." Janet backed away. "I'll be in touch if I need anything else." She walked numbly out of the shop into the cool shaded alleyway and caught her breath. There could absolutely be another William Brooks. But tall and handsome...and named William Brooks? She cringed. Why was Jason's father stealing credit cards and using them to drink coffee and eat muffins? And what in the hell was she supposed to do with this information? Call the cops on her own semi-permanent house guest?

"Jason," she growled, and dug her phone out of her bag again and tapped his name when it came up on her screen. "If you don't answer this time, I will personally see to it that—"

"Janet! How are you, darlin'?"

"You're there!" she said, so shocked that he'd finally answered the phone that she forgot her anger for a moment.

"I know, I'm sorry it's been so crazy—again—but Mike is almost up to full speed, and then we'll really be cooking with gas. This job is bigger than they thought—"

"Jason, wait." She filled him in on the stolen card and then waited through a long pause on the other end of the line.

"Can you give me a bit to figure things out?"

She bowed her head and breathed out a quiet sigh. "Will you talk to him? I don't want to get in the middle of this, but Jason, maybe he's not doing so well with the divorce and he's just acting out?"

"Maybe."

"Or, and I don't want to pry into his business, but he's gotta be in financial straits. I mean, divorce is expensive, and he bought that stinker of a boathouse that he can't even live in until spring, but I'm sure he's already paying on it—"

"I said I'll take care of it, okay?" Jason snapped.

She bit her lip and stared at a seam in the sidewalk. This was uncharted territory, and she didn't want to overreact, but...

Jason sighed. "I'm sorry. This is just a stressful time. I promise, I'll look into it. I—I've got to go."

Before she could answer—or reply at all—he disconnected. She slipped the phone into her pocket and marched toward her car, when her phone buzzed against her butt. She grabbed it and tapped the screen without looking. "It's okay—I'm stressed, too, okay?"

"What are you talking about?"

Not Jason. She pulled the phone down and frowned. "O'Dell, sorry, I—I thought you were someone else."

The detective's voice was clipped, short, when he spoke again. "We've got another missing girl. Smith wanted me to call you and let you know."

Janet's eyes snapped up and scanned the street, as if she might see the girl if she looked fast enough. "Does she think it's related to Lola?"

"Yes."

O'Dell's single-word answer sent chills up Janet's spine. "What do you need me to do?"

"Just hang tight. I'll be at the Spot in ten minutes."

Janet dropped her phone into her bag and hustled to her car, wiping beads of sweat from her brow even as she smiled. If O'Dell wasn't *already* at the Spot, then at least for once, the crisis at her bar that Cindy Lou had texted about earlier had nothing to do with police.

CHAPTER FOURTEEN

When Janet pulled up to the Spot, the situation outside had taken a surprising turn for the worse. Not only was half the lot inaccessible due to the large construction vehicles and the workers, but an overflow of cars crammed into the other half. It was only one in the afternoon—way too early to be so overrun with customers.

She wedged her beat-up car into a non-spot so close to the excavator that if the construction vehicle moved even an inch it would demolish her ride.

Good riddance, she thought, glaring at the setup. Bruce probably had enough insurance to rebuild her entire bar if things went wrong.

She approached the building and counted fifteen people waiting listlessly in a line that bloomed out from the front door.

"They're not ready to start yet," a voice called from the back of the line.

Janet's head swung around. A scrawny guy glared back at her as she walked into her bar.

"Why are those people waiting outside?" Her eyes swept the

room. William was gone, but Cindy Lou and Faith were there, along with one customer. "Why is everyone waiting outside? Are we open or not?"

Cindy Lou adjusted her bra strap and avoided eye contact, only lifting one shoulder and dropping it back down.

Janet lowered her voice as she got closer to her assistant manager. "What's going on?"

Cindy Lou raised her chin toward the corner booth. Faith clutched a clipboard and seemed to be taking notes as the man across from her spoke in fits and spurts. She strained to hear the conversation and then narrowed her eyes when she caught a stilted recital of the man's work history.

"What is she doing now?"

"Interviewing," Cindy Lee muttered out of barely opened lips.

"Interviewing who?" Janet's voice was loud. And when Faith and the stranger looked over, she spoke louder yet. "Who are you interviewing, Faith?"

Faith and the stranger locked eyes for a moment, then stood and shook hands. He left, and Faith looked longingly after him before sucking in a deep breath and heading toward Janet.

"I'm interviewing for the new cook position, of course." Faith looked up at Janet with wide, innocent eyes.

"Whose cook?" Janet crossed her arms over her chest and narrowed her eyes. But it was lost on Faith, who was happily checking off lines on her clipboard.

"For your cook. I know *you* don't want the job, based on what Jason and William say happens in your own kitchen. Am I right?" Faith looked up at the sound of Cindy Lou stifling a gasp. "What? Am I wrong?"

"Faith, while I appreciate..." Janet tapped her foot and tried to unclench her jaw, but she couldn't think of a single thing she appreciated about Jason's mother just then.

Faith grinned victoriously. "This shouldn't take me but a day, Janet. I've got a whole process set up here. Got some great candidates from the ad I posted online. We should have somebody up and ready to start by the first of the month."

Cindy Lou jabbed Janet in the side with her elbow. It was just what Janet needed to snap out of her shock at Faith's complete lack of boundaries.

"This is completely unnecessary."

"I know, but you don't have to thank me, Janet. I've been doing this for a lot longer than you have, and I know—"

"You misunderstand me, Faith. This is completely unnecessary because I have already hired a chef."

"A *chef*?" Cindy Lou asked, the surprise in her voice colored with awe.

"That's right." Janet nodded slowly, the idea taking shape with every passing second. "I—I've already hired a chef. And he'll be ready to start in the food truck as early as tomorrow." Janet nodded and uncrossed her arms, but her fingers wouldn't stop fidgeting as she wondered how she was going to make her last statement true. "And that should bring us into compliance, at least with serving food, with plenty of time to spare, while I figure out what to do about our parking lot."

Faith's shoulders slumped before she straightened her back and dropped the clipboard down to her side. "I had no idea. I wouldn't have gone to all this trouble—"

"Yes, please don't...ah, go to this trouble again without checking in with me first."

Faith stepped back as if Janet had pushed her, and after a long moment, she tucked the clipboard into her bag.

"Well, I guess I'll let you tell everyone outside there's not a job. Boy, will they be disappointed! I better go check in with Bruce. He might need my help with decisions outside."

Janet and Cindy Lou watched silently as Faith headed out

the back door into the alley. For the few seconds the door was open the sound of jackhammers filled the air, then muted again when the door closed.

"So. Who are you going to hire?" Cindy Lou asked, a sly smile on her face.

"I guess I'm gonna run outside while Faith isn't looking and ask those job applicants who can start work tomorrow."

"It's okay to let her do this for you. Gives her something to do, keeps her out of your hair at home...I don't know, it sounds like a win-win to me."

Janet shook her head. "That woman has no boundaries. If I don't shut her down now, who knows where it'll end."

Cindy Lou shrugged and went back to prepping the bar. At the same time, Janet crept to the front door and peered through the glass until she spotted Faith. When the other woman walked around the back of the building with Bruce, Janet ducked outside and called the remaining job applicants over.

"Thank you all so much for coming on what I can only imagine was short notice—"

"I saw this job posting last week! What do you mean, short notice?" It was the same scrawny man who'd yelled at Janet when she'd walked in her own bar just minutes earlier. Janet frowned but was glad for the information. It was good to know that Faith had been planning to hire a cook for Janet for a week, long before she got to Knoxville—and long before she presented Bruce Hobak's services as a win-win. That woman was a schemer, and Janet would have to keep close tabs on her for the remainder of her time in Knoxville.

She cleared her throat and addressed the group in front of her. "My name is Janet Black and I am the owner of the Spot. Who is available to start tomorrow?"

Amidst the general grumbling, the scrawny man from before said, "The ad said the job would start on the first of the month! I wouldn't have wasted all this time coming out here to this crappy part of town if I'd have known tomorrow was the start date." As many turned to leave, one man slowly raised his hand.

"I can start today, if you need me to."

"It wouldn't be until next week. I was just weeding out the applicants." Janet frowned, not realizing she'd weed them out so thoroughly with one question. "What's your name?"

"Cameron."

"Well, Cameron, call me at this number in twenty minutes. I can't talk to you now." She looked over her shoulder and saw that Faith and Bruce were still out of sight behind the building. "I want to ask you a few questions before I make this job offer official."

Cameron's brow wrinkled and he looked around uncertainly. "Can we just do that now?"

"I'm sorry, we can't. It's complicated, but if you'd like the job, call me in twenty minutes."

She watched him walk away, wondering what else Faith might have set into motion from Memphis. But she didn't have long to think, because as Cameron drove away, O'Dell's car pulled into the lot.

CHAPTER FIFTEEN

O'Dell stared across the bar—but not quite at Janet. More like at her shoulder. He refused to make eye contact. "Are you seriously telling me that you don't care that Lola's best friend has been missing since last night?"

Janet pursed her lips and stared back, willing O'Dell to meet her eye. He didn't. "I'm telling you that Amanda Rhodes's parents haven't hired me to look into her disappearance. What's Smith doing, anyway? Why are you working this case?"

"Everyone steps up for a missing kid, Janet. We're not all so heartless."

She blew out a sigh. "I'm not heartless! I just have a full plate. I haven't even really dug into the Lola Bridges case yet—a fact that Quizz won't let me forget. And I'm up to my ears in staffing issues here, plus a new state investigation! I mean, if we all stick to our own jobs, we'll be much happier in the long run."

O'Dell stuffed his hands into his pockets and frowned. "I just never thought I'd wonder what kind of person you were. Huh." He shook his head as he backed away from the bar, then nodded tersely at Mel—who'd just arrived for her shift—and Cindy Lou. "Ladies."

Janet groaned. "Dammit, O'Dell! I'm not heartless. I just don't have time to do Smith's job. And you shouldn't be doing it, either!" she called.

His step slowed and he glanced back at her. "Come on, Janet. Help a guy out, huh?" His wheedling tone was so unexpected that a grin spread across her face.

She laughed, although, based on how Cindy Lou's nose wrinkled, it might have sounded more like a giggle. The thought brought her up short and the smile vanished from her face. "Why do you think I'll be able to help, anyway, O'Dell?"

"You can speak their language. I'm a cop—they'll go running from me. Smith, too. But you? You're like their cool older sister. I mean, you own a bar—you can get alcohol whenever you want. That's some serious credibility in their eyes. I want to use you shamelessly to get some intel on Amanda. These first few hours can be really important in finding someone—young girls especially." All the humor left his face. "You hope it's their choice to be out of communication, but that's not always the case. In fact, it's *often not* the case."

A knot of genuine concern balled up in her stomach.

Cindy Lou nudged her in the side. "I can handle things 'til you get back, boss. Get outta here. Go find that girl."

Janet tucked her ID into her back pocket and tossed the rest of her purse on a shelf under the bar. "Fine. Let's go, O'Dell—but you owe me."

Their fingers brushed when they both reached for the door at the same time. He cleared his throat and motioned that she should go first. "I'm pretty sure you still owe me from over a year of investigations here, but sure. I owe you."

"I met her."

O'Dell looked over, his eyebrows drawn together.

"Amanda. I met her out at the high school, asked her about Lola. She seemed genuinely confused about where Lola could be. Also made it sound like the boyfriend was no good."

"What'd she say?"

"Just that she'd never met him, but didn't like how Lola described him." She shrugged. "Not much to go on, huh?"

O'Dell shook his head.

"So what happened?"

"Parents said they last heard from her yesterday morning, when she left for school. She sent a text at the end of the day like usual. Nothing seemed out of the ordinary, but she wasn't home when her mom returned from work. Mom went through her room and noticed that her overnight bag was gone—and her school backpack hung in the closet instead. So she definitely planned to go somewhere."

"Boyfriend?"

O'Dell flicked on the turn signal and headed north through town. "Uh-huh. He's from another school, and his parents haven't seen him since yesterday, either."

"Oohhh." Janet nodded knowingly. "So they're together somewhere...planning their future? Ugh. Kids are so dumb."

"No—they're naive. Big difference."

A billboard advertising the zoo, just a mile ahead, touted their new cage-free enclosures. For some reason the sign made her think of Jason's father. Did he feel caged in after the divorce? Trapped? They passed the beautifully manicured zoo entrance, with tall, yellowed grasses swaying in the late afternoon breeze. It would be terrible to feel that way...but breaking the law? Doing what basically amounted to petty theft for free coffee and muffins? She pressed her forehead against the window, her eyes glazed, barely seeing what they passed as she wondered when Jason planned to talk to his dad. Or if.

"Hey—you still there?"

She blinked back to the car. O'Dell's hand rested just inches from her thigh, as if he'd reached out to tap her and thought better of it at the last minute.

"Oh, sorry. Just thinking."

"When you answered the phone earlier, you said 'It's okay. I was stressed, too.' Are things okay?"

She looked away from O'Dell out the window again. He was always so observant when it came to her. It was nice...and also stifling.

O'Dell took the on ramp onto 40 East, and she turned back to face him. "Where are we going?"

He smiled, recognizing that she wasn't going to answer him. "A friend of Amanda's thinks they might be holed up at a motel in Kodak."

"Then why didn't you just go?"

"You think they're going to open the door to a cop? Never. And I can't go breaking the door down—kids might die of shock. No, you go in, act like housekeeping or something, and talk to them. Get them to come home. Their folks are worried. They probably can't see past tonight, you know?"

"I am not the right person to talk to them about a responsibility to their parents, O'Dell! I wouldn't even know where to begin!" Janet's mother had been dead for years, and she'd only connected with her father recently, after a lifetime of thinking that he'd abandoned her mother when he found out she was pregnant. He'd tracked her down recently and claimed her mother had never even told him she was pregnant.

"Do your best. Pretend it's your kid, Janet. I'm sure something will come."

When the motel loomed large in front of them, she turned to

her partner for the day. "And if I manage to talk sense into these two idiots, what then?"

"Then you bring them out and we take them home."

"No charges?"

"They're minors. We'll let their parents take care of punishment."

Janet thought about that while O'Dell went inside the office to get information from the front desk. He was out a few minutes later with a key and a smile.

"The housekeeping cart is on the second floor. The manager said it's all yours. They're in room 215."

She crossed her arms. "You seem to be enjoying this a little too much. Why isn't Smith here? This case is right up her alley."

"Kids have only been gone fifteen...twenty hours. Not a missing persons case yet. But Mr. Adler asked if I could help. What can I say? I wanted to."

"Mr. Adler? You mean the school principal who wanted to have me arrested? Great. So glad to be doing *him* a favor." She harrumphed but snatched the key from O'Dell and climbed out of the car. "Ridiculous. Housekeeping, my ass. I'm about to walk into two teens boinking each other with nothing more than a cart of towels to cover my eyes."

"Do your best, Janet. Talk some sense into them."

She huffed up the metal staircase to the second floor and swiped the housekeeping cart from the nearest hallway. Since when was she ever the voice of reason? She was just as likely to be the one gallivanting off with her boyfriend under her mother's disapproving glare as the one trying to end a secret tryst.

Nevertheless, she reached out and knocked on the door to room 215. A muffled giggle was followed by a warbly voice saying, "No—no thank you. We're good."

She pinched her lips together and knocked louder this time. "Open up," she snarled, then cleared her throat and tried to lighten her voice. "Uh, building maintenance here. There's a problem with the uh...plumbing in the bathroom. Should just take a minute." She inserted the key into the lock and entered the room.

The drapes were drawn, the room dark. "Amanda? I have a message from your mom. Can I talk to you for a minute?"

CHAPTER SIXTEEN

At a red light, Amanda caught Janet's eye from the backseat through the rearview mirror. "Would you say my mom is super pissed, or more like...super worried?"

Janet looked to O'Dell to answer. He shifted sideways with a frown. "Did you hear your boyfriend's dad?"

Amanda swallowed hard and nodded. "Uh-huh. He was really angry."

"Right." O'Dell faced front again when the light turned green and eased off the brake. "I think your mom is going to be more worried."

Amanda pressed her forehead against the window. "I'm sure the anger will come later."

Janet snorted. "Well, I mean, you did leave your mother's house to get laid, without having the courtesy to leave a note, call, let her know you were safe, and now you have the *gall* to complain that she might be angry? Uh...yeah! She's pissed. Of course she is."

"Janet," O'Dell admonished, and reached out to touch her leg.

She smacked his hand away. "O'Dell! I'm serious. Can this girl try and put herself in her mother's shoes?" She craned her neck around to look at Amanda. "Imagine that *you're* at home after school one day, and your mom never comes home from work. No call, no note, nothing—just a complete no show. Would you be able to fall asleep, not knowing what had happened to her?"

Amanda closed her eyes and her bottom lip trembled, but Janet didn't let up. "Or maybe you'd call the cops? Her friends? Maybe you'd start with her boss, to ask if she knew what happened?" Janet's face felt hot and her voice was too loud, but she couldn't rein in her emotions as she rounded on the teen in the backseat. "Would you try the hospitals to see if they had any accident victims? Call the highway patrol for the same reason?"

Unshed tears shimmered in the teenager's eyes when she opened them, and O'Dell shot Janet a look. "What? You told me to act like she's my kid. And now suddenly I'm pissed!" O'Dell stared ahead and she shrugged. "I'm just saying, she better go in there groveling for forgiveness."

Janet wrinkled her nose, Amanda continued to stare out the window, and O'Dell looked at her like she'd lost her mind. She squared her shoulders and caught Amanda's eye through the mirror. "Don't do drugs."

"Huh?" Amanda's wide eyes stared at her blankly from the backseat.

O'Dell snickered and she glared at him. "Isn't that just always good, solid advice?"

They pulled up to Amanda's house and the teen tried to shoot out of the car, but there weren't any handles in the back and she groaned and threw herself against the seat. "Can *she* stay in the car, please?"

O'Dell hid a chuckle behind a cough. "No, we'll both escort you inside, in case your mom has any questions."

His shoulders shook with unaired laughter and Janet ignored him completely as she stood and opened the back door.

Amanda climbed out of the car and made to move past Janet, then stopped and searched her eyes. "She was lonely. Like, really, terribly lonely."

"Who?"

"Lola. You asked me back at school the other day if there was anything I wanted to tell you that might help bring her home. Her mom just started dating that loser Paul, and wasn't spending any time with her. And I...well, I guess I abandoned her at the same time with my new boyfriend. I didn't mean to, it just—it happened." She looked over her shoulder when O'Dell cleared his throat. "Anyway. I just wanted you to know that. She might have decided to leave because there wasn't anything keeping her here, you know?"

Amanda sniffled loudly and then squared her shoulders and walked stiffly up the front walk.

The front door flew open and an unexpected figure ran onto the porch and down the steps.

"Mrs. Bridges?" Amanda said.

Lola's mother hugged her. "Oh, Amanda! We've been so worried!" Her eyes darted behind her to the cop car parked on the street. "Is—we thought that you might not be alone..." She dropped her arms down to her sides. "Was Lola with you, too? You can tell me. I won't be mad at her, I promise!"

Amanda's face fell, and she stammered down at the sidewalk. "I'm sorry, Mrs. Bridges. I don't know where Lola is."

Misty covered her mouth with her hand, her eyes bright, and nodded rapidly. "Of course not, dear, I don't know what I was thinking. Get in the house, your mother's been sick with worry."

Amanda glanced at Janet one last time and then walked with heavy steps up to the porch. O'Dell followed. Before they disappeared inside, a woman cried out, "Mandy! Oh, thank God!"

The circle of light that cut across the dark night shrunk to a mere sliver before disappearing completely as the front door swung closed.

Suddenly, Janet found herself alone with Misty, both women teetering on the edge of an emotional breakdown.

"I thought—I-I hoped that Lola might be with her. Maybe they'd planned just to get away for a few days. You know how kids are—they like to do things in groups, and I...I guess..." She shook her head violently and crossed her arms over her chest, as if physically holding herself together. When she looked at Janet again, her face was closed off, hopeless. Her eyes shifted to something behind Janet as she said, "No news, then?"

Janet shook her head. "I'm going to the Annex Friday night." She tried to clear the emotion out of her creaky voice with a cough. "Amanda thinks that Matt, the guy Lola might have been dating, hangs out there. I thought we're more likely to get some answers on their turf, you know? Away from school."

Misty stepped closer to Janet and reached out to touch her arm. "Are you okay, dear?"

"Of course—yes, I just...thinking about you and Amanda's mother...it just—I'm fine."

Misty's lips pressed together and her breath stuttered in. "You'll keep us posted?"

"Of course. I'll call you as soon as I find out anything new."

Lola's mother nodded again and walked past Janet down the walk to a car parked across the street. Janet watched her drive away, filled with a new resolve to bring Lola home.

"What happened back there?" An hour later, O'Dell put the car in park and turned to face her; the overhead lights in the parking lot of the Spot cast a yellow glow on the lower half of his face.

"What do you mean?" Janet studied her folded hands, resting on her lap.

"Well...you got pretty animated with Amanda."

"Uh-huh."

"So...who did you lose?"

She leaned against the head rest and blew out a sigh. "I bounced around a lot after high school, and a few years ago, I'd moved back in with my mom. We kept out of each other's way, mostly. But one night she didn't come home from work. I found out later that she'd had a heart attack while driving home." She turned to look at the front door of the Spot. "It took days to find her. The car went into a ditch—it was completely covered by overgrown scrub brush. They were..." Her breath caught and she sniffed loudly. "They were long days."

O'Dell reached out and placed his hand on hers. "I'm sorry, Janet. That must have been very difficult."

Her nose tingled and her eyes felt full from unshed tears. "God, this was years ago, but something about tonight just brought it all back for me. To do that to someone on purpose? No one should have to lay in bed at night wondering where her family is."

"You helped bring Amanda home." O'Dell squeezed her hand. "And hopefully we'll do the same for Lola."

She frowned—she hadn't managed to do anything for Lola's mother yet.

"Do you want me to walk you in?"

She moved her hand from under O'Dell's and shook her head. "I'm fine. Good night, O'Dell."

He sighed and leaned away. "Good night, Janet."

CHAPTER SEVENTEEN

"I feel like we all should've had a say in this hire." Cindy Lou's big blue eyes looked at Janet reproachfully as she signed for a delivery at the cash register. Several days had passed since Janet had returned Amanda to her house.

The bar had been open for an hour, but it was still early, and no customers were there—although that was perhaps due to the raucous noise from the construction crew outside.

Now that Bruce Hobak's employees had finished digging up the area of the parking lot where the covered eating area would go, a dozen workers gathered to assemble the framework for the pergola addition. Hammers, both manual and powered by batteries, were going non-stop.

"I mean, it's like adding a member of the family. Don't you want to know what we think about him?" Cindy Lou opened a pair of scissors and sliced open the tape holding the cardboard box closed, then lifted out another box, heavy by the way she moved.

"What's that?"

"I think..." She opened the interior box and squealed. "Yes! I

thought so!" She grinned and lifted out a bright red fire extinguisher and added, "I got two! One for each exterior door!"

Janet rubbed her temples and took a deep breath, then
poured herself a vodka. She picked up the soda wand, but when
two pneumonic hammers hit at the same time, she placed the
wand back in its cradle, opting for a lime wedge instead.

Cindy Lou walked the larger extinguisher out and set it down
by Mel's usual seat by the door, then came back and eyed the
back door doubtfully. "I'm not sure where to put this one. It
doesn't look like there's room to hang it because of the juke box."

"Let's just put it under here for now," Janet said, shoving the
bright red canister under the bar. "And thanks. I'd forgotten all
about what Bruce said."

"Luckily you've got me, lurking in the background taking
notes." Cindy Lou grinned. "So...about Cameron..."

Janet smirked. "I know we are a small staff, but I really think
he's going to fit in with everyone here."

Mel stopped taking chairs off a table nearby and turned.
"Where did you find him again?"

Faith turned the page of her newspaper loudly and didn't
look up, but Janet could almost see her ears tuning in to the
conversation from a few seats away.

Janet bit her lip, unwilling to admit that she'd hired him from
Faith's pool of potential employees from a few days earlier. She
squared her shoulders and got up from her stool. "What's important is that he'll be here any minute. And I want us to welcome
him into the Spot family."

"The Spot family?" Cindy Lou tilted her head to the side. "I
like that."

A jingle caught everyone's attention. Amidst the chaos in the
parking lot when she'd first met Cameron, Janet hadn't really
taken stock of her new employee. So the man who walked into
the bar was shorter than she'd remembered, barely five-foot-six,

and had stocky, wide shoulders and slim hips. His white blond hair caught the light just as the door swung closed behind him and when Janet stepped forward, she saw Cindy Lou looking longingly at his naturally pale hair.

"Cameron, nice to see you. I'd like you to meet a couple of your coworkers. This is Cindy Lou, my assistant manager," the two nodded at each other, "and this is Mel. She works the door for us on busy nights, and sometimes helps out at the bar when we're in a pinch."

"She's your bouncer?"

As Cameron assessed Mel critically, the bouncer leaned forward and rested her chin on top of her hands, which were folded on top of the mop handle.

A short stand-off between the two followed, which finally ended when Mel pushed the mop roughly around the floor without taking her eyes off of the new cook. "I could bounce you or anyone else out of here whenever I want. Don't you forget it." Her eyes narrowed and she stared at Cameron until he looked uncomfortably away.

Janet forced a laugh. "We've got a real nice crew here, Cameron. I can't wait for you to get to know everyone." She shot a look at Mel, who only pursed her lips in response, and pushed Cameron back the same way he'd just walked through the bar.

"I didn't mean to—"

"Never mind. She'll be fine."

"I've just never heard of a girl bouncer."

"She's *a woman*, and I said I understand. But I'd say it's time for you to open your mind."

Cameron looked taken aback, but Janet straightened her back and continued to guide Cameron out the door. This was her first hire in ages, and she was hanging a lot on it being successful.

"Here it is." She gestured grandly to the food truck. The new layer of red paint didn't entirely cover the old logo, the letters for

Timmy's Taco Truck still raised slightly against the rest of the panel. "What you think?"

"I guess I'm wondering where Timmy is?" Cameron scratched his forehead and his eyes settled on a rusty spot of the frame by the front tire.

"You and me both. It's my truck now, and you mentioned on the phone you are familiar with fry baskets. I think that's all the expertise we need for this job. Let's head in and check out the set up."

She pulled out her keyring and unlocked the back door to the truck, then motioned that Cameron should go first.

Janet climbed up three steep steps to get into the truck and immediately crossed the small space inside and forced open the service window. Every surface, even the floor, was made of stainless steel. Cool air drifted into the small interior, and dust motes danced in the early afternoon sun.

Cameron drew a fingertip across the closest counter. "Pretty dirty."

"And that's why I'm giving you a few days to clean the inside, test everything out, and let me know what I'll need to purchase to get things up and running by Saturday. That's going to be our grand opening of the restaurant."

"What's it going to be called?"

"What?"

"Are you renaming the place now that you'll be serving food?"

"Huh." Janet leaned back against the nearest countertop, stumped. "I hadn't thought about it." She tried to shift, but her back pocket was now attached, via some unknown sticky splotch, to the counter. She twisted her hips to break the seal, then ripped a paper towel square from the roll hanging behind her and draped it over the sticky spot. When she looked back up

Cameron was eyeing the door like it was an escape hatch. "You got something in mind?"

"Sure. Cameron's Canteen."

Her brow wrinkled and she tried to come up with a diplomatic way to say, "Who the hell do you think you are?" Before new words came, a sly grin lit up his face.

She chuckled. "If we make any changes, it'd be something like Janet's Joint." He ducked his head and she led the way out of the truck. "Come on. You'll need to fill out some forms and then you can get to work. I have a bunch of cleaning supplies left over from a situation with the Beerador a while ago. You can start with those." She led the way through the bar and into the office and pointed at a bank of small lockers on the wall adjacent to the door.

"The locker on the top left is open. That's where you can put your stuff when you get to work every day. We have a strict no-phones policy when you're on the clock. I'm not paying you to play games or text with friends. If you don't have food to cook, there's always going to be something that needs cleaning. If you can't find something to do, I'm more than happy to give you a job."

Cameron nodded, then took the seat Janet motioned to and picked the pen up from the desk. "Come on out when you're done and we'll get you set up out there."

She let the door close with a bang and sidled up to Cindy Lou. "Well?"

"Well, what? You hardly let us say two words to the man before you ushered him to safety."

"I thought Mel was going to break him in half."

"Could have if I wanted to!" the bouncer called from across the room.

"Well, don't! We need him."

Cindy Lou leaned in toward Janet and lowered her voice. "That woman has ears like a damn moth!"

"A moth? Don't you mean a bat?"

"That'd be like saying someone is as strong as an ox."

"What's wrong with that? Ox are strong, right?"

"An ox is the third strongest living animal. You should say strong as a gorilla."

"Right again!" Mel called with a grin.

Janet shook her head, then looked around the space, still empty of customers. "Where's Faith?"

"Oh, she left in a huff about five minutes ago. Muttered something about all her hard work not being appreciated anywhere she goes." Cindy Lou popped one fist on her hip and shook her head. "You'd think she might take the hint, but I'm guessing she's gonna keep right on 'working hard' for you, hon."

Janet grimaced. She had no doubt Cindy Lou was right.

"What's this?" Janet picked an envelope with her name on it up off the bar.

Cindy Lou's brow furrowed. "I don't know. I'd swear it wasn't there just a minute ago."

Mel put the mop away and cruised closer. "That lady from the other day dropped it off. Asked for you, but said she couldn't wait."

"Misty Bridges? The missing girl's mother?"

Mel nodded and Janet tore the envelope open. Inside, a new, more recent picture of Lola. This one was a candid shot, with a group of friends in the background.

Amanda sent me this, and I wanted you to have a copy. Today is Lola's birthday. Thanks for all your help bringing my baby girl home.

A sliver of guilt slid down Janet's throat, making it hard to swallow. She hadn't done much since Misty had hired her. But that would change tonight at the Annex. Janet's plan took shape in her head.

"Mel, can you show Cameron where the cleaning supplies are? Tell him to take a few hours today to scrub out the truck, and then have him write out a list of supplies he'll need. I can pick everything up tomorrow morning."

"No problem, Janet." Mel rubbed her hands together in a way that made Janet worry for Cameron.

"Go easy on him, okay?" she admonished, then grabbed her purse from the shelf under the bar. She peered inside the massive bag and made sure Lola's phone was there, then she dug her keys out.

Cindy Lou turned at the jangle of noise. "Where are you going?"

"To the Annex."

Mel planted her elbows on the bar and leaned forward. "Isn't that a high school make-out spot? What, ah...who are you meeting there...and does Jason know?"

Janet smiled without humor. "Not that he'd have time to meet me anywhere lately." She moved out from behind the bar and headed toward the door. "I'm going to find out who Lola's boyfriend is, and see if his friends know where he might be. He and Lola have been gone for too long."

CHAPTER EIGHTEEN

The sun was already setting in the cool late-winter afternoon, but it was still too early to find anyone at an outdoor hangout spot, so Janet made an unscheduled stop by Quizz's office.

Her mentor's feet rested on her desk, and she leaned back in her office chair and looked up with a grin when Janet laid out her evening plans.

"You want to take me to the Annex?" Quizz smiled. "I think at some point you got the wrong idea about me, Janet." She chortled at her own humor, but made no attempt to move from her desk chair. "I don't think so."

Janet leaned against the door jamb. "There's something creepy sounding about a woman in her thirties roaming around Lookout Point alone. But *two* women in their thirties?" She wagged her eyebrows comically. "Totally legitimate, right?"

Quizz picked up a pen and clicked it open and closed a few times while she thought. "You think you'll find this Matt guy there?"

"No, but I think we'll finally find some of his friends, learn more about him—where he lives, what grade he's in, where he hangs out. And all of those facts might help us track him and Lola down."

"Police haven't been able to identify him."

"Right. But what kid's going to talk honestly to police—especially when they think their friend is going to get into trouble? Not many. But we're just a couple of cool chicks." She tried to use O'Dell's logic to make her argument, but Quizz wasn't buying it.

"We're going to stick out like sore thumbs, and someone will probably call the cops on us for even being there."

"No way. No one's supposed to be there. If anything, we'll just ruin the night for some super cool kids who won't feel comfortable smoking their weed or drinking their illegally purchased beer in front of us."

Quizz clicked the pen slower and slower until she stopped altogether. "I hate cool kids."

"Right? They're the worst."

A wide grin stretched across Quizz's face. "Yes," she hissed. "Why didn't you open with that? I'm in. Let's go ruin the night for some cool kids!"

"It's not exactly Lookout Point, is it?" Quizz eyed the ramshackle barn warily. Only the thumping bass to an unknown song made it out to the road where they stood. The rundown structure was lit in the distance by car and truck headlights and a campfire.

"I guess the darkness is part of its charm."

"Just part of it?"

"Hmm, good point. It might be *all* of the charm." A breeze blew across the field and Janet lifted her nose into the air and sniffed. "Well, that and the weed."

They left the car alongside the road, figuring they'd have

better luck approaching the teens on foot. Closer to the barn, figures came into sharper relief, and the familiar tune of an old punk rock song took shape.

"Looks like two groups—you want to split up?" Quizz asked.

"Then we're right back to creepy old single lady wandering amongst the teens."

"Together it is. Follow me." Quizz made her way to a scrawny teen hunched over an open laptop. When he saw them, his eyes darted down to his computer; his fingers snaked out and soon a new song echoed from the speakers.

Quizz cocked her head to the side, listening. "Is that 'Warning' by Green Day?" His double take was comical. "We're not cops, okay? Not here to arrest anyone." Nearby, engines fired, a stampede of people intent on leaving.

"Not cops?" the boy asked, eyeing a set of car keys on the table next to his computer.

Quizz reached out and covered the keys with her hands. "Nope. PIs. Just want to talk. Can you tell your people to abort the exodus?"

He grinned appreciatively, then tapped a button and a different song replaced the last. He produced a microphone from the table and announced, "False alarm. Back to business." Then he looked at the two women. "Don't screw me over, okay?"

Janet sat down on a folding chair across from him. "What's your name?"

"Kyle Bronstal."

"You all go to Holderside High?" He nodded, and she held Lola's picture out. "You know Lola Bridges?"

Kyle leaned in and studied the picture, then shook his head. "Never seen her. She a freshman or something?"

Janet shook her head. "No. She goes to Boulder Ridge, but she's supposed to be dating some kid named Matt from your school."

He shrugged. "Don't know any Matts."

Quizz frowned. "Not police, remember?"

Kyle lifted one shoulder and dropped it. "Fine. There's a Matt in that truck over there—but I'd make some noise as you approach, unless you want to see all of him, you know?"

"Why are you up here all alone?" Janet asked.

He shrugged again. "Lookout. Plus I like to mix the music. It's kind of my thing." He looked up at Janet. "You sure she's not your daughter?" He motioned to the picture with his chin. "She looks just like you."

She pressed her lips together, more offended than she should be that this kid thought that she was old enough to have a seventeen-year-old daughter.

He donned a pair of headphones and turned his attention back to his computer.

Quizz shot Janet a look that said, *you owe me so big,* then led the way to the truck.

Janet was relieved to see that the vehicle was not, in fact, rocking, but she still cleared her throat and coughed as they approached. She tapped on the passenger-side window. "Looking for Matt?"

A girl stared at her without moving.

Quizz had gone around the back of the truck and now knocked on the driver-side window. "Hello!"

The pair sunk down in their seats, trapped, and then both windows lowered automatically.

"Hey, listen, we weren't doing anything wrong, okay, and you can tell my mother that when you drop us off. Don't impound my truck, man. Last time it cost two hundred and fifty dollars to get it back and my dad was supper pissed—"

"We're not cops!" Janet said loud enough that Matt's girlfriend flinched and shrunk away from the window. "We're looking for this girl. Do you know her?"

The girl's eyes narrowed and she crossed her arms over her chest when she looked from the picture of Lola to Matt.

"I don't know her, Wendy, I swear!"

"Unbelievable!"

Janet jumped out of the way when Wendy shoved her door open and stalked toward the circle of light around the barn.

"Thanks a lot," Matt said with a frown.

Quizz wrapped her hands around the window frame and leaned in. "Listen, Matt, I don't have a lot of patience for teen angst. This girl, Lola, is missing. You know anything about her?"

He threw his hands up. "Don't know her! Never even met anyone with the name Lola, okay? God!" He threw himself back against the seat and pulled a face.

Quizz and Janet's eyes locked through the cab of the truck. The kid seemed put out that his girlfriend was pissed, not because of anything to do with Lola.

"Are there any other Matts at your school?"

Matt stared ahead with a pout, but Janet had nowhere else to go. She would happily wait him out. He must have sensed it, because he blew out a loud breath. "I don't know. There are, like, a ton of Matts, aren't there? It's not exactly an uncommon name."

"Any of them dating Lola?"

He shrugged, and Janet lost her temper. She reached into the cab of the truck and picked up a wine bottle. "I'm sorry that we messed up your plan for the night—which I'm guessing included wooing your girlfriend with a swig of Strawberry Hill Boone's Farm straight from the bottle and hoping she forgot about the smell of pig shit in the air so you could get to second base, but we're looking for a missing girl, and her parents are worried. Now, look at this picture and tell me what you might know!"

Matt's cool-guy attitude dropped like a rock and he shrunk away from Janet, a look of defeat on his face. "I'm sorry about this girl, but I don't know her. Ask Kyle. He knows everything about everybody at the school."

She whirled around to look for the DJ, but the table was empty. He was gone.

CHAPTER NINETEEN

Janet bolted down the poorly lit path toward the main road. When the light from the barn had all but disappeared, she caught sight of a hunched figure, moving fast.

"Kyle!" she called. "Kyle, just a few more questions!"

Quizz huffed and puffed behind her, trying to keep pace. "Suddenly you're an Olympic-caliber sprinter?" she muttered.

But the sprint was short-lived, because up ahead, Kyle tripped over a loose rock and fell to the ground, his bag of electronics flying off of the path into the dark mass of unmown pasture grass. He swore colorfully and creatively and when Janet finally reached him, clutching the stitch in her side and gasping for breath, he looked up at her, rocking back and forth on his haunches.

"Do you have a flashlight? Where's your cell phone, dammit? I've got to find my stuff!" He crawled forward on his hands and knees, reaching out blindly for his beloved electronics.

By then Quizz had joined them, loudly hacking as she caught her breath. Janet held her phone up, lighting the closest section of the field. Soon Quizz did the same. After he'd collected his belongings, he stood and clapped dirt off his pants.

"Thanks." Kyle clutched his messenger bag to his chest and took an unsteady breath. "Took me two years working at McDonald's to save up the money for this stuff."

Janet and Quizz kept their cell phone lights trained on the path in front of them, and they took a more leisurely pace to the road.

"Where were you going?" Janet asked when they finally got to the line of cars parked on the shoulder. She followed Kyle to his car, a beat-up Ford Escort, and memorized his license plate in case he ran off again.

"I know you said you weren't the cops, but I'm not really supposed to be out tonight. I don't know, it seemed like as good a time as any to just head home." He unlocked his car and gently set his bag down in the backseat. "Did you find anything out about your girl?"

Janet shook her head. "Matt said that he didn't know her." Kyle made to get into his car, but she held out a hand. "Matt also said that you might know if any of the other Matts at Holderside were dating Lola."

Kyle made a face. "Matt doesn't know shit. Excuse me, but it's true. He's thinking of Kyle Richardson. That dude is always up in everybody's business. I'm the music guy, right? The tech guy. I don't have time to get into everybody's personal relationships. Jesus," he added under his breath, "I'd make time for my own relationship first."

Quizz snorted and Janet had to force the smile off her face as well.

"So you're a tech guy?" She rummaged around in her bag, finally pulling out Lola's cell phone. "My boyfriend's a tech guy, but something struck me as I was out here tonight. We are old, and *old* and *tech* go together about as well as Matt and Wendy, am I right?" Kyle snickered and she continued. "So can you take a look at this phone, tell me if you see anything that Lola's mother and I might have missed?" She punched in the password that Jason had discovered earlier at the bar then handed the unlocked phone over to Kyle. He swiped through the screens, then made an appreciative sound in the back of his throat.

"Yep, here it is." He held the device out so Janet could see the face of it, then pointed to an innocuous-looking app.

"What are you showing me—she liked maps? What does that have to do with anything?"

Kyle shook his head. "It *looks* like a maps app, but this is actually an app of subterfuge. It's like a Snapchat you can hide from parents. Parents are so tech dumb that she probably didn't really even need to have it on her phone, but it's kind of fun."

He tapped the app open and Janet was less than impressed when a familiar-looking directions page filled the screen. She shrugged. "So...what am I looking at, exactly?"

Kyle grinned and nodded. "I don't know, maybe I was wrong. Even when it's open you're not seeing it."

Janet's eyes narrowed and she took the phone from Kyle's outstretched hand and held it close to her face. That's when she saw it. In the upper left corner of the directions page, a small transparent envelope icon faded in and out. "Right here?" She pointed to the icon. He nodded, and she tapped it with her finger. Suddenly the interface of the app changed completely, and a chat session opened with one question:

Continue chat with Matt?

"Bingo," Quizz breathed, reading the screen over her shoulder.

Janet held the phone out like it was a bug. "Argh! What do I do? I don't want Matt to know that I have Lola's phone!"

She slid the phone into Kyle's hands like it was a time bomb. He tapped the screen three times rapidly, then handed it back to her. "Here's their conversation thread." He swiped up and whistled low. "Looks like they'd been talking a lot. Hey, I've really got to go. My mom's going to kill me. I said I was going to work, but McDonald's closed an hour ago."

Quizz thanked him, because Janet's head was bowed over Lola's phone. The screen glowed brightly in the dark night, and Janet scrolled down to read the last few lines between Lola and Matt.

"He asked her to visit him..." She scrolled up. "Looks like a couple of weeks ago. Ugh, he said, 'I can't stand being apart.' Is this guy even in high school?"

"I'm guessing not." Quizz sighed.

"Oh my God, he wants her to get on a Greyhound bus—"

"A Greyhound? To where?" Quizz asked sharply. "I thought Matt went to another school in Knoxville. Is he from another town—another state? Oh, Jesus, this is going to mean informing the FBI if she moved across state lines. I never should have let you take this case—"

"Hold on, hold on..." Janet continued reading the messages until she found the answer. "Memphis. He asked her to meet him at a restaurant in Memphis."

"Well, I guess that's better than a motel. But what are we supposed to do now?"

Janet looked up from the phone and squinted in the sudden darkness until she found Quizz. "I guess we're going to Memphis."

"I don't have time to go to Memphis!"

"Tomorrow. We'll have to leave tomorrow. This can't wait."

CHAPTER TWENTY

"I cannot believe that you talked me into doing this." Quizz shot a disgruntled look at Janet before hiking the strap of her bag over her shoulder. "Our client's sure not going to pay for this. I'm not going to pay for this. So who's going to pay for this? Remind me again?"

"We're going to mark this down as a business expense and you'll get a big fat tax break for the year." Janet turned toward Quizz. "Hey—it'll pay for more advertising!"

"More? What are you talking about? I don't do any advertising. Who's got money for that?"

"Oh—I thought...Hmm." Janet had remembered Misty Bridges saying she'd found Quizz's agency through an ad, but she must be mistaken. She looked up to compare the departure time on the overhead board to the time displayed on the digital ticket on her phone. "Looks like we have forty-five minutes until we board."

"And remind me again why we're not driving?"

"Because then we'd have to get a hotel room and pay for gas

and more meals. I think we'll end up coming out ahead here, especially flying standby like we are."

Quizz's silence was tacit acknowledgement that Janet had found a great price on their tickets. After a moment of silence, she said, "But we'll have to rent a car."

"I got a great deal on a crappy car. We're all set."

"But then we can't split up! And we only have six hours on the ground."

Janet stared at Quizz for a long moment. "Well, you know what they say."

"What?"

"Teamwork makes the dream work."

Quizz chuckled and started walking toward their gate. "Come on, Black. Let's get this over with."

The flight was uneventful and within three hours they were sitting in their rental car while Quizz called up directions on her phone.

A smile ghosted her lips, but she didn't look up when she said, "I can see why you got a steal on this car."

"Turns out they don't give deals on Mercedes or BMWs."

"Guess not. At least it's clean."

The old Chevy Metro was indeed clean, the vacuum tracks still visible on the upholstery in the backseat.

"Can you turn off the heat? I'm starting to sweat."

Janet fiddled with the controls, but all she could do was change the air from hot to cold—there was no way to turn it down from full blast.

"Now we know why it was on sale."

Janet cranked her window down, hoping the cool winter air

might counteract the intense heat blowing from the registers, and put the car into drive. "Which way?"

"Looks like Monahan's, the restaurant where Matt and Lola planned to meet is just northwest of where we are now." Quiz studied the map on her phone and added, "We'll need to go north on 55."

They were quiet as Janet navigated the unfamiliar streets, with Quizz occasionally adding directions to the voice on her phone's map program until they got into the correct neighborhood in South Memphis and started looking for parking.

Quizz turned in her seat to face Janet. "I hate to be blunt—"

"No, you don't."

"But how are we going to get a line on this guy—are we going to ask the other customers if they know a dude with a Hawaii-shaped birthmark near his belly button? I could be wrong here, but we might get the cops called on us. Especially if this guy's a minor." Quizz shivered, despite the heat blowing on them.

"I brought Lola's picture along. I'm hoping we'll get a hit on her before we have to resort to the birthmark." Janet handed a spare picture of the girl to Quizz.

Her mentor grumbled but kept her mouth shut until they climbed out of the car. "I'll work the front of house. You head around back and see who's chatty in the kitchen."

Janet raised her eyebrows, but Quizz didn't look back as she disappeared into the front of the restaurant. Alone outside, Janet gingerly made her way to the alley between buildings and peered around the corner. Though it was daylight, this wasn't the kind of neighborhood she'd usually care to wander through on her own. The smell of day-old grease hung heavy in the air and she stepped over a puddle of questionable liquid as she headed toward the back of the restaurant

A screen door hung crookedly on its frame. Meat sizzled, metal spatulas clanked on the griddle, and Janet stopped to listen to the short bursts of speech that issued from within. "Lucy, order up! Jonesy, order up! Got to get this food 'fore it gets cold, now. Order up, order up!"

Footsteps pounded toward the door, and Janet leapt aside to avoid getting smacked as the screen slammed against the brick wall.

The cook had a cigarette clutched between two fingers in his right hand and a lighter in his other. "Entrance is around front." She nodded but didn't move, and his head tilted to the side. "What are you doing out here?" He stopped just a foot away from Janet and kept an eye on her while he lit his cigarette.

"Getting clogged arteries just by proxy." Janet leaned closer and looked hungrily at the cigarette. She'd quit smoking years earlier, but still loved the smell.

The cook grinned and held the stick out toward Janet. "You need one?"

Janet blew out a slow breath and leaned away. "No. Thanks, though. I'm looking for someone. A girl from Knoxville's gone missing—maybe came here." She reached into her purse and pulled out Lola's picture. "You recognize her?"

"Nope." He took a deep inhale.

"Can you look at the picture before you answer?" Janet stepped closer. "She's only fifteen. Her mom's worried, man."

He took another deep drag, then cut his eyes sideways at Janet as he exhaled. "Fine. Everybody looking for someone lately. Give it here." Janet put the picture in his outstretched hand and watched his eyes as they scanned Lola's face. "Maybe."

Her eyes narrowed and she tried to squash down the flicker of excitement in her gut. "When?"

"I don't know. There was a girl. Maybe a week ago? She mighta been here with Matty—but like I said, I don't know. She was blond, that's about all I could say for sure."

"Matt! Yes. We're looking for him, too. Do you know him?

Last we heard he asked this girl to meet him here, at this restaurant."

The cook blew out a slow breath that had nothing to do with his cigarette. "Shit. He's one weird dude. How old you say she was?"

"She *is* fifteen. How—how old is Matt? Is he in high school?" As soon as the question was out of her mouth she knew the answer was "no." The cook looked to be in his thirties. No way he'd know a high schooler dating another high schooler by name.

"Lola." He rolled the name around in his mouth and then looked over at Janet, a question in his eyes.

"Yes—yes, that's her name. Did you meet her?"

"I don't know, man. A lotta chicks come and go up there, okay?"

"Where? What's Matt's last name?" Janet pulled out a notebook and was still feeling around the bottom of her bag for a pen when the cook smacked his lips.

"I don't know. I mean, I don't hardly know the dude, okay?"

"But you might have seen her? What did they order? You're not going to get in trouble! We just want to bring Lola home. So what's Matt's last name?"

The cook tossed his cigarette down onto the uneven asphalt and ground it out with his heel. "My break's over. They didn't come into the restaurant—at least, not that I know of. I saw them heading up there." He pointed to a rickety fire escape ladder that looked like it hadn't passed a city inspection in decades. "I only know Matt because sometimes we out here taking smoke breaks at the same time. His apartment's up there."

He looked sidelong at Janet again before disappearing back into the kitchen.

Janet texted Quizz, and minutes later the other woman rounded the corner into the alley. "I'm glad you got something.

The hostess couldn't seem to get past my being a PI to actually answer any questions. Do you think Lola's up there?"

"Only one way to find out."

Quizz nodded and followed her to the base of the ladder. "Let's do this."

CHAPTER TWENTY-ONE

The fire escape creaked when Quizz placed her foot on the bottom step and she looked back at Janet with a scowl. "You do not inherit my business if I fall off this ladder and die. You hear me?"

"Loud and clear, boss. You want me to go first?"

"No. I want you to be my soft landing if the metal fails."

Janet started to chuckle, but as she heaved herself onto the ladder behind Quizz, it shuddered and screeched and the laugh died on her lips. "There goes the surprise factor."

Quizz looked up from the steps at the two large windows facing the alley. "I don't think surprise was ever in the cards."

By the time they completed the dangerous journey to the first level of the fire escape balcony, all the blood had drained out of Quizz's face, leaving her pale. She crept closer to the apartment wall and only acknowledged Janet's "You going to knock?" by reaching out with a shaky hand toward the metal fire door.

Janet narrowed her eyes. "Are you scared of heights?"

"Of course not." *Knock, knock, knock.*

The sound was timid, and when nothing happened, she tried

again, pounding loud enough that the cook downstairs stuck his head out of the screen door and yelled, "You tryin' to wake the dead?"

Janet breathed, "God, I hope not."

She took her lock pick set out of her bag and went to work on the doorknob, Quizz barely moving to the side, so that the woman was breathing down her neck. "A little space, please?"

When Quizz didn't move, Janet looked up to see that the other woman's face was still pale, and now a sickly sheen of sweat covered her forehead.

"I'm not scared of heights. I just..." She sighed. "I just don't like it that much. Now move," she snapped. Janet stepped back. "There's a reason I'm called the mentor, and you are called the apprentice." She turned her back on the railing behind and straightened her shoulders, as if leaving her fears behind. She set her oversized shoulder bag down by her feet, unzipped the main compartment, and pulled out a crowbar.

With a splintering crack, they were in. The cook shook his head and scurried back inside the kitchen. Quizz used her elbow to push the door open and Janet peered over her shoulder into the dark room beyond.

"Don't touch anything." Quizz snapped on a pair of gloves and reached into the apartment, feeling along the wall for a light switch.

As soon as she flicked it, a blue-white overhead light illuminated the entire space. Janet took in the entire small efficiency apartment with a glance. What she saw kept her glued to the metal landing outside.

In a low voice, Quizz said, "Oh my God."

Janet's eyes didn't know where to land. The kitchenette took up the back wall; the refrigerator and a foot-long stretch of chipped linoleum countertop led to the undersized two-burner stove. But it was the small lacquered wooden table that left her wide-eyed and unblinking. A stack of old VHS tapes took up half of the table. Three rolls of duct tape were stacked with precision next to them, with two great strips of the silvery tape hanging off the close edge of the table and fluttering in the slight breeze coming through the open door. Several zip ties jutted through the jagged plastic opening of a package, and as Janet finally stepped into the apartment, she couldn't help but wonder to what use the rest of the package had been put.

"Ugh." Quiz pulled her sweatshirt up to cover her nose and mouth. Janet looked down at her useless V-neck, wishing she could do the same. The smell of spoiled milk or meat made her think no one had taken the trash out for days.

"What's this?" Quizz stepped close to the wall leading to the bathroom and passed her gloved hand over what looked like brown paint splatters.

"Paint? Dried blood? I can't tell."

Janet grimaced. Had a crime happened here? She looked down at the duct tape and zip ties as she wondered. That's when the first VHS cover came into focus. She cringed.

"Oh my."

"What?"

She lifted her lock pick up—still gripped tightly in her hand— and used it to tip the top VHS case over, revealing another porn tape underneath. "There must be twenty different movies here."

Quizz frowned. "What is this place?"

Both women continued to catalog the space.

The only other place to sit—or sleep—was a futon, shoved against the adjacent wall and covered with piles of clothes.

Beyond that, a narrow wooden door stood half open just three steps away. "Bathroom?" Janet's voice was barely more than a whisper.

"Think it's empty?" Quizz's voice was also low.

Janet's heart rate quickened at the thought of what might be lying on the other side of the door. Was there a bathtub? Was it occupied?

She raised her face and sniffed the air. Nothing could compete with the smell of spoiled food. She took a few cautious steps forward and, following Quizz's lead, used her elbow to push the bathroom door open. Her eyes swept the tiny space and she slowly raised one hand to cover her mouth.

Behind her Quizz held up her phone. "Do I call 911? What's in there?"

"Nothing. But this bathroom hasn't been cleaned in months." It wasn't until the words left her mouth that her shoulders slumped forward in relief. She backed away from the bathroom and when she turned, she found Quizz staring at her, a funny expression on her face.

"What? It wasn't until I saw the bathroom was empty that I realized how worried I was that we'd find Lola here, dead!" Janet heard the warble in her voice but couldn't help it; you could hardly fault someone for feeling jittery in a stranger's apartment with duct tape, zip ties, and the smell of decay.

"No, it's not that." Quizz's eyebrows drew together and she searched Janet's face for a long moment, then picked a picture frame up off the coffee table at her thigh. From where they'd entered just inside the door, a pile of laundry had obscured their view of what sat on the table. But now that they were across the small apartment, a framed picture—a big one at that—seemed to take up all the surface area.

It was a silver decorative frame, almost a foot tall, with white matting surrounding a professionally taken eight-by-ten picture. Quizz handed her the frame. Dread cracked like an egg over the top of her head and slid down the back of her neck until her body convulsed with a bone-jarring shiver.

Her legs felt weak, like jelly, and she placed the frame carefully back on the coffee table, setting it down next to a stack of bills. Her eyes zeroed in on the top page. It was an electric bill, but that's not what caught her attention. The customer name, listed right above the PO Box address, was William Brooks. She slipped the paper out from under the picture frame and, hands shaking, tucked it into her bag, then backed away from the futon, away from the blood splatters, and out of the apartment into the bright winter sunshine outside. Quizz followed her out and pulled the door closed as best she could with the splintered wood and broken lock.

After they made their way back down the rickety ladder, Quizz stepped in Janet's path, forcing her apprentice to look her in the eye. "What's happening here? What's your connection to this Matt guy?"

Something bad was going on, but there was no way she was going to tell Quizz that *Jason's father* was paying the light bill at that duct tape-zip tie-porno house apartment...but that wasn't all. She swallowed down the acidic taste at the back of her tongue and looked up at the apartment door with a grimace.

"Janet, we don't know who he is, but he's got a framed picture of you next to his bed. I don't know where we go from here. Do you?"

CHAPTER TWENTY-TWO

At the airport, Janet excused herself to the bathroom. She needed a minute alone to think. They had a problem, and Quizz only knew the half of it. Why was Jason's dad renting that shitty apartment, and why did it look like a frat boy's dark sexual fantasy had played out there? And why did he have a framed picture of *her* next to his bed?

The obvious explanations were too ridiculous to even consider, and yet...was it possible that William was involved in Lola's disappearance?

She thought back to his behavior—not just since Lola went missing, but in the weeks before that.

He'd been moody, difficult—on edge. But she'd chalked it all up to Faith's looming visit, and the emotions dredged up from a decades-long marriage ending in anger.

But what if it was more? What if he'd been unable to adjust to his new reality?

And what about this Connie woman he'd been dating? No one had met her or seen her during his entire alleged relationship. Did she even exist?

What if she didn't—what if Connie was just a front for Lola? She shuddered. Someone knocked on the stall door.

"You okay?" Quizz's voice was tinged with concern.

Janet cleared her throat. "Yup. I'm almost done." She reached back and flushed the toilet for show, then walked out of the stall and washed her hands.

"What's going on?" Quizz leaned up against the hand dryer and studied her.

"Nothing. I mean, that apartment was just jarring, you know? What do we do now?"

Quizz frowned. "I don't think it's enough to call O'Dell with. I mean, the cook didn't even know for sure if he recognized Lola —and there wasn't any sign that she'd been inside that apartment. Plus, we broke in...so...I think we keep this to ourselves for now."

Janet nodded, her throat suddenly dry. That was fine with her, because at this point, any kind of investigation might lead police right to her own house. A rush of hot fear and cold dread ran through her at the same time, leaving a trail of goose flesh up and down her arms. She rubbed them roughly and avoided Quizz's eye in the mirror.

"Flight's about to board." Quizz looked at her watch. "I'm going to buy some Red Hots. You want anything for the flight?"

She shook her head. After Quizz left, she pressed her hands against her temples, trying to steady her mind. Out in the terminal, she found a quiet corner and called Jason.

The call went straight to voicemail, but just hearing Jason's strong, steady voice was a comfort. "I can't take your call right now. Leave a message, or please call my associate, Mike, if you need immediate help."

How could she possibly summarize her last three hours in a voicemail? "I need you to call me. Like immediately! I'm in Memphis about this missing girl case, and...something strange came up with—" Her voice faltered and she fell quiet. It wasn't exactly voicemail material, accusing his father of child abduction and possibly murder, was it? "Just please call me," she finished weakly.

"Who was that?" Quizz was back, chomping on the cinnamon candy, her cheeks already red from the spice.

"Just trying Jason again."

"No luck?"

Janet shook her head.

"What's going on with him?"

"What do you mean?" she shot back.

Quizz's eyebrows met her hairline and she chewed the candy in her mouth thoroughly and swallowed before answering. "I just mean he's been MIA lately." She studied Janet, clearly noting her jumpy, defensive tone.

Janet forced herself to relax. Quizz didn't know. Jason didn't know. Only *she* knew about William's connection to that apartment. "He's been really busy with a new job." Quizz went out of focus as her brain made a connection. Busy with a job in Memphis, in fact. Huh.

"Now boarding flight 5039 to Knoxville. All silver medallion passengers, welcome aboard."

Quizz popped another candy into her mouth and then pulled her boarding pass up on her phone. "Never been so happy to leave a place, you know?"

They barely spoke on the trip home. The only words Janet uttered were to the flight attendant when she ordered a vodka straight up with lime. She was headed home—to the home she shared with Jason's father. Did she confront him, or wait for Jason? And just how long would Jason keep her waiting, anyway?

Not ready to face her house or William, Janet dropped Quizz off at her office and then drove to the Spot. The bar was crowded; the parking lot was full, and even the street was lined with cars for blocks. Janet ignored the construction barrels and drove around the caution tape to park alongside the Dumpster in the back alley.

She ducked past Mel and spotted O'Dell and Detective Smith at the bar. Seeing the other cop set Janet on edge even further. Smith was actively looking for Lola, and now she had information on the case. Information that she wasn't going to share with police just yet. Her body tensed as she approached the pair.

O'Dell smiled when he caught sight of her and stood to offer Janet his seat. Smith didn't move, but kept a steady, if not completely unfriendly, stare on her face.

Janet didn't sit. She locked eyes with Cindy Lou and leaned across the bar to order a vodka with lime. "Make it a double, Cindy Lou."

Janet felt Detective Smith's eyes boring into her and she resolutely continued to face forward, downing half her drink in one gulp. *Steady,* she told herself.

O'Dell continued to hover at Janet's elbow, and Smith finally leaned forward and tapped her on the arm. "Have a seat, Janet."

"No thanks."

Smith and O'Dell exchanged a look, and the other woman stood. "I've got to go to the bathroom. I'll be back in five minutes."

They watched her walk away, then O'Dell pulled Janet into the open seat and sat lightly in the seat next to her. "What's going on, Janet? You seem jumpy or something."

She needed to talk to someone about what she'd discovered in Memphis, but chatting with a police detective probably had consequential side effects. She took a small sip of her drink, already feeling the warm flush of the alcohol branch out from her chest. "O'Dell, what are your job requirements?"

He looked blankly back. "What do you mean? I investigate murders and then arrest people. What's not to understand?"

"No—I mean, if you hear about a..." Her voice faltered, and O'Dell's brow wrinkled. She plucked the lime wedge from the rim of her glass and squeezed it over her drink to keep herself focused and calm, then tried again. "If you hear about a possible crime, do you have to move it up the chain? Or can you sit on it for a while?"

He scooted his stool closer. "What's going on?"

"Seriously, O'Dell, if I tell you something—"

"Can I just say that if *you* know something about a crime and don't report it, *you* could be found guilty of a crime."

"What?" Her eyes darted up to the cop, but she couldn't take the weight of his stare, and she looked back down at her drink. It was empty. Dammit.

"And the same is certainly true for me. I'm a mandatory reporter. However..." He fiddled with the label on his beer bottle, then downed the remainder of his drink in three great gulps. "However, I'm willing to listen to something as a friend, not an officer of the law." He leaned closer. "What happened?"

She met his eyes and saw nothing but raw truth gazing back at her. She could trust him. But before she could launch into the story of what she saw in Memphis, Detective Smith was back from the bathroom.

Instead of waiting for O'Dell to stand up from her seat, Smith slid onto his lap and wrapped her arm around his neck. "So, Pat, are you done here, or do I need to go back to the bathroom?"

Janet's shock at seeing the two of them *together* must have come across, because a flush rose up O'Dell's face. "Janet...I, ah, I wasn't sure if you knew, but Kay and I have been dating for a couple of weeks now."

"And I intend to make sure Patrick doesn't get in any trou-

ble." Detective Smith looked at Janet with a smile that didn't
quite reach her eyes. "Can we help with anything, Janet?"

Janet stood and backed away from the stools—from the happy
couple—and forced a smile onto her face. "Yes, of course. I—I
hadn't heard, so...that's great news. Really, really great." *Jesus,
stop saying great.* "We're done here. You two have a great night."
She cringed and then turned, walking fast along the bar before
ducking under the service area. She didn't breathe again until she
was standing next to Cindy Lou, their backs toward O'Dell and
his girlfriend.

"Crazy-good business tonight!" Cindy Lou looked over to
Janet as she waited for two pints to fill at the taps. "Cameron's
doing a great job out there—but God, the paper plates sure fill up
our trash cans fast. Faith was in here, talking 'bout having Bruce
add an outdoor kitchen to the lanai plans? You'd better keep her
on a short leash, huh?"

Janet didn't answer, just stared around her bar with flat eyes.
She'd never felt so strange and out of touch with her own business as she did just then. Like she shouldn't even be there. But
the alternative—going home to face William—was even less
appealing.

Cindy Lou babbled on, too busy to notice Janet's mood.
"Everybody sure does seem to love the food. I think you were
right to keep the menu simple. Hard to mess up a cheeseburger,
ya know? It's funny, ain't it? You get so used to how things are,
you can't even see that change is a good thing sometimes, huh?"

"Yeah. Change is so great." Janet turned away from a
customer's order and instead filled her own glass. Whether she
liked it or not, change was here. She pounded the shot and
poured herself another, the action finally catching Cindy Lou's
attention. Her assistant manager frowned, but Janet ignored her.

Change was here, all right; she just never imagined she'd be
navigating the changes on her own.

CHAPTER TWENTY-THREE

The last customers left only after Mel flipped the overhead lights on full. With a grumble, the group of girls walked out into the night, a white cloud of breath following them through the parking lot.

"Finally!" Mel twisted the deadbolt after them. "I'm beat, Janet. Okay if I leave the mopping until tomorrow? I'll come in early." She looked hopefully across the room.

"That's fine, Mel. Thanks for all your hard work. See you tomorrow."

When the bouncer was gone, Cindy Lou set the glasses she'd been cleaning down on the drying rack and turned to face Janet. "You ready to talk yet, or you wanna keep brooding silently over there like dad-gum Batman?"

Janet hardly smiled at the joke.

"Well, now I know it's serious. Are you okay, hon?"

She couldn't exactly spill the secret of William's Memphis apartment to Cindy Lou, but she was touched that her longest-tenured employee cared enough to ask. "I guess I'm just feeling kind of...adrift."

"Because Jason's been gone so much?" Cindy Lou nodded sagely. "It's a change, isn't it? Weird when it's the change you *wanted* that's making you feel so alone." She picked up two more dirty glasses and turned back to the glass washer in the sink. "I think this new setup's just going to take some time to get used to. I don't know." She tossed a smile over her shoulder. "Does it help or hurt having Jason's family breathing down your neck? You'll never be alone as long as William's living in the upstairs of your house."

She laughed lightly and turned back to the glassware, but Cindy Lou's words sent a chill down Janet's spine. The last thing she wanted was to go home and face William on her own. How could she possibly be alone in the house with him and not bring up his Memphis apartment? But did she really want to know why there was porn, duct tape, and zip ties? Or find out why he even had that apartment at all?

No wonder he couldn't afford his own place in Knoxville—he was already paying for a place somewhere else.

She closed the lid on the condiment container and slipped it onto the middle shelf of the Beerador, thinking. Maybe asking William some questions wasn't a bad idea. After all, what would Jason know? He'd been busy for the last seven or eight days, hardly home, barely checking in.

Her stomach clenched just thinking about an interview. Then again, it clenched thinking about not asking him, too.

She and Cindy Lou walked out to the Dumpster with the last two bags of trash. A light spilled out the food-truck window onto the dark pavement.

"Cameron?" Janet called. She'd forgotten that the cook was even there, let alone still working.

He stuck his head out the window and smiled. "Just cleaning up out here. Busy freaking night."

"How'd it go in there?"

"Good. We ran out of buns with about an hour to go. I just used lettuce leaves and called them our low-carb special, and no one really complained too much."

Janet snorted. "I guess we need a process for keeping track of how much to order of everything. You should have let us know in the bar about the problem. Maybe Mel could have gone out to buy more from the grocery store."

"Yeah—there's really no way to get anyone's attention. I could hardly stay on top of the orders as it was! I would have texted, but I had to put my phone in my locker, you know?"

"Hmm." Janet pulled a face as she considered Cameron's dilemma. With him outside, removed from the bar, it really didn't make sense for him to not have any way to reach them except for leaving his post—which was far busier than she'd expected. "I guess I either need to run a phone line out there, or have you keep your cell phone, huh?"

He smiled and ducked back into the truck. Seconds later he pulled the windows closed and the lights flicked off as the back door opened. "Do we lock it up?" he asked.

"I'll get it." Janet stepped forward with the key ring.

"Let's go get our stuff and get outta here, Cameron." Cindy Lou yawned and pulled the door back open. While Janet was in no hurry to leave, everyone else clearly was, because before she could make it back inside the building, Cindy Lou and Cameron were already out the front door and gone for the night.

Mel and Kat's half of the duplex was dark when Janet drove up, but her side looked like a midnight madness sale at the mall. Light shone through the blinds from every window, including her bedroom.

The bass of music greeted her as she walked up to the front

door, and when she pulled the door open, the heavy smell of cinnamon wafted out of the kitchen, mostly covering a sharp ammonia scent that lingered in the front room.

William dropped a scrub brush into a bucket when she stepped in and mopped his brow with a cloth. "Whew. I'm beat, how about you?"

She looked blankly at the freshly scrubbed windows. "Were you...cleaning?"

"Funny how something hits you and you've just got to get it done that minute! That ever happen to you, Janet?"

"Uh...sure."

"Is that Janet?" Faith called from the kitchen.

"What is Faith doing here?"

William grunted as he climbed down from the stepladder. He carried the bucket of cleaning water to the sink in the minibar—but before he hefted it up to drain, he changed his mind and plucked a rocks glass from the shelf, then turned the faucet on all the way, cranked it over to the hot water side, and pulled out a bottle of whiskey along with some other ingredients.

"I got the oven set up in there today, and I told Faith she needed to make sure it works! She's making cinnamon rolls, and I just decided this minute to make a hot toddy to celebrate. You want one?"

Janet flinched when the chef's knife sliced down into a lemon with a *whack!* Juice sprayed the mirror in a pattern not unlike the blood spatter in the Memphis apartment.

"N-no thanks, I'm just about ready to turn in." Suddenly she didn't want to ask him any questions. About anything.

He shrugged, a suit-yourself expression on his face, then added some steaming hot water to his mug. He shut the faucet off, then twisted the cap off a bottle of whiskey and slugged some into the already steaming liquid. He stirred in honey straight from the squeezy bear and then pinched a lemon wedge between his finger and thumb before dropping it into the mug.

He lifted the cup to his lips. "Mmm." He took a long sip and then cruised to the couch and looked up at Janet, still frozen at the threshold. "How was business tonight?"

Janet admonished herself to *get it together* and walked stiffly to the couch across from him and took a seat. She made a conscious effort to relax her body. "Good. Surprisingly busy, actually." Faith walked into the room with a plate of fresh rolls and set them on the coffee table between Janet and her ex. "We ran out of hamburger buns, if you can believe it."

Faith pulled a roll apart from the rest and sat next to William. "Maintaining the right balance of wholesale ingredients is one of the hardest parts of running a restaurant."

Janet took a deep breath and tried to ignore Faith's superior tone.

"Well, it's a big learning curve for us this week, but the food truck worked amazingly well," she embellished with a smile, feeling no remorse. "Another day or two, and we'll have paid off the truck completely. Won't be able to say that about the outdoor dining addition, will we?" She pressed her lips together. This was not the start she'd planned in the car on the drive home. Riling Faith up would not result in getting answers to any of her questions about Memphis and William. She pressed her shoulders down and tried for a friendlier tone. "Anyway, there are definitely some bugs we need to work out—including how much of what to order. Maybe you'll be able to help me with that, Faith? You certainly seem like an expert in that area."

Faith tried to hide her satisfied smile in her pastry but failed. "I'd be happy to help, Janet. All you need to do is ask."

Janet suppressed a sigh. She felt like she'd just done that, but Faith wasn't going to capitulate so easily. Before she could say something else she'd regret, she turned to William. "Quizz and I made a quick trip to Memphis today."

He choked on his hot toddy, and the next several minutes were spent cleaning sticky honeyed whiskey off the table and leather couch. When all was quiet again, she tried again.

"Yes, we had a tip that whoever Lola was dating might actually be from Memphis."

"Any luck?" Faith's eyes never left her cinnamon roll; her focus on pulling the layers apart was unlike anything Janet had ever witnessed. And it might have been her imagination, but it sure seemed like Faith's body went rigid with her question.

"Uhh...not exactly. Just a dead end that left a lot of questions, you know?"

"Well," Faith replied briskly, "I guess a dead end is better than a dead body."

"What?"

"I-I—I just mean that dead ends are a kind of closure unto themselves, aren't they?"

"To be honest, it all made me think about Connie." Janet turned to face William again. His face, moments ago red from his coughing spell, had drained of color.

"What about her?" he asked with genuine surprise.

"Isn't she from Memphis? When are you going to see her again?"

"William, didn't you tell her?" He shook his head but didn't speak. After several long moments, Faith blew out a breath and said, "William and Connie broke up. He said he just didn't see it working out, you know, in the long term."

"Well...it's a shame we never got to meet her," Janet said as diplomatically as possible, even as her insides squeezed as if she'd turned into the honey bear.

"Whatever are you talking about?" Faith asked, relaxing back into the couch. "I'm glad we didn't waste any time on her, to be honest."

William chuckled, though it sounded forced to Janet's ears. She excused herself as soon as she was able, and found when she was alone in her room, she couldn't quite catch her breath.

A bloody apartment with William's name on a bill, and now he'd apparently told Faith that he and Connie had broken up.

Was that true? Or was Connie dead?

She covered a scream when a sharp knock issued from the other side of her door.

"Janet?" William asked.

She crept to the wood separating her from Jason's father as quietly as she could, and then pressed the toe of her sneaker against the lower corner of the door, knowing that simple physics would be on her side if William tried to force it open.

"Uh-huh?"

"Just wanted to let you know that Jason called—he said he's busy as all get out, but will try and call you tomorrow at the Spot."

"O-okay. Uh...thanks, William."

"Good night."

"Good night."

His footsteps echoed on the floor as he made his way back to the couch. She didn't move from her spot—instead, she leaned forward until her head rested against the unforgiving wooden doorframe. She was exhausted, but probably wouldn't sleep a wink. She'd never be able to turn her brain off, to stop from wondering whether she was living with a killer.

CHAPTER TWENTY-FOUR

Janet hardly slept that night; every time a floorboard creaked, she was convinced that William was sneaking around the house, doing something bad. And somehow, even though Janet had been holding her phone all night, Jason managed to sneak in a call that went straight to voicemail. She was convinced he was avoiding her, using a technology trick to keep her phone from ringing. But why?

She must have drifted off to a hard sleep sometime after five in the morning, and she awoke to the shrill ringing of the landline in her room, late-morning sun slanting through the curtains.

She reached blindly for the receiver. "What?"

"I hate to call you with this problem right now, Janet, but we've got a real situation here at the Spot." Cindy Lou's breathless voice had Janet leaping out of bed.

"What? What's happened now?" She clutched her chest and searched the floor for her pants from the night before, hopping into them and just barely keeping her balance. "Are the cops there? What's wrong?"

Cindy Lou gasped. "Oh, good Lord, no! It's just that—you

know we're hosting that big FOP dart tournament tonight? Well, I told Cameron to come in early, and don't you know, he's two darn hours late! I can't get ahold of him. I don't know what to do. But there's got to be a load of prep work for tonight and someone needs to get started."

Janet fell back against her bed with a groan. Planning gone awry for the Fraternal Order of Police dart tournament was not a crisis—at least, not according to her new sliding scale for disaster. No blood? No psycho killer? No crisis. "I'll be right in. Call Mel and ask if she can come in early. I'm sure he just overslept." She buttoned her jeans and plopped back down onto the mattress. "Hopefully he'll show up, but I'll be in soon, too." Janet hung up with a frown, then pulled on her T-shirt and tucked her cell phone into her back pocket as she walked out of her room.

"Jesus, Mary, and Joseph!" she yelped, when she came face to face with Jason's father. His arms stretched high over his head, and an awful expression contorted his face. She leapt back and managed not to scream, only because as his arms dropped, it was clear he was stretching—not launching an attack. "What are you doing? Did you—" She looked behind William at the blankets and pillow stacked on the couch. "Did you sleep out here?"

"Faith decided it was too late to drive back to the hotel, and I thought I'd give her the bed and sleep down here."

"But there's another guest room upstairs—"

"We didn't want to cause extra laundry for just one night, you know?"

"Oh...sure." She slunk past him to the kitchen—absentmindedly admired her new working stove—and then dumped some grounds into the coffee machine and waited while it percolated. Was she nuts? How could Jason's father—so polite that he didn't want to make extra dirty laundry—also be a part of that house of horrors she and Quizz found in Memphis? There must be another explanation, but she couldn't for the life of her figure out what it might be.

She wanted to keep Jason's parents close, keep an eye on them, monitor their behavior. Suddenly, she knew just how to make that happen.

"William! I might need you and Faith to help out in the food truck tonight!"

"This really was a great idea, Cindy Lou." Janet surveyed the huge crowd and watched as Mel carted a new keg out from the back cooler. "Right in there, Mel, thanks."

She moved the empty keg onto the cart after Mel heaved the new one into place. The five dartboards that Cindy Lou had purchased at a real-estate foreclosure sale for peanuts hung on the back wall of the bar, and the twenty people who'd entered the tournament mingled with the other patrons as the tournament got underway.

"Finally don't have to worry about the cops showing up, huh?" Cindy Lou asked with a smile.

Janet chuckled, but the sound died on her lips when William walked in the alley door.

"I can't get the damn stovetop to keep the heat!"

Janet made to move out from behind the bar, but Faith stood up with her hand up. "I'm on it, Janet. William, let's go."

She watched Jason's divorced parents chat comfortably as they made their way back outside.

"They sure have come to an understanding recently, haven't they?" Cindy Lou stared after them as she wiped a glass with a dry towel and set it back on the shelf. "I wonder what changed?"

Janet looked thoughtfully at the door through which Faith

and William had disappeared. "It's almost like they're going to get back together."

"I've got to hand it to Faith," Cindy Lou said, tapping her lips with a finger, deep in thought. "She sure does have him by the balls, don't she? Like, she swept into town and suddenly he's ended things with his girlfriend and is giving up his bed so she can sleep comfortably? She's got it."

"What?"

"That enviable ability to hook a man." Cindy Lou sighed and then snapped to attention when a customer asked for a frozen margarita. She winked at Janet, then looked across the bar. "No problem, sweetheart. One fantastic frozen margarita, coming up."

Janet's phone buzzed. She looked at the screen and groaned inwardly. Quizz wanted to talk. But before she could answer the call, O'Dell tapped her hand.

"Can I have a word?"

She slipped her phone into her pocket—she'd call the PI back later—and grabbed a pint glass, avoiding O'Dell's eye. "Sure. Need a drink?"

"N-no. I'm good, thanks." He held up his beer bottle and she felt her cheeks heat up at the mistake.

"Oh, okay. So...what's up?" She set the pint glass down and assessed the other customers at the bar to see who was ready to order.

"I guess I just wanted to explain about Kay and me—"

"O'Dell! You don't have anything to explain. I mean..." She scrubbed the counter between them with a wet rag. "I'm dating Jason. You're free to date anyone you want."

After a long pause, he hummed out a sound, then said, "Okay, we won't talk about it." He reached out and touched her hand, forcing her to stop scrubbing and look up. "But I also wanted to follow up with you after last night. You wanted to tell me something?"

"Oh—no. It's fine. Everything's just fine." She pulled her hand away, and filled a glass with beer, just to give her something else to focus on.

"Are you sure? Because you can still count on me as a friend, Janet. I'll always be a friend to you."

She set the full pint glass down on the bar and stared at the thin layer of foam on top. O'Dell was a friend...and she surely felt like she needed someone to talk over everything she'd uncovered lately. She looked up and stared into his engaging bright green eyes. She could trust him; of course she could. She opened her mouth, but someone else spoke first.

"What are you drinking, hon?" Detective Smith came to a stop by O'Dell's side. "Ooh, I'll have the same, Janet. Pat, did you see Rivera got two doubles and then a dang bullseye? You've got to watch his next turn. Come on." She held her credit card out for Janet. "I'll just start a tab. Thanks." She linked her arm through O'Dell's and took the bottle before pulling O'Dell away.

Janet turned her back on the happy couple, but there wasn't time to worry about O'Dell, because Mel materialized at her side.

"I think you need to get out there to the food truck, Janet. I don't want to say they're going to kill each other...but they've got sharp knives, hot oil, and a lot of poorly resolved anger issues."

"Are they fighting?"

"No, but they're backed way up, and don't seem to be handling the stress very well."

Janet hurried through the crowd inside the Spot and climbed into the back of the food truck outside. Faith stood at the griddle with two dozen burger patties sizzling away. Meanwhile, William hoisted a basket of black fries from the hot oil.

"Dammit, Faith, I told you to tell me when the timer went off. I can't hear it over everyone shouting orders at me. Now we've got to toss all this oil 'cause it'll taste like burnt food!"

"Well, I can't hear the timer when you're over there yakking away with the customers like we ain't got five hundred things to do back here, *William!*"

"Hey guys. Looks crazy out here. What can I do to help?" Janet stepped between the two.

"Oh, she wants to help now, isn't *that* delicious," Faith muttered, tossing cheese squares onto half the patties.

"You leave her alone, ya old hag. Janet," William's eyes sparkled as Faith sucked in an injured breath, "we need another bag of frozen fries. I set them in the ice machine when we came in from the store this morning. Can you go get them?"

"I'm on it," Janet replied, ignoring Faith completely. She skipped back down the steps and entered the Spot through the alley door to avoid the crowds.

O'Dell smiled at her, but she pretended not to see him as she headed for the walk-in cooler. Kegs were stacked two tall right by the door, and she had to pick her way past even higher stacks of cases of bottles to get to the ice machine along the back wall. "What a mess," Janet grumbled. Cameron must have moved things around earlier in the week when he'd been prepping the food truck. She'd have to tell him—if he ever came back in—that part of his job was to leave the cooler as neat as he found it. She stepped around a messy pile of broken-down boxes and reached out to lift the lid of the ice machine when she pulled up short. An open hand rested on the concrete floor at the base of the machine. The skin had an unhealthy bluish pallor that left a smattering of goosebumps across her shoulders. Janet's eyes moved along the lines of the woman's outstretched arm, the blond hair, the camisole and jeans.

The blond hair.

Was it Lola?

She reached out to touch the wrist, but the skin was icy.

Whoever she was, she was dead.

CHAPTER TWENTY-FIVE

Janet stumbled back toward the door, then stopped and turned back. She crept forward again and lifted a lock of hair that covered the woman's face. Small crow's feet stamped the outer edges of the woman's eyes, her thin lips were parted slightly, and a drip of blood came from the ear closest to the ground. A small puddle of it pooled just below her chin, and the blond hair on that side matted into the blood.

Definitely not Lola. But there was something oddly familiar about the woman's face.

She backed out of the room and walked directly into O'Dell's chest. He grabbed her by the shoulders to steady her. "Whoa there! You okay?" Janet turned around and locked eyes with the homicide detective.

"Yes, Patrick, of course she's fine," Detective Smith snapped from somewhere to Janet's left. "It's your turn, come on. You're holding up the tournament. I'm sure Janet has things to do tonight."

But O'Dell didn't drop his hands. "Janet? What's wrong?"

Suddenly she was shivering uncontrollably, and it had nothing to do with the temperature. "B-b-body. There's a body."

"What body?" O'Dell asked.

"Patrick, really!" Smith snapped.

William stuck his head inside the door just feet away. "Janet? You got those fries? I got a dozen hungry cops out there just a-waitin' on you, now!"

Janet looked at William, then back at O'Dell. Her lips felt tight, as if she couldn't move them, but with everyone looking at her, she forced the words through. "There's a dead woman in the cooler."

"What'd you say, Janet?" William stepped all the way into the building, and his lips tilted down into a frown. "Who's dead?"

Janet pointed wordlessly at the door to the walk-in cooler, and William made to charge in.

Smith's arm shot out, nearly knocking William off of his feet. Her earlier irritation was immediately replaced with cool, calm authority. "Janet, where exactly is the body?"

"Against the back wall. By the ice machine."

Smith pushed William against the wall and O'Dell dropped Janet's arms and stepped around her, then pulled open the door to the walk-in cooler. The cops nearest him put their darts down, somehow aware through body language alone that the tone of the night had shifted dramatically.

"Secure the entrance," someone said.

Janet made a half-hearted attempt to head to the door when Smith barked, "Not you! Stay there."

Rivera propped the door open with his foot as O'Dell disappeared into the dark interior.

He was back out less than a minute later, his cell phone pressed to his ear. "Homicide at the Spot, down on Retreat Road. Rivera and I are already here, but I'll need an evidence crew as fast as you can get them here." He slipped the phone into his pocket and then lifted something in his other hand. His eyes squinted as he read off the small rectangle. "The victim had an ID in her back pocket. Connie Hutchings." He looked to Janet. "Do you know her?"

"Connie," Janet repeated slowly, and couldn't keep herself from turning to look at William, still pressed up against the wall by Smith.

"Connie?" His ragged breathing almost swallowed the name.

"Is that your girlfriend?" Janet couldn't keep the accusation out of her voice.

The lights flicked on across the room, and the people farthest away from the cooler squinted around, confused.

Smith pushed William to the corner booth. "Who is she?"

William's already pale face drained of any remaining color. "She was my—my girlfriend. I mean, kind of. We'd been taking a break."

"Is that right? And why's that?"

"Well, she'd stopped returning my calls, but also, well...Faith thought it was best."

"And who's Faith?" Rivera asked, his voice calm, friendly.

"My ex-wife."

"And where is she?"

Janet didn't like the direction of this line of questioning. "Hey, Rivera—"

Smith stalked forward and grabbed Janet's arm, steering her toward the bar, away from William, away from Rivera. She still heard William's answer.

"Well, she's in the food truck, just like I was."

Rivera nodded to another cop and he headed for the door.

"What's going on here?" Janet asked, shaking free of Smith's grip and turning to face the cop. Smith was unusually short, and it felt satisfying to stare down at someone for a change.

The cop smiled humorlessly. "What's going on is that your future in-laws are the best suspects we've got in what looks like a murder investigation. Take a seat. You're not going anywhere, either."

Because her calls had gone unanswered for days, she sent a text message to Jason.

Dead body at the Spot. Police questioning your parents. CALL IMMEDIATELY.

Seconds after hitting send, a text came in from an unknown number.

This is Mike. I'm contacting Jason ASAP. Hold tight.

"Hold tight? What the—"

"Hold what?" O'Dell appeared by her side, his eyebrows drawn together.

Janet tucked the phone back into her pocket. Had Jason turned his phone over to his colleague? She'd have to investigate that question later. She looked up at O'Dell. "Nevermind. What's going on?" She motioned to William, still sitting in the corner booth. The color had returned to his face, but his vacant gaze was unsettling.

"Something's not right here, Janet. Why would he be holding back?" O'Dell crossed his arms over his chest. "Do you think he'd protect Faith?"

"You think Faith killed Connie?"

O'Dell rubbed a hand roughly across his face. "Too early to say. But she's completely unaffected by the death, and William's acting strange."

Janet looked across the bar at the other corner booth. Faith sat at the table, studying her nails.

"Any idea yet on when Connie was—" She pressed her lips together, unable to finish the question.

"The temperature inside the cooler complicates the time-line. The coroner doesn't want to say until she gets the body back to her lab. But best guess—around twelve to twenty-four hours."

So when Janet was lurking around a Memphis apartment, Connie—from Memphis—was likely killed.

O'Dell cleared his throat and sat down next to her. "I need to ask you a few questions."

"Shoot."

His eyes narrowed.

"I just meant go ahead."

"When was the last time you were in the walk-in cooler today?"

Janet blew out a sigh. "I was in there before we opened today, but just grabbed a couple cases of Bud closest to the door. I'm not sure I would have noticed if Connie was—if she was already lying back there."

"What about last night?"

She shrugged. "Cindy Lou or Mel might know more. I'm sorry."

He nodded. "I believe you."

Some of the tension leached out of her shoulders and she slumped over the table, until O'Dell's next question caught her completely off guard.

"Where was William last night?"

"At my house. I was tossing and turning all night and heard him working in the kitchen on and off."

O'Dell's mouth tilted up on one side. "Still not done?"

"So close I can taste it. There was a measuring issue with the countertops and they had to be sent back. We're just waiting on them and we'll be ready."

"So what was William working on?" The question was casual, but Janet felt the intensity behind it.

She looked up from her hands and narrowed her eyes. "He's still working on the cabinet trim and baseboard pieces. He can only do so much at a time because of his knees."

"Arthritis?"

Janet nodded.

O'Dell made to stand. "Please thank Mel for us. She corralled all the customers inside and kept them from leaving until we could take down everyone's names. She was a real lifesaver."

"You heading out?" Janet stood with him. They were close. O'Dell didn't step away when she moved next to him, and she instinctively looked around for Smith.

"She left. And yes, I'm leaving, too. Not enough evidence to bring anyone in, but we'll make sure William and Faith know they're not to leave Knoxville city limits."

Janet nodded. They weren't going anywhere, anyway.

As O'Dell pushed away from the table and headed over to talk to Faith, her phone buzzed and she took it out of her back pocket to see a final text from Mike.

Can't reach Jason. I'm coming in tomorrow. I have some questions.

Janet set the phone down on the table and slid it away from her like it was a grenade about to go off. Was Jason missing, too? It seemed the only reasonable explanation for why he wasn't calling her back, or responding at all to her last text. But Mike was coming in. What did he have to say to her that he didn't want to say over the phone?

She tried to steady her breathing, but could only manage short, shallow gasping breaths. It didn't feel like there was anywhere safe to go tonight. Janet rested her head on her folded hands on the table.

Another night in her house with Jason's parents, who may or may not have killed Connie in cold blood and then dumped her body at the bar. Suddenly, William's story about having an inexplicable urge to clean her windows left her feeling cold and clammy. Was the reason behind the cleaning so innocent? Or was there something else to hide?

CHAPTER TWENTY-SIX

Faith rolled her suitcase to the bottom of the stairs and turned to look accusingly at Janet. "This night has been one of the worst in my life!"

"Pretty bad for Connie, too," Janet muttered, hanging her coat in the closet by the door.

When she turned back around, Faith's sharp eyes matched the tone of her voice when she said, "What?"

Janet stalked across the room and headed for the minibar. Last night she hadn't felt safe in her own home. Tonight, she was officially pissed off. She was angry with Jason for disappearing when she needed him most. She was angry with his parents for acting shady when she needed stability. Hell, she'd take plain sanity just then. "I said it was a pretty bad night for Connie, too."

"Oh." Faith bowed her head and took a step back. "You're right. How thoughtless of me."

"William, what happened to her? What happened to Connie?" Janet narrowed her eyes and studied his reaction.

Jason's father's expression darkened. "I have no idea, Janet. And you'd better watch who you're asking what."

William moved to the bar and Janet had to step out of his path—she wasn't at all sure he wouldn't bowl her over if she didn't. She and Faith ignored each other, both women watching him fix a large pour of bourbon.

After he placed the bottle back on the shelf, Janet cleared her throat. "I haven't talked to Jason tonight. Have either of you?" Again, she watched both of their faces like a hawk. She wanted—no, needed—to believe that none of them could get ahold of him.

"Nope," William said slowly after he'd drained his glass.

"Nothing here, either," Faith added.

William put his glass next to the sink and turned around. "When I talked to him yesterday, he said he was still in Memphis for work. Weren't you just there, too?"

Janet didn't answer. She felt adrift; as far from Jason as she'd ever been—and not just physical distance. She'd never felt so unconnected emotionally from him, either. What was he up to?

"You never said what part of town you were in, Janet." Faith's tone made it clear she thought Janet had let her down with the omission.

"Some kid at a local high school helped me crack into that missing girl's cell phone, and she'd agreed to meet her boyfriend at a place called Monahan's Restaurant."

Janet studied Faith's oversized red suitcase and stepped forward. "Bummer about the hotel not having a room for you anymore, Faith. Want me to bring your bag upstairs for you?"

When Jason's mother didn't answer, she looked up and found Jason's parents staring at each other. The tension between them took her breath away. She didn't like the way Faith was looking at William—anger, mixed with fear and anxiety—and she didn't want to be anywhere near it.

Janet grabbed Faith's bag and made her escape.

She ignored the dust bunnies that swirled around her feet on the steps, her heart heavy. Life felt out of control, and she hated that feeling—it reminded her of her wayward younger years, when she was angry, rudderless, and irresponsible. Now she was a business owner with a boyfriend, but the same internal chaos swirled up inside of her.

She dumped the bag into the empty guest room and headed back down the hall. Tense, angry voices floated up the stairwell.

"Where is my son, William?" Faith's terse whisper meant she was trying to be quiet, but the soundwaves bounced along the wooden floors and drywall like they were being amplified by speakers.

Janet froze at the top of the staircase.

"I don't know where he is," William answered, and Janet had to strain to hear him. "But we do know that Jason's looking into things. It's going to be okay."

"How can you say that?" Faith snapped. "I've never felt like things were worse!"

"Not now, Faith!" William whispered, then he called up the stairs, "Janet, need any help up there?"

Her cheeks flushed with the feeling that she'd been caught, but she clomped heavily down the stairs and beat a hasty retreat to the safety of her bedroom with an unconvincing excuse about being exhausted—even though her body vibrated with nervous energy. After she closed her bedroom door, she stood just inside her room, her ears straining to hear the rest of Jason's parent's conversation.

It wasn't long before they continued with their conversation.

"...can't be the problem..."

"...But what if that's what he's looking for?"

William's low bass got lost in the HVAC system, but Faith's pitch was just high enough that it was easier to hear through the door.

"We said we'd washed our hands of him. And we have to hold firm to that."

Whatever William said in response angered Faith.

"We're not abandoning him. You know how he is! You can't reason with him. He's safe as long as he can keep his spot at the home. He's safe there!"

William's voice raised in accordance with his temper. "I'm telling you it's all quite suspicious. And I think that's what Jason's looking into. He didn't go to Memphis for work, no matter what he's telling us. And that must mean he's worried about her. And I am, too. Look what happened to Connie—and we weren't even serious. Jason *loves* her! What do you think he's going to do about that?"

Faith shushed him and the floorboards creaked as the pair made their way upstairs.

Janet leaned against the wall in silence for a long time. By the time she wearily made her way across the room and dropped into bed, she knew two things with certainty. Faith and William knew —and maybe Jason did, too—who'd killed Connie, and they weren't going to tell the police a thing.

———

"Inspection day," Janet said as soon as her assistant manager walked in the door. "What are our odds?"

Cindy Lou plopped her bag down and then propped her hip against the countertop. She tilted her head to the side and, ticking them off on her fingers, listed out her thoughts. "*One* murder case is now open here, *two* fry baskets melted right into the hot oil last night in the food truck when Faith came in to see what was taking William so long and the cops pulled both aside for questioning and no one remembered to turn the heat off until smoke started billowing out of the windows, *three* of the food truck tires are now completely flat, and *four* people might have gotten food poisoning from the frozen interior of the burgers that Faith served." Her eyes narrowed and her lips crowded to one side of her face. "So I'm thinking we have a shot."

Janet's brow furrowed.

"Oh, I'm sorry, did I say we had a shot? I meant we have no chance in hell of passing this inspection."

Despite her foul mood, Janet smiled. She'd never heard Cindy Lou cuss before. "What has you so riled up?"

"I was in the darn walk-in cooler twice yesterday *with a dead woman*! I sure wish people would get their act together around here. You can't go shoving dead bodies into this bar! That's twice now! What is wrong with people?"

Janet had to agree; they'd had more than their fair share of death at the Spot. But there wasn't time to question the universe just then. The inspector's appointment was coming up in just half an hour.

"Did you call the clean-up company?"

"Yes, and they said we get the frequent customer discount. Ten percent off for repeat clients."

Janet's nose wrinkled. "So we'll be able to open today?"

Cindy Lou crossed her arms and nodded. "The medical waste crew will be here in fifteen minutes."

"And we've got thirty minutes to clean up that food truck. Since Cameron seems to be a no-show—"

"Again!"

"Would you mind keeping an eye on the bar while I head out and assess the damage?"

"No way!" Cindy Lou said. "I am not staying in this bar alone. You stay here, *near the murder closet*. I'll go clean that darn truck."

"Uh—you're going the wrong way!" Janet called after her when she went in the opposite direction of the food truck.

"I have to put my bag away first!" She flounced off into the office with her bag. A minute later, she was back. "Janet?"

Her tone caught Janet by surprise and she looked over. "What now?"

"I think you'd better come see this."

Janet glanced at her wristwatch and sighed. They didn't have time for any other surprises, and frankly, she didn't have the energy for anything else just then. But she followed Cindy Lou into the small office space. Cameron's locker door tilted open.

"I didn't mean to open his locker, but you know how sometimes if you slam one of the doors, the others kinda open up? Well, I just put my purse into my locker, but I was a little irritated about how this day is starting off, so I might have closed my door with more force than normal."

"So? Just close it back up, Cindy Lou. It's not the end of the world." She reached forward to do just that, when a wisp of blond hair made her snatch her hand back. "What the..." She leaned forward and lowered her voice to a whisper. "What's in there?"

Cindy Lou shook her head hard. "I'm not touching anything."

Janet groaned and, swiping a pen off the desk, she nudged the locker door open.

"Good Lord," Cindy Lou breathed. "Is that the next victim?"

CHAPTER TWENTY-SEVEN

"Are you going to call Cameron?" Cindy Lou asked when Janet picked up her cell phone. They were back behind the bar, and by unspoken agreement weren't going to separate again.

"No." Janet's lips pinched together and she tapped O'Dell's name, then waited impatiently for him to answer.

"If you're calling for an update, I'm not at liberty to discuss anything with—"

"No. I'm calling with information," Janet interrupted.

"What kind of information? I know you'd like to believe that Faith and William are innocent, but just because they're Jason's parents doesn't mean we're not going to take a long hard look at their possible involvement."

"It has nothing to do with them. My new cook Cameron is a no-show at work again today, and Cindy Lou and I happened to look in his locker, and we found a lock of blond hair in a little baggie, and a picture of a blond girl. I just thought...well, with Lola missing, and Connie dead...it sure seems like someone's going after blonds."

"Do you have Cameron's contact information?"

Janet relayed his cell phone number and his address, as he'd marked down on his employment papers.

"And the picture—the hair?"

"I'll keep it safe for you here behind the bar." Janet gingerly picked up the zip-top bag, then shoved it and the five-by-seven picture on a shelf below the counter.

While she did that, O'Dell heaved a great sigh. "It probably won't do us any good, especially since you moved it from his locker, but we'll run some tests on the hair at least; rule out Connie and Lola."

Janet grimaced but nodded.

A silence between them stretched, and she turned away from Cindy Lou.

O'Dell finally spoke. "Are you all right?"

"Mm-hmm. Just been a crazy week."

He barked out a laugh. "That's one way to describe it. I'll swing by Cameron's place, see if he's home. If he is, I'll bring him into the Spot. We can both ask him a few questions, okay?"

"Sounds good." Janet's breath hitched as a surge of emotion hit her, and she blinked quickly to clear it away. O'Dell—though just a friend—was a lot more reliable than Jason lately. She hated to wonder why that was.

She disconnected and slipped the phone into her back pocket. When she turned around, Cindy Lou was studying her intently.

"I know this isn't my place, but if you're going to make a change, do it now. He's not too interested in that Smith lady, but he might be if they spend more time together. You know?"

"Don't be ridiculous, Cindy Lou." Janet squared her shoulders and grabbed a spray bottle. "We'll wait for Mel to get here to do the cooler—"

"Praise Jesus!" Cindy Lou chirped.

"That means we have time to wipe down the tables right now." Evidence techs with Knoxville Police hadn't cleared the scene until after four that morning. It had been far too late to clean anything. But now they had to get ready for a full night of business.

The bell over the door jangled, and a gorgeous brunette walked in.

"Hey, hon, we're open, but barely. Food service doesn't start until...later." Cindy Lou finally came up with a time frame that was technically true.

The woman moved like a cat, slinky and sure of herself. She glided past Cindy Lou and came to a stop by Janet. "Are you Janet?" Her voice was like an FM disc jockey: low, throaty, sexy.

"Who's asking?" Janet immediately felt on the offensive. She ran a hand through her hair—which she'd washed, but let air dry on her way into work that morning. The woman standing opposite her looked like she'd just had a professional blowout, with contoured makeup and designer clothes.

"I'm Mike. I've been working with Jason, and I have some questions for you."

"*You're* Mike?" Cindy Lou's voice cut through Janet's shock and she snapped her mouth shut. She ripped her eyes away from the goddess in front of her when Cindy Lou spoke again. "What in the hell is wrong with Jason?"

Janet nodded along with Cindy Lou's question, wondering the same damn thing when Mike cleared her throat delicately.

"I haven't been able to get in touch with him for days. He hired me, trained me briefly, then set me loose on a project and I haven't seen him since. I just don't feel comfortable with the setup."

Janet snorted. "I'm right there with you, *Mike.*"

Mike's eyes narrowed. "It's short for Mikaela, but I've gone by Mike since middle school. You got a problem with that?"

Cindy Lou stepped between them. "No. No problem here. I'm afraid Jason's not here. We haven't seen him for days, either."

Mike's expression hardened. "Well, he's missed my first pay day, and I'm not inclined to keep working for him. I'm in high demand in this area, if you want the truth—"

"I believe it," Janet muttered.

"And I don't take lightly to being treated this way." She tossed a 9x12 yellow clasp envelope down on the table between them. "Here's some information I found interesting. You can tell Jason I expect to be compensated properly if he expects to keep me as a contractor." She pivoted and stalked out of the bar.

When Janet recovered enough to look at Cindy Lou, the other woman was fanning her neck with the envelope. "Is it me, or was that woman H-O-T hot?"

Janet's lips twisted into a snarl. Janet didn't like it one bit that Jason hadn't fully explained the hire. The factual omission stung worse than an outright lie.

Cindy Lou nudged Janet's shoulder with her own as she picked up her spray bottle and cloth. "I guess now we've got to figure out where in the heck Jason is! He's not here, he's not with Mike, so what's he been doing while the world crumbles down around us?" Cindy Lou's head jerked up as she realized that she'd spoken out loud. "Oh, I mean, well, you know what I mean, boss. I just...where is he, right? I'm sure he'll be back home with you soon enough. And really, good news that he *wasn't* with Mike, right? That's got to be a good thing. I wouldn't want my man near that man-eater if she was the last computer expert in the world!"

Janet winced and turned away from Cindy Lou. She sprayed cleaning solution on a table and swiped at it angrily. Where *was*

Jason? His father mentioned that he'd been in Memphis when Janet was there. Was he still there? Was he ever coming home?

Her phone buzzed and she ripped it out of her pocket—but it wasn't Jason. O'Dell's text was short and to the point.

Taking Cameron downtown. Meet us there.

Well, at least she'd get answers to one question today.

CHAPTER TWENTY-EIGHT

Janet clutched the zip-top bag with the picture and hair in one hand and scrolled through her phone with the other. There wasn't even a seat in the waiting area of the downtown police department, so she leaned up against the wall. O'Dell had never minded keeping Janet waiting in the past, and today was no different.

When the door that lead back to the detectives' section finally opened, it wasn't O'Dell who stepped through.

Smith, though small, looked down her nose at Janet. "Let's go. He's waiting for you in the back."

Janet brushed aside the urge to stay right where she was and followed Smith down the hall. "Anything new on Lola?"

"Nothing. We've re-interviewed all of her friends, the principal, her teachers, her parents. Everyone knows about a boyfriend, but nobody knows who he is."

Janet's step slowed down until she was several doorways behind Smith. She needed to tell Smith about Matt, about Memphis, the apartment, William. "Ummm...the boyfriend—that's the kid everyone's calling Matt, right?"

Smith looked over her shoulder at Janet. "That's the one. Doesn't seem to go to any nearby schools, either; at least, not that we've found. This way, Janet." She pushed open a door on their left and walked in.

Janet followed slowly, still mulling over how she needed to proceed. But this was going to be tricky, and almost anything she shared could lead to William going to jail. Maybe Faith, too. Did she really think them capable of murder? Her lack of sleep the last two nights were a testament to how unsure she was.

"Well?" Smith stared at her expectantly.

"Uh—sorry. What was that?"

"Did you bring the picture and the hair?"

Janet reached into her bag and pulled out the items from Cameron's locker.

Smith assessed the picture quickly, then scrutinized the hair, her nose scrunched. "Not Lola, but that's the only thing I know."

"How can you tell just by looking at it?"

"Lola dyed her hair. This is untreated hair." She looked up with a grin. "My mom was a hair stylist. I spent a lot of long days at the salon with her when I was growing up."

Janet nodded stiffly and Smith took the evidence and left the room. When she was alone, Janet frowned as she surveyed the space. The room was plainly furnished: a small table, a large dark window, and two hard plastic chairs. She sat down and crossed her arms, realizing belatedly that she was more put out by Smith's anecdotal story about her childhood than by being alone in a police interview room. She didn't like knowing anything that made Smith seem more human. She didn't like to think about why that was.

When the detective came back empty-handed, Janet asked some questions rapid fire. "What are we doing here? Is O'Dell going to bring Cameron here? This room won't hold all of us, that

much is clear." Even just the two women in the small room made
for a tight squeeze.

Smith pressed a button on the underside of the table, and the
dark window lit up to reveal the room next door. "O'Dell thought
you could watch him interview Cameron from in here."
Cameron sat at an identical table and chair setup in the other
room. He leaned back in his seat, aggressively chewing a wad of
gum, and Janet had to wonder how long he'd been sitting there.
"We're ready," Smith said into her walkie-talkie.

Moments later, the door in the other room swung open and
O'Dell walked in. "Sorry to keep you waiting. We sure do appreciate you coming in on such short notice."

"No problem, man. But I don't have a lot of time. I missed
work the last two days, and I really need to go in today and grovel,
you know?"

"As it turns out, I did know about that. We had a situation at
the Spot last night—"

Cameron's groan cut O'Dell off. "The dart tournament? Oh,
man, I'd completely forgotten about that dang thing until just
now." He groaned again and ran his hands roughly through his
hair. "I'm sure I'm totally fired." He groaned again.

"Where were you?"

The cook sprawled back in his chair, one arm hanging down
by his side, the other still grasping a tuft of hair at the crown of his
head. "Unbelievable. Family problems will come looking for you,
no matter how far you try and get away, man. I was just dealing
with some family drama. It's over now, but not soon enough, man.
Not soon enough."

O'Dell nodded sympathetically. "Your parents? Siblings?"

"My parents. I had to run to Memphis for a crisis that just
never seemed to end."

O'Dell's eyes flicked over to the two-way mirror, and Janet's
gut clenched. Cameron had been in Memphis?

"Where in Memphis were you?"

"My parents live in Cooper-Young. I just got back last night—but late. Too late to go into work."

"Probably for the best," O'Dell said, leaning against the table on his elbows.

"Oh yeah? Why's that?"

"Janet found a dead woman in the walk-in cooler."

"What? Holy sh—I mean...was it someone...was it someone they knew?"

Cameron's voice shook on the last word, and Janet and Smith both leaned forward instinctively.

"It wasn't a stranger, that's for sure. While we were investigating the scene, we found this in your locker. Care to explain?" O'Dell held out the lock of hair and the picture.

The color drained from Cameron's face. His lips pinched together, and he suddenly became interested in a rip in the knee of his jeans. When he looked up, his face was set, his expression grim. "Am I under arrest?"

O'Dell leaned back in his chair, crossed his arms over his chest, and rubbed his lips with his hand. "Is there a reason you think you'd be under arrest?"

Cameron didn't take the bait. With a screech of metal against tile, he pushed his chair back and stood. "You know where to find me, obviously, but I have to go. I'm late for work."

O'Dell nodded, but didn't move, just watched Cameron walk around the table and out the door.

Janet crept to the door and eased it open in time to see a patrol officer disappear around the corner with Cameron, headed out toward the lobby.

O'Dell stepped into the hall and looked past Janet. "What'd you think?"

"I think he's hiding something, but not anything to do with

Connie Hutchings' death," Smith said succinctly from behind her.

"Agreed." O'Dell's gaze sharpened as he focused on Janet. "You?"

"I'm not sure I want to be at the bar with him. Something didn't add up there. Whose hair is that? Who's the girl?"

O'Dell shrugged. "Maybe he'll tell you." He held up the zip-top bag. "I'll have this tested, see if we get a hit in the system. But I agree with Smith—this has nothing to do with Connie."

Janet frowned, but before she could answer, a commotion at the end of the hallway made all three turn.

Lola's mother fought her way through the door into the detectives' section. "You!" She pointed at Janet, her expression torn. "You told me you'd keep me updated! But I just heard—I just heard that there was a body found at your bar. A blond girl, that's all anybody's saying. Was it my Lola?"

Smith stepped forward, around Janet and O'Dell, reaching out toward Misty. "Mrs. Rivers, you should have called. We don't have any news of Lola." When she got close, Misty gripped her arms for support. "Come with me, ma'am."

They disappeared down the hallway, leaving O'Dell and Janet staring after her.

"Surprised she hasn't turned up, yet," O'Dell finally offered.

"Yeah. Me, too."

"Doesn't bode well, does it?"

"No." Janet turned toward the exit. "It doesn't."

CHAPTER TWENTY-NINE

O'Dell escorted Janet out to the lobby, and they stood together by the front door, O'Dell not turning to head back inside, Janet not walking away.

"Tell Misty to come to the Spot when she's done here, okay?"

O'Dell nodded, searching her face for something.

Janet gulped under his scrutiny. "You looked over when Cameron mentioned Memphis. Why?"

"Quizz called me. Said there's something going on there."

"Did she tell you what happened?"

O'Dell shifted, then looked down at the ground to watch the toe of his loafer scrub a black mark off the tile. She didn't think he was going to answer—he just kept looking at the damn tile floor—but he finally blew out a sigh.

"She told me enough that I can see that you're connected somehow. I don't know how, but you are. So I'm working some back channels down there, keeping everything on the down low until I know that you're safe."

Janet blinked. "But what about Lola?"

"Whatever happened to her already happened. And I'll work

to make sure that her family finds justice. You're my priority now."

The words hung heavy in the air as Janet tried to make sense of what he was telling her. He thought Lola was dead. He thought Janet was in trouble.

"Where's Jason?"

She blinked again, hating that he kept catching her off guard. "I wish I knew. He's been MIA for over a week now. Just a few text messages and voicemails so I know he's alive."

O'Dell frowned when she opened the door. "Be careful, okay?"

She drove to the bar, feeling unsettled. She wasn't in danger. Obviously if William was going to kill her, he'd had ample opportunity over the last five months of living in her house. But what was driving him? And what was Jason's role in all of it? What did Faith know? What was Cameron hiding? Was anyone else at the Spot in danger?

Cindy Lou waved happily from behind the bar when Janet walked in. "I canceled the kitchen inspection because of unusual and unplanned chaos. That's actually one of the reasons listed online—and boy, does it fit our situation! They said they can push it back for a week, but they'll just pop in when they have time in their schedule. Hopefully we'll have a chance to get those new fry baskets in!" She lowered her voice. "The walk-in's all cleaned up, too. I wrote a check from the office account and put the receipt in the lockbox. Now there's a business expense you didn't plan on using twice. Bet you get audited." She shot a sympathetic look over the bar and Janet mustered up a smile.

She sent Cindy Lou home to get some rest before they opened for business later that afternoon.

But when she was alone, she couldn't settle into any task while she waited for Lola's mom to come in.

Finally the bell over the door jingled, but it wasn't Misty who walked in.

"Let me just set a few things straight with you right now." Quizz cracked her knuckles as she glided to a stop directly across the bar from Janet. Her lips curled as she spoke. "You are not a PI. You are not legally allowed to investigate anything on your own without me. *You are an apprentice*, and that means you have to do what I say or go find another PI dumb enough to try and mentor the one woman *on the planet* who already knows everything there is to know about everything!"

Janet tried for a conciliatory smile. She must have failed, because Quizz's snarl deepened.

"I have left you no fewer than four messages, demanding that you call me back. Have you called me back?"

Janet meekly shook her head.

"No, you have not!" Quizz pounded her fist against the bar with each word. "I have information that is pertinent to your missing-girl case, and if you cannot find the time in your *very busy schedule*," she looked scornfully around the dead empty bar and paused for effect, "then I suggest you make the time to prioritize the case that you signed my firm up for *on your own and without consultation from me*, so that we can find Lola and move on to taking cases that will make us actual money to keep the lights on at Quizz Bexley Investigations. *Do I make myself clear?*"

Janet blew out a slow breath and nodded. "Yes."

Quizz blinked. "Yes...you understand?"

Janet nodded again. "Yes, and I'm sorry I've been out of touch. It won't happen again."

"Oh." Quizz slapped the bar with her open hand and pulled out the barstool she'd been hovering over. "Good. I'm glad we've got that straight."

Janet poured the other woman an iced tea and set it on a coaster. "So what's the news?"

Quizz took her time stirring the ice cubes around in the tall skinny glass and taking a long, steady sip before answering. "I got some information about that apartment in Memphis."

"Oh yeah? What?"

"Not so fast." Quizz tilted her head to the side and studied the tightness around Janet's eyes. "What's been keeping you so busy?"

Janet set about making herself a Long Island iced tea, needing to keep her hands busy so her brain wouldn't lock up with information overload. "Well...let's see...Jason's father's ex-girlfriend was killed...and her body was left in the walk-in cooler. The new cook I hired has a weird obsession with blond girls and keeping locks of their hair...so *that's* nothing to worry about, obviously. And my boyfriend has been MIA for so long that his new employee Mike—who's pretty much the most gorgeous woman I've ever seen, by the way—came into the bar to tell me she's quitting. So, you know, just a regular week, really."

Quizz sat frozen with her lips still clamped around the straw. "You haven't heard from Jason? In how long?"

"I guess it's been..." Janet looked at her watch, as if it was minutes or hours she was dealing with. "Yeah, going on a week now."

"And not a word?" Quizz breathed.

"An odd message here and there, but my texts are going unanswered and he won't pick up when I call. So yeah. Something's going on."

Quizz shifted uncomfortably in her seat and stirred the ice cubes around her empty glass.

"More tea?"

"No. No thanks. I'm not sure how to say this, Janet, but... well, that apartment in Memphis? With the porn and the duct tape and zip ties?"

Janet kept her eyes on the cocktail shaker. She poured in

vodka, then rum, but even as she tried to distract herself with the task, her stomach clenched. She was certain that she didn't want to know what Quizz was about to say, but she nodded anyway, and the PI continued.

"I made some calls to some contacts I have in Memphis after we got home. Let me tell you, nobody wants to talk about anything until they know why you want the information. I finally connected with the real-estate firm that owns that building."

Janet's vision went hazy, but she picked up the tequila and gin and poured them in at the same time. "Uh-huh?" Her voice hitched on the short syllables and she cleared her throat roughly. Quizz leaned forward and tried to catch her eye. Janet refused to look up.

"Well, here's where things get strange. Apparently that unit failed inspections several years ago because of the fire escape—no surprise there. So as far as their records indicated, no one's allowed to live there—the unit was supposed to be empty."

Janet twisted the cap off the triple sec and glugged some into the shaker, then squeezed in some simple syrup. She shook the whole concoction, then poured it into a tall glass filled with ice, added a splash of coke and a lemon wedge, and sucked half of it down through the straw before setting the glass carefully on the countertop and looking at Quizz for the first time.

"And?"

"It took some smooth talking, but I finally got a helpful person over at MLGW."

Janet's nose wrinkled.

"Memphis Light, Gas, and Water."

"Oh. Good idea." Janet was momentarily distracted from the mounting sense of dread, impressed with Quizz's investigation.

Quizz's chin jutted up. "They're not supposed to share customer information, of course, but I can be very persuasive when I want to be." Her proud expression slid off her face as quickly as it had appeared, and she seemed to brace herself for what was coming. Janet did, too. She already knew the answer, but what would happen when it was out in the open? Who else would they have to tell?

"And did they tell you who was paying for the power?"

Quizz shook her head, then reached across the bar, pushed the straw aside in Janet's Long Island, and took a pull straight from the glass. "The customer information was missing—in fact, my source was blown away, because the name had been wiped clean out of their database." Janet's mouth went dry, but Quizz wasn't finished. "But here's where things get really strange. They made a note in the system that someone else called, asking for the same information. Janet, Jason Brooks called two days ago asking about that apartment. How is Jason involved in this?"

Quizz searched Janet's face, but Janet was saved from answering when the chime over the door jangled.

"Janet, Quizz, thank God you're both here!"

CHAPTER THIRTY

Misty crossed the bar and fell into a seat next to Quizz. Her boyfriend, Paul, hovered behind her, resting his hands on the back of her barstool. "Detective Smith told us all about the body here. And I just feel awful. I didn't realize that your family was suffering a loss, too."

Janet winced at the assumption that she'd been close with Connie but didn't want to correct the other woman and lose the sudden surge of goodwill.

Quizz saved her from having to create a narrative.

"Mrs. Bridges, I'm sure you're frustrated by the lack of progress in your daughter's case."

"We are!" she said, including her boyfriend. "We just can't believe that nobody knows anything! I mean, her friend made it twelve hours before they were found out. I can't help but think it doesn't—" Her voice caught, but after a moment she soldiered on. "It doesn't bode well for Lola."

"As I told you on the phone after you first met with Janet, these cases are tricky at best, and downright awful and intractable at worst. We're doing our best, and following up on leads, but at this point, like Smith has surely told you, there's just not much to go on."

"What about the phone? Did you get anything from the phone? Detective Smith wasn't happy that I gave it to you and not her, but I told her that you seemed to be taking it more seriously than her department. I don't know, maybe it was a mistake."

Janet came out from behind the bar and took the seat on Misty's other side, forcing her own turmoil over her boyfriend's possible involvement in a murder to the very back of her brain. "Mrs. Bridges, we are doing everything we can to find your daughter. Quizz and I have been following up on leads since last week. We were able to crack Lola's password and discovered that she'd been exchanging messages with a guy named Matt. They planned to meet up in Memphis."

Misty sucked in a gasp and her hand covered her mouth. "No! Why would she do that? How?"

Janet stared over Misty and Quizz's heads. That was a good question, and one Janet had skipped over in her haste to go to Memphis and investigate. Would the girl have gone? She didn't have the funds to fly, didn't own a car. Minors couldn't buy bus tickets on their own.

"The reason we haven't been in touch is because we just can't tell if she went or not," Quizz said, covering for Janet's silence. "We showed her picture all around, and the good news—at least, we think it's good news—is that no one really recognized her. The closest we got was a cook at a nearby restaurant remembering a blond girl—hardly definitive. Maybe she never left town at all."

"But if she's still here, why wouldn't she have gotten in touch? It doesn't make any sense!"

Quizz's head dropped and Janet cleared her throat. "All I can promise is that we'll keep working on finding Lola, Misty. We'll keep looking for your daughter."

Paul held a handkerchief out to his girlfriend and she clutched it against her eyes for a brief moment before heaving a great sigh and pushing back from the bar. "Thank you. I guess that's all we can hope for."

After the couple left, Janet sagged against the bar. It was too much. Her business in chaos, her personal life turned upside down. Trying to find a wayward teen was going to push her over the edge. Janet turned to Quizz. "I want off this case."

Quizz's eyes bulged, and blood rushed to her face. "I don't give a great goddamn what's going on in your personal life. You just sat here and promised Misty that you would work to find Lola. And that's exactly what you're going to do!"

Quizz swiveled away from Janet and stalked to the door. "I want an update on what you've done to find Lola tomorrow. My office, nine a.m. *sharp!*"

———

By the time Cindy Lou got back into work an hour later, the door to the bar was locked, the lights were off, and Janet lay across the small uncomfortable threadbare couch in the office with an ice pack over her eyes.

"What are you doing?" Cindy Lou crossed her arms and leaned against the doorframe, just a shadow, illuminated from behind by the bar lights she'd flicked on when she crossed over to the office.

"Sulking." Janet's head pounded. Her heart felt like it was shrinking in her chest. She didn't know what to think about everything that had happened over the last forty-eight hours.

Why was Jason looking into that Memphis apartment? Was it a good sign? It meant he surely knew—or at least suspected—that his father was involved in Connie's death, and maybe Lola's disappearance, too. But then why wasn't he back home, telling her what was going on?

But worst of all, Quizz thought she was going to keep working on the missing-girl case? Janet couldn't keep going in so many directions at once. Not only did she not have any brain space left for someone else's crisis when she was so fully mired down in her own, but she was failing at nearly everything she attempted! Misty needed a pro—not an amateur.

Cindy Lou interrupted her internal struggle with a reminder that even more chaos was coming. "Hey, don't forget the FOP rescheduled the dart tournament for this weekend."

"What?"

"I thought you might have forgotten. Friday night? I told them we'd pay for the pizza, in light of...well. Just seemed the least we could do, you know?"

Janet must have groaned in response. She pressed a hand over the ice pack covering her eyes and wished she was anywhere else. But Cindy Lou was determined to cheer her up.

"You need a trip to the salon. I've got the perfect girl for your hair. I'll make the appointment. Let's go."

"No." Janet didn't move from the couch. A blowout was not going to make her feel better—and more importantly, she didn't *want* to feel better. She *needed* to feel all these terrible things swirling around her body in order to figure out what to do next.

"You're not going to just lay there like a sad sack."

Janet groaned, and Cindy Lou glided over and pulled her up with surprising ease for someone in three-inch stilettos. "Let's go. You'll be able to think better after a conditioning rinse."

"Cindy Lou! No! I'm not over here moping. I'm processing a lot of shit right now. William might have k—" The words died on her lips. Impossible. She just couldn't see it happening. Now, Faith...that was another story, but what did it all mean? She groaned again and Cindy Lou jumped back like she'd been shot.

"Sorry! Sorry, I'm—I just..." She looked around the small space and suddenly felt like she was stuck inside a pinball machine. If she had to stay inside the Spot for even a minute longer, she was going to explode. But she couldn't go home. Jason's mother and father were there. What was their connection to the Memphis apartment, to Connie's murder?

"Fine. Let's go."

Cindy Lou jumped again, this time in delight, and she clapped her hands together as she steered Janet out of the office, through the bar, and toward her car in the parking lot.

Janet slid into the tiny red convertible. Maybe Cindy Lou was right; maybe she'd be able to think better in a place where she wasn't surrounded by memories of Jason, by his smell, his touch. She rode in silence, which allowed Cindy Lou to ramble on without interruption about everything from her son Chip to her cat Bubbles.

When they arrived at the salon, Cindy Lou ushered Janet in like she was a celebrity client. She and the stylist put their heads together for what felt like a long while, and then the stylist, Tracey, instructed her to lay back against the sink while she put on a conditioning treatment that would "make your hair shine like this morning's sunrise."

Janet almost backed out then, but Cindy Lou sighed in pleasure as she took the seat at the sink next to her while Tracey walked away to collect the product. A different younger girl came back a few minutes later and introduced herself as the intern. Cindy Lou's headphones were in, her eyes closed. Some new age music wafted toward Janet and she shuddered. She'd rather have silence than listen to that.

The intern got to work on Janet first, squeezing something out of a tube and rubbing it all over her head. Her eyes watered, and an unfamiliar sharp smell tingled her nose. "Do you have headphones, too?" the intern asked.

Janet nodded and reached into her bag. Maybe her brain could work out a way that it wasn't Jason's family who'd killed Connie and lured Lola to Memphis. She cued up a heavy metal song and zoned out to the drum beat as she prayed that some other scenario would come to her. Anything that might mean the people she loved were innocent.

CHAPTER THIRTY-ONE

"I am so incredibly, terribly sorry." Tracey met Janet's eyes mournfully through the mirror, then shot a look that could kill at her intern. "I was clear that Tammy was to work on Cindy Lou, as she's a return client, and I was going to work on you. Then I got a phone call from my daughter's school, and I'm afraid there was a mix-up."

Janet tilted her head to the side and took in the new color of hair on her head. It wasn't blond...more like orange at the tips and just *without* color near the crown of her head. "I—I still don't understand. What happened?"

Tracey shuddered before answering and Janet flinched. It must be bad if Tracey didn't even want to utter the words.

"Cindy Lou just loves that white blond hair that so few people naturally have. So on Cindy Lou, we do a bleach treatment, then pre-tone and she's good to go."

Janet looked blankly back through the mirror, but she could see the color that was so clearly missing from her hair now rising in her cheeks. Her natural brown hair was ruined. Was this woman saying she couldn't get it back? Before she could ask, Tracey spoke again.

"So the reason I was gone for so long that *this,*" she pointed at Janet's head, "was allowed to happen, is that after I got off the phone with my daughter's school, I discovered a situation with our color wheel."

Janet's brow wrinkled. What did that have to do with her?

Tracey covered her eyes with her hand and took a deep breath. "The shades from light auburn all the way to black are ruined. One case exploded, and now we just can't trust any of them—"

"What are you saying?" Janet roared. "Get my hair back to brown! It can't be that hard!"

Tracey bit her lip. "Well, that's just it. We're out of color. I can make you blond, but I can't do brown—not until we get our new shipment of color in next week. Maybe in two weeks. It just depends on our supplier!" she added hastily when Janet let out an aggrieved groan.

"Blond! How is it that you have the product to do that?"

"Well, that's just it; the blond contains bleach, and they're packaged in stronger materials, so they're just fine. No exploding packets. But everything else has to be sent back to the manufacturer. Not safe to use."

"Not safe—not safe—" Janet spluttered, but Tracey didn't stop long enough for her to really get going.

"So what we'll do," Tracey plodded on gamely, "is a second round of bleach to get the color evened out." She took a lock of Janet's hair into her hands and peered at the roots. "Definitely needs a treatment, and a pre-tone, and then add a really gorgeous yellow undertone to give you some depth of color." She looked up with a smile. "I mean, really, a lot of women would pay a ton of money for this—ah—obviously, we'll be doing it for free because it's not what you initially requested, but don't be surprised if you decide to stick with it in the end." Her smile slid off her face when she took in Janet's mutinous expression and she beat a hasty retreat to the color station.

Words failed Janet completely. Cindy Lou had taken her headphones out around the halfway mark of Tracey's explanation and she smiled brightly. "Everybody goes blond eventually, Janet. It was just your turn." She rested her head back against the sink basin and closed her eyes. "Sounds like you'll be here for hours. Don't you worry, hon. I'll head right into the Spot when I'm done and get everything up and running. I'm not the assistant manager for nothin', after all." She stuck her headphones back into her ears and fell quiet, a small smile on her lips.

"William, Faith, I wasn't expecting you two to come in today." Janet walked nonchalantly past Jason's parents and headed behind the bar. She tried to ignore the deafening silence that met her greeting, along with the four sets of eyes she felt were glued to her head.

She grabbed a rocks glass and filled it halfway with the sticky, syrupy frozen margarita and held the icy glass against her forehead for a moment before taking a small, refreshing sip. "I hate to say it, but you were so right about this machine, Faith," she called to Jason's mother across the room. Faith's brow furrowed, and Janet grimaced and looked down at the tiny beads of frozen drink, then swirled them around her glass before taking another sip. She closed her eyes and then tilted her head back, reveling in the cool liquid making its way to the back of her throat.

"Well, I think it looks great," Cindy Lou said, her voice as syrupy as the drink now sliding down to Janet's belly. "I mean, really, really like...not exactly *natural*, you know, but like you spent a whole lot of money on the job."

Mel barked out a laugh. "Cindy Lou said there was a crisis, but I didn't realize it was a...I mean, a *life* crisis."

"This is why I came in?" Quizz's plaintive whine was enough to finally draw Janet's eyes away from her glass.

"I wouldn't call this a *life* crisis, Mel." Janet tried to brush off her disgruntled feelings. "It's a mistake that I have to live with, but not for long."

"Are you going to change it?" Cindy Lou asked, dismayed.

Janet ignored her. She didn't blame Cindy Lou for her hair, but she didn't want to chat things over with the woman, either. Instead she looked at Quizz. "Why are you here?"

"I'm asking myself the same question."

Mel chortled, "I called her and Jason's parents in after Cindy Lou said—and I quote, 'The shit is about to go down.'"

"I really thought you were going to murder Tracey. I mean, I know that you knew it was that intern's fault, not Tracey's, but the look you had in your eyes! I've never seen anything like it."

Janet threw back the rest of her drink, then squeezed her eyes closed and pinched the bridge of her nose when the freeze headache struck, like a dagger was cleaving her head in half. When she blinked back to awareness fifteen seconds later, her eyes landed on Faith and William, heads bowed together at the corner booth. Faith's hands moved animatedly above the table, and William's expression dropped into a scowl.

Janet's heart lifted—were they fighting? Were things back to normal? But before she could celebrate, William dropped his head into his hands and Faith reached forward to stroke his shoulder. The pair stood and walked quickly to the exit. "We'll see you at home, Janet," William called.

Faith stopped and turned to look at Janet. "I don't think it looks too bad, hon. I'm sure we'll all get used to it."

Mel chuckled as the pair walked out into the parking lot.

Janet turned away and met Quizz's eye. The PI had seen the

strange touching scene between Jason's parents, too, and wasn't going to let it lie.

"I just got off the phone with a friend of mine in Memphis. She's with the Shelby County Sheriff's office. She told me that Connie's family reported her missing eight days ago, but they hadn't actually heard from her in a couple of weeks."

"Hmm. That lines up with when William said she stopped returning his calls."

"Are you sure?"

Janet's nose scrunched up as she searched her mind. "Well, no. I guess not. I mean, he told us that Connie'd stopped returning his calls—that was back when I hired Cameron, maybe... a week, week-and-a-half ago? I heard William tell Faith that he was ending things with her. I guess I just assumed that they talked that day and officially ended things. But...well, I don't know if that happened."

"What did he say *exactly*?"

"Faith said it was time to end things. William said, 'Don't worry, it's taken care of.'" She looked up at Quizz, her eyebrows so close together they were practically touching. "But he didn't mean—I mean, there's no way he meant that he ended *her*."

Quizz didn't answer, only took a long, slow sip of her sweet tea.

Janet rinsed out her sticky glass and set it in the dishwashing sink. "When did her family last see her?"

Quizz looked down at her notebook. "Just over two weeks ago."

Janet's stomach dropped, like she'd just noticed a deer in the road and wasn't sure her car was going to stop in time. "The sixth? That's the same day that Faith arrived in Knoxville. That's the day she drove in from Memphis."

CHAPTER THIRTY-TWO

Quizz left, and Cindy Lou, complaining of a stomachache, went home, too. So only Janet and Mel were working for the few customers who sat sprinkled throughout the bar.

Because there wasn't a huge need to check IDs at the door, Mel was doing an inventory count in the walk-in cooler. She walked out with a clipboard in one hand and a bottle of beer in the other. "We're just about where we should be. I'm celebrating by drinking this bottle, so now we're one short of what we should have." She clapped the clipboard down onto the bar and twisted the cap off her beer in the same second. She took a slug, her eyes never leaving Janet's. "What's going on? Kat and I haven't seen you around the house in a while. Or Jason, for that matter."

Mel and her partner Kat lived in the other half of the duplex that Janet and Jason owned. The unit was a mirror image of hers, and the women usually chatted over morning coffees or anytime they sat on the porch. Not lately.

"I don't know." Janet absently continued dusting the liquor bottles on the shelf next to the Beerador and stared off into space.

"Is there anything I can do?"

"I wish there was. But it doesn't seem like there's anything anybody can do."

"I gather that Jason's acting strange?"

Janet snorted. "That's an understatement. I haven't heard from him in over a week. He's hiding something, Mel, and I don't know what."

Mel shifted on her feet and studied the peeling label on her beer bottle. When she looked up, her expression was pained. Like she didn't want to say what she was thinking.

"Spit it out." Janet wasn't in the mood for games.

"It's just—I mean, how much do you know about Jason?"

"Well..." Janet set her rag down and crossed her arms. "I mean, I've been dating him for years, his father lives with us, his mother's practically moved in. I feel like I know him really fucking well."

Mel nodded, unaffected by Janet's misdirected anger. "That's good. But I mean—do you know anything about his past? His history?"

Janet's arms flew up. "Of course I do!" She pinched her lips together and dropped the dusting rag, then wiped her forehead with the back of her hand. She closed her eyes, her hand still resting against her head. When she pried her eyes open again, Mel was taking another sip of her beer, and after a minute Janet sighed. "I mean, no. Not really much at all."

"Maybe that's a good place to start?" Mel walked away, and Janet stared after her until she disappeared into the walk-in cooler.

Her shift at the Spot had never felt longer. Business was slow, but not slow enough to close early. She and Mel easily handled the crowd, but when it was finally time to go home, closing down the bar took twice as long without Cindy Lou's help.

Despite O'Dell's best guess, Cameron hadn't come in begging for his job back, so Mel had manned the fry baskets and griddle for the three people who ordered food.

"I guess it's time to hire a new cook, huh?"

Janet grimaced. The last thing she cared about was hiring another cook to work at a food truck she didn't want that hardly any of her customers were ordering from. "I guess I should have let Faith make the hire in the first place."

"Hey, one less thing for you to worry about, huh?"

"Sure."

Mel grinned.

"What?"

"You just don't want anyone to think that you need help. Nobody does it all on their own, you know. That's no way to live."

Janet dumped ice into the sink from the lower compartment of the condiment container, then closed the lid and set the whole thing on the lower shelf of the Beerador. "Sure, sure. I know. I'd just *rather* do it all myself. Other people only end up letting you down. Easier to not let them step up in the first place."

"Ouch!" Mel grabbed her heart dramatically.

"Oh, Mel, you know what I mean. I'm completely happy to rely on you for all bouncer- and friend-related issues. Let's start right now, with this trash can." She laughed when Mel groaned.

"That's not what I mean, and you know it. But I did toss the lettuce and tomatoes out there. They were way past their prime." Mel heaved the trash bag up out of the can and tied the ends closed. "Hardly worth having the food available if none of the customers are going to order anything."

"No lie," Janet said, adding *buy produce* to her list of tasks on the notepad by the cash register. "I wonder when they'll come for the inspection. I hate having to be ready all the time. I guess our menu isn't enticing enough." She ran a finger down a copy of the closest menu. *Hamburgers. Cheeseburgers. French fries.* "I mean, what else could we add that won't break the bank? Hot dogs?"

Mel shrugged. "What about those fried cheese stick things? They can't be too expensive."

Janet wrote it on her list so she'd remember to think about it the next day, and the two walked out into the dark parking lot together. Mel tossed the trash into the Dumpster while Janet locked the door. "See you at home!" Janet called.

"I'm heading to the grocery store," Mel corrected. "Kat says there's no food in the house."

"It's three in the morning! What kind of food do you need?"

Mel laughed. "I don't know. I only know if it's not there, I'll be starving until morning."

Engines started up and Janet flicked the radio off so she could think on the drive home. Since Jason wasn't answering calls or texts, she was going to work on William and Faith as soon as she got home. Wake them up, if necessary. After all, they were staying in her house. It was time to stop being polite and start being herself. She smiled grimly at the thought.

Ahead of her, Mel turned off toward the twenty-four-hour supermarket, and she idly wondered while she waited for the light to turn green what midnight feast Mel was planning.

When she turned down her street, it took her an extra minute to notice that Jason's truck was in the driveway. She turned off her engine and sat in the dark as her exhausted body tensed up and a hot flush worked up from her belly. When she realized she was girding her loins, stalling for time, she launched out of her car and up the front path to the door. She twisted the handle and pushed, but the door was bolted shut.

She fished her keys out of her bag and jabbed the correct one into the lock. It didn't work.

She pulled the key back out and inspected it—definitely the right one. She tried again, and nothing happened.

Janet pounded her fist against the door.

Bam, bam, bam.

"Jason, are you in there?" She tried to keep the anger from her voice, but didn't think she succeeded, especially when her fist hit the door even louder the second round of knocks.

When the door finally flung open, Jason stood at the threshold, a scowl on his face. Her heart fluttered, and despite her anger with him, her own body couldn't hide how glad she was to finally see him.

"Your key won't work. I changed the locks."

"You—you what?" She looked at him blankly, confused by his words, his expression. She was supposed to be the angry one —not him.

His scowl deepened, and he stepped forward, forcing her back down the front steps. His broad shoulders filled most of the doorframe, so that she could barely see around him into her house.

"Move, Jason! You have a lot of explaining to do! Where have you been? Why haven't you been returning my calls?"

His jaw locked, and he crossed his arms. "You can't come in. In fact, you need to leave. Mom packed your stuff today." He motioned to the side of the porch, and Janet gasped when she saw three suitcases stacked on top of each other. "Goodbye, Janet."

A sudden chill settled in the base of her stomach. Jason was kicking her out of the home they owned together?

Her face froze, and after an indeterminate amount of time, she reached up and touched her lips, parted in shock.

Jason had been gone for weeks, out of touch, not communicating, and now he was telling her that she had to go? She had to leave?

She shook her head, trying to make sense of the very few but confusing words that Jason had uttered. She was out, *but his parents were in?*

Her boyfriend stared at her, his face a mask, completely void of emotion. She reached out toward him tentatively and he didn't move away. Then, with a strength that surprised even her, she put her hands on his chest and shoved him out of the way and stalked into her house.

"My belongings don't fit in three goddamn suitcases, Jason. And you don't get to kick me out. This is my house just as much as it's yours."

CHAPTER THIRTY-THREE

The silence inside the house was palpable. It felt like a bass drum beating in Janet's heart, her ears, her head. She prowled around the main room, passing Faith, William, Jason—but no one would even look her in the eye.

"Where have you been?" She glared at Jason, but he only stared at the wall behind her, unblinking. She swung her gaze over toward his parents. "What about you two? What are you up to at all hours of the day and night, heads together at the bar? You're up to something. What?"

Faith stared at Janet—not with confusing anger like her son. It was another emotion that simmered just under the surface, one that Janet couldn't quite name. William stared at the floor; whereas Jason and Faith's faces were red, William's was pale. Like he'd just learned some terrible truth.

"I don't understand, Jason. This is my house! This is my—" Her voice broke, and she couldn't get the words out. She couldn't say that this house and everyone in it just then, were her life—her family. She could no more leave them than she could cut off her hand.

Faith's face twitched. William—pale already—turned a shade of light green, and he swayed on his feet. Only Jason remained impassive, staring at her, completely unmoved.

"You have to go, Janet." His lips pressed into a flat line, and the muscles in his arms—crossed tightly over his chest—were strung tight like a bow.

Janet's eyes narrowed. "I'm not leaving. You can leave. In fact, you can all leave! But I'm staying."

"Go!" Jason's yell was so unexpected, so loud, that she and Faith jumped. He moved toward her, propelling her toward the door before she could command her own feet to stop moving. And even then, he physically lifted her over the threshold and barred her from walking back in. "Go, Janet. Go now. Please." His voice broke on the last word, and it was that sound—the emotion that seeped into his voice that broke her out of her own rage. Her shoulders dropped, and she leaned toward Jason. His eyes were tired, sad, like he'd just learned something awful.

She reached out and rested her open palm against his chest. He didn't move away, and she took a shaky breath. "Jason, why? What are you doing? I don't—I don't understand what's happening. Where do you want me to go? It's—" She shook her head, then motioned to the darkness around her. "It's three in the morning! Just let me stay. Let me help you work out whatever's going on. Jason. Please." The crinkles around his eyes softened; he reached up and pressed his hand into hers, and her heart lifted. He looked like he might be thinking about letting her in, might be considering telling her what in the hell was going on.

But then, red and blue flashing lights lit up the street behind her, and a voice called into the darkness. "Janet?"

Jason's eyes hardened, and he pushed her hand away from him. "Your ride's here. Goodbye, Janet."

And with that, he closed the door in her face. The last thing she heard was the *thunk* of the deadbolt sliding into place.

O'Dell tossed her bags into his trunk, then hustled around to the driver's side of the car and climbed in. He looked at Janet, pale, fighting off tears, and then closed his door and started up the engine. "Uh...where to?"

Janet took in a deep breath through her nose and then blew it out her mouth. When she looked over at the cop, he quickly looked away. "Why are you even here?" she spat out.

"Well." He shifted in his seat, still staring at the road ahead. "Jason called me about fifteen minutes ago. Told me I needed to come get you."

"What?" she exploded. "And you listened? Since when did you two become friends?" O'Dell didn't answer, and she forced herself to turn and face forward, then took a minute to calm herself down. "I'm sorry. I'm not angry with you. I'm just—God! I'm just angry!" She took another deep breath and focused on modifying her tone. She couldn't find friendly, but managed to drop anger. "What else did he say?"

O'Dell looked at her sideways and cleared his throat. "He said that you'd need somewhere to stay, and that I should come pick you up. Now—now wait just a minute," he added quickly when Janet's thin grip on composure started to slip. "Not like that. He said you were going to need a friend. And we're friends, aren't we, Janet?"

She pressed her fingertips to her eyelids. No matter how many deep breaths she tried to take, she couldn't seem to fill up her lungs with enough air. "I'm not sure I'll be able to sleep tonight, O'Dell."

"Well. You'll need somewhere to stay, anyway, and I have a guest room all ready for you. Can't be wandering around town at this hour. Nothing good happens after midnight, that's the truth."

She nodded. Couldn't argue with that after the last thirty minutes of her life.

"Here comes Mel," O'Dell announced. Sure enough, Janet's bouncer was headed their way, grocery bags clutched in her hands as she made her way toward them.

Janet rolled down her window and tried for a smile. "Hey."

"What's going on? I heard yelling, then I saw O'Dell, and damned if that didn't make me more worried. No offense." She looked past Janet and frowned. "If you need a place to stay, Janet, our guest room is open."

Janet blinked back what could only be tears, finally making their way to the surface. How could she be suffering through the greatest emotional turmoil of her life and find out, at that exact same time, that she had somehow acquired some really great friends, despite her best efforts to be cranky and mean?

As she considered Mel's offer, Jason opened the door and stared out at them. She wasn't close enough to see his face clearly, but she could feel the anger rolling off him in waves. He was waiting for her to leave—waiting for her to be across town, not just across the thin drywall separating their unit from Mel's house next door.

"No, thanks, Mel. I'll head to O'Dell's place. He's been kind enough to offer me his guest room while I figure out what...what I should do next."

Mel nodded soberly and stepped back onto the sidewalk, hitching the bags up higher in her arms. When O'Dell put the car into gear, she called to Janet, "Hey. I'll see you at work tomorrow."

Janet nodded and watched her in the sideview mirror until she shrunk into nothing. Mel was telling her that while her home life might be exploding into a fireball of disaster, nothing else had changed. Janet could still count on her. She reached out, without looking, and grasped O'Dell's hand.

"Thank you."

He didn't answer, just squeezed her hand as he drove through the darkness.

CHAPTER THIRTY-FOUR

Sunlight squeezed through the blinds and Janet buried her head deeper under the covers. O'Dell had shown her to the guest room and left her alone—but not before looking at her worriedly like she might dissolve into a pool of emotion.

When the bedroom door had closed, she'd thought she might do just that. But in the end, a sense of overwhelming so deep and complete enveloped her, leaving her unable to feel anything at all.

Eventually she'd kicked off her shoes and crawled under the covers. But now her brain was turning on along with the day, and she groaned, her throat dry and scratchy. She poked her head out and saw a bottle of water on the nightstand. She chugged half of it down, then leaned back against the pillows. She hadn't been in a state to notice anything the night before, but now, in an effort to not think about her life or her boyfriend (*ex?*), she studied her surroundings.

No doubt she was in a man's house. The bedroom set was made of dark wood, the walls were painted a smoky blue, and the only decorations were two hockey sticks crossed into a "x" hanging across from the window. Cheap mini blinds that weren't closed all the way were to blame for letting in those cheerful rays of light, and Janet was eyeing them suspiciously when a light tap on the door interrupted her investigation.

She made to pull the covers up, then realized she was still fully dressed from the day before. So she climbed out of bed, ran a hand through her hair, and opened the door.

O'Dell smiled at her like they were at a funeral. "How—ah... how ya doin'?"

She smiled thinly back. "No one's dead...so that's a start."

He held out a mug of coffee. "You like it black, right?"

She blew on the surface as a sudden chill started at the base of her spine. She wrapped her hands around the mug. O'Dell noticed her discomfort and stepped past her into the room, opening the closet adjacent to the hockey sticks. "You need another blanket in here?" He pulled down two and tossed them on the bed. "I'm sorry. I should have gotten you more set up in here. I just—I mean, it was all pretty last minute, and—"

"How last minute? When did Jason call you, anyway?"

O'Dell looked down at the floor. "It was just a few minutes before I came to get you."

"You were just—what? At home? And he called you?"

"He called me on my cell."

"How did he have that number?"

"I was going to ask you." O'Dell rubbed the back of his neck with one hand and took a sip from his own mug. "I sure didn't give it to him."

"Neither did I!" Janet's brow furrowed. "You were at home?"

"No. And apparently neither were you. He, ah...he said you would be on your way home, and I should get there in fifteen minutes." O'Dell turned away from her and busied himself with reorganizing the extra sheets in the closet. There was something else, something he wasn't saying, but he was happy to ignore her completely. Of course, Janet wasn't. She stepped closer.

"What? What aren't you telling me?" He didn't answer and she took the fitted sheet out of his clumsy hands and shook it out, then started gathering the corners together. "What does Smith think about me being here?"

He shrugged, and his eyes narrowed as he watched her hands. "What are you doing there? I've never understood how to fold these damn things."

She lowered her hands. "O'Dell. What does Smith think?" She finished folding the sheet and handed him the tidy square packet.

He looked at her like she was a magician. When she crossed her arms, he grimaced. "I explained to her that we were just friends."

Janet raised her eyebrows. "And?"

He took the sheet from her and shoved it back onto the shelf along with the rest of the unfolded crumpled-up set. "And...she didn't really care for the plan. So...we broke up."

"I—I'm sorry. She knows...I mean, surely she knows that nothing's going to happen here." She stared hard at O'Dell. "Nothing." She didn't want there to be any expectations. His eyes darkened and she backpedaled. "I just mean—argh!" She turned away and stalked to the other side of the room. "I shouldn't even be here. I don't know why Jason arranged this— this thing! It just—I mean, nothing about it makes sense! I should be at a hotel. This is—it's not your problem—"

"Calm down." O'Dell's commanding tone did the opposite of soothe her.

"I am calm," she snapped. "And I'm leaving."

"Stop! I don't know what's going on with your boyfriend, but he made it clear to me that he didn't want you on your own."

"What?"

"Whatever's going on, he thinks you need protecting."

"That's bullshit. I don't need—"

"And for some reason, he doesn't feel like he can do it, but I can. And I will," he added grimly. "Now let's go get breakfast."

He stalked out of the room, and Janet fell back onto the bed, feeling more confused than ever. So Jason thought she was in danger, and was happy to push the job of keeping her safe onto somebody else without even discussing it with her? She was so irritated that she couldn't even begin to think about eating. O'Dell pounded on the door. "Let's go. I'm starved."

"I am not a child," she muttered to herself, "who needs to be coddled."

"Now!" O'Dell barked in his cop voice and she jumped up from the bed and hurried to the door.

"Dammit! Stop doing that!"

He grinned and tossed a hat to her. "It's cold out there. Better bundle up." He walked down the hall ahead of her and she smiled against her will. She *wasn't* hungry, but she might as well eat. She'd need energy, strength, for whatever lay ahead.

She must have been in a haze the night before, because now she walked through O'Dell's house as if for the first time. The short hallway opened up into the main room. A television took up most of the far wall, and a cluster of black leather theater seats formed a half-circle facing the screen. An old barn door, hanging on casters across a heavy steel bar, was open, revealing a small but tidy kitchen. Janet's eyes zeroed in on the coffee pot, gleaming under an overhead light on the countertop, and she took another sip from the mug still clutched in her hands.

"I'll drive." O'Dell tossed back a grin. She always thought he was handsome, but here in his element, with day-old whiskers and a casual T-shirt stretching across his chest, she felt a stab of guilt that she was responsible for his relationship ending.

He didn't bother locking up when they left the house, and as he navigated the streets of Knoxville, she found herself wondering what had happened to make Jason race home, only to kick her out and ask his least favorite person to watch over her. What had Jason found out while he'd been in Memphis? What scared him enough to send her packing?

She was determined to find out.

CHAPTER THIRTY-FIVE

"Have you ever been here?" O'Dell eased into a spot on the street and pulled open the change drawer next to the steering wheel. "Ah! Four quarters. That should do it if we don't dawdle." He slipped the quarters into his palm and opened his door. "You coming?"

She squinted at the restaurant across the street. "Morning Glory? Is it any good?"

"You ever heard of a Dutch Baby?" Janet shook her head. "It's like a cross between a pancake and eggs. Greatest thing I've ever tried. But you gotta wait for it—I'll put the order in right when we get in, and we should be fine."

"I'm not even hungry," Janet said, realizing it was true as the words left her lips. Her stomach was so full of confusion, there wasn't any room for eggs—or anything else for that matter.

"You need food. You have a busy day ahead of you." O'Dell walked around the hood of his car and opened her door.

"I do?" She felt sluggish, like her brain couldn't make any decisions. She hated that feeling.

"You do." O'Dell steered her across the street by her elbow

and then held the door to the restaurant open. "You have to see what your boyfriend's been up to."

She leveled O'Dell with a stare. "And how am I supposed to do that? You know Jason! He can get phone numbers without asking for them. He can tap into computers near and far. What can I do?" O'Dell greeted the hostess and followed her to their table, and Janet finished talking to herself as she followed him. "What can I do, for real, except pour drinks and be irritated with people?"

"What was that?" O'Dell waved the menu away and instead, placed an order for two Dutch Babies and a pot of coffee. "You want juice, too, or anything?" Janet shook her head and he took his time moving utensils around after the hostess left. "Janet. You have work to do today."

Her shoulders dropped. "I can't do anything, O'Dell. I don't even want to."

He spread the paper napkin across his lap and rested his elbows on the table. "You have to find out what Jason's working on. What he doesn't want anyone else to know."

Janet blew out a sigh but waited for the busboy to fill their waters and walk away before responding. "There's nothing I can find out that Jason wants me to know—and obviously he doesn't want me to know anything, which is why he kicked me out of my own house."

"Janet." O'Dell shook his head. "You're not thinking this through! Jason's not worried about anyone else. He's sure as shit not worried about me. He's not worried about Detective Smith. But you—he knows that you can figure this out if you stay close, and he's not going to let that happen. So what can you do that we can't?" She shrugged again. "Well...figure it out. And then do it. I mean, think! His father's girlfriend goes missing—winds up dead —right as he starts acting strange, aloof. It might be connected." He drained his coffee and then picked up the carafe to refill it.

"Happy to help if you need it." He looked up earnestly. "I'll always be here for you."

She blinked when tears sprang up unexpectedly. His horrified expression was enough to drive them away, but he handed her a napkin and looked across the restaurant while she composed herself.

"Thank you. For everything. And I'm sorry that I've managed to mess up things between you and Smith."

"It wasn't serious. It was probably time to end things anyway."

"Why?"

He leaned back, but his eyes never left Janet's face. "I just wasn't really ready to dive in with anyone right now."

"Oh." He held her expression and her stomach did a flip-flop that had nothing to do with hunger. She looked down at her lap. "You deserve to be happy, O'Dell."

"I know." She looked up in time to see a sly grin cross his face. "I will be."

She was saved from having to answer by a cackle of laughter from the other side of the restaurant. Her eyes narrowed. She'd know that laugh anywhere. "Cindy Lou?" O'Dell shrugged and she scanned the room. Had her assistant manager gone home sick the day before only to be enjoying a cozy brunch this morning? The laugh rang out again.

It sure didn't sound like someone recovering from an illness.

Her eyes zeroed in on Cindy Lou at a booth across from the kitchen. Her employee was wearing full makeup and a bright sunny outfit that attracted all the light in the room. But it was the cowlick on the back of the head of the man across from her that had Janet leaping up from the table.

She stalked across the room, nearly taking out an unsuspecting waiter with a full load of plates on a tray over his head.

"What's going on here, Jason?" Janet snapped as she came to

a stop at the edge of their table, crossing her arms and staring down at the table full of half-eaten biscuits and gravy, eggs, and bacon.

Cindy Lou's big blue eyes looked up and the laugh died on her lips. "Oh, hey, Janet."

"Hey? Hey? What's going on, Cindy Lou?" Her voice was louder than she'd intended, and her assistant manager flinched slightly. She could hardly bear to look at her boyfriend, but when he remained silent, she was forced to turn her eyes on him. "And what about you, J—" The man sitting across from Cindy Lou was not Jason. "Oh my God, I'm so sorry! I thought you were..." In a panic, she looked back at Cindy Lou, whose confused expression turned sunny again.

"Janet, I'd like to introduce you to Jeff—" She touched her lips and another laugh trilled out. "I can't believe I'm going to say this, but I don't even know your last name! Oh my stars, isn't that so embarrassing?"

Janet couldn't take her eyes off the man sitting across from Cindy Lou. It wasn't Jason, as she'd been so certain from her table, but it was easy to see how she'd made the mistake. This stranger, Jeff, had the same coloring and the same cowlick in his hair. But this man's features were more delicate, his lips thin and unfriendly. Cindy Lou's words finally wormed their way into her brain, and instead of apologizing, she felt herself getting angry all over again.

"What do you mean you don't know his last name? Did you just meet this morning?"

Cindy Lou blushed and looked down at her coffee. "Well, no...although I think we got to know each other a little better this morning, Jeff, wouldn't you agree?"

Janet threw her hands up in the air and a girl sitting alone at the adjacent table picked up her book and scrambled away from them toward the exit. "Unbelievable! Cindy Lou, when are you going to learn that you can't hop in bed with any man who wants to? You don't even know his last name!"

"I know, but like I said when we met, there's just something so familiar about him—"

Janet snorted. "I'll bet. It's called his big, giant d—"

"Janet!"

She jumped at the closeness of O'Dell's voice and turned to face him. "What?"

"Let's leave Cindy Lou alone to enjoy her breakfast. I think it's time for us to go."

He grabbed her under the elbow with a firm grip and steered her out of the restaurant. He stopped and faced her out on the sidewalk. "What is wrong with you?"

"What's wrong with me? She's in there with another stranger, doing God knows what—"

"I think we all know what they did, and she's a grown woman. She doesn't need you judging her just because you disagree with her life choices."

"Well, that's just—I can't—" Janet spluttered into silence, hating how obnoxiously reasonable he sounded. She turned back to look through the window.

"You really cleared it out in there," O'Dell grumbled. "But we were only halfway to our Dutch Babies; you'd have never made it."

She squinted at the empty table next to Cindy Lou's.

"Leave her alone," O'Dell barked. "Stop staring at her like that."

"No—it's not that."

The change in her tone—no longer uptight and angry—was enough to pull O'Dell out of his breakfast lament. "What?"

"The girl—I think the girl sitting next to them—the one I scared away? I think that was Lola."

CHAPTER THIRTY-SIX

A phone chirped from the depths of O'Dell's pocket and he winced when he read the screen. "It's Kay—Detective Smith. I've got to take this." He held the phone up to his ear and turned away from Janet, heading toward his car.

Janet took the opportunity to head back into the restaurant to see what she could find out about the girl who looked so similar to Lola.

Cindy Lou and the stranger were gone, a waiter clearing their half-eaten plates away as Janet approached. But the girl from the next table had come back! She was digging around in her wallet, staring at her bill. She looked up when Janet stopped, and her eyes went wide. She leapt up, spilling her coffee across the table in her haste to get away. She didn't look back as she hustled out of the restaurant, with Janet hot on her trail.

"Lola!" she called, certain the girl in front of her was an exact match for the picture in her purse. "Lola, wait! Your mom is so worried about you!"

But the girl shot a terrified look back at Janet that was so fear-ful, so frightened and panicky, that Janet froze in her tracks. She watched the girl run across the street and flinched at the screeching tires of a car that narrowly avoided slamming into her.

Lola didn't slow down, just shot one last scared look over her shoulder as she disappeared between buildings.

O'Dell stood uncertainly at his car, his cell phone grasped in one hand, one foot in the car, the other on the pavement as if he hadn't been able to make up his mind on whether he should get out and chase after the girl or not. "Who is that?"

Her frown deepened as she thought back to Lola's look of terror as she ran away.

"I think—no, I *know*—it's Lola. She looked like she was terrified—of...of me!"

O'Dell's voice was clipped, short, when he spoke. "Stay here. I'm going after her."

As she watched him disappear into the same alleyway, her brain made a connection that had been missing up until just then. As Lola ran away, she didn't just look haunted. She looked hunted, like an animal running from a hunter in the woods.

What had made the girl so terrified of Janet? Or who?

———

"No trace at all?"

"None. It was like she just disappeared," O'Dell answered, slowing at a light before turning right.

"I don't like it," Janet said.

"We don't even know that it was Lola. In fact, the more I think about it, the less sense it makes. Why would she be here in town—on her own, I might add—and not let her parents know?"

"It was her." Janet stared out the window, her voice low. "I know it was."

"Well." O'Dell shrugged, and kept driving.

Janet glanced over. "You can just drop me off at my car. I

don't want to take over your life."

"I think that's already happened," he said, but he didn't frown, just said it matter-of-factly. "And I'm not worried, so don't you be worried."

Her chest felt tight, and she turned away from the detective. O'Dell was being so nice, but she knew that this wasn't fair. She'd roared into his life the night before like a hurricane, ruining his relationship, messing with his weekend. And she knew—she wondered if he did, too—that she'd blow out just as furiously as she blew in.

"Looks like a party," O'Dell muttered as he pulled up to the house. Mel and Kat stood on the front walk, in the middle of an animated discussion that stopped as soon as they saw Janet climb out of the car.

"I decided I'm not leaving." Janet attempted to smile when the women looked over, but it felt more like a grimace when it made it to her face. "I mean, after all, I pay for half. Jason can't just kick me out."

Neither woman responded, and Janet turned away from their confused faces to find the door to her house standing wide open, the inside so dark, the open door looked like a yawning black hole.

"What—" She raced up the porch steps and gasped, not daring to cross the threshold. The furniture was gone. Even the pictures had been taken off the walls.

The house was empty. Deserted.

"What happened?" She whirled around to face Mel.

Her bouncer shrugged. "That's just what Kat and I were discussing. I have no idea. We were home all night and didn't hear a thing."

Kat looked unhelpfully back, then bent down to pick a wine-key up off the cement path. She held it out to Janet. "Is this yours?"

Janet dug her hands into her pockets, refusing to take it—refusing to believe that the only possession she had left, besides three suitcases of clothes at O'Dell's house, was a cheap wine key from a shitty bar in Montana.

O'Dell had been hanging back by the car, but he pushed off the passenger door and walked past the trio, heading right into Janet's place. He was only inside for a couple of minutes, but not a word was uttered until he came back.

"Everything is gone." He looked past Janet and asked Mel, "Where did they go?"

Her lips were pressed into a thin line and she shook her head back and forth.

Finally, Kat spoke. "We don't know. We were home all night and didn't hear anything, until the moving van fired up and pulled out this morning before six. If I hadn't looked out the window and watched the taillights disappear, I wouldn't have known that they were here at all."

"What was the moving company?" O'Dell was in full detective mode now. He slipped a notebook out of his back pocket, but Kat shook her head. There wasn't anything to write down.

"It was dark—and—and hard to see. And, you know, the truck was really dirty. I didn't see the name—or maybe there wasn't a name. I'm so sorry, Janet." She looked back and forth between O'Dell and Janet, not sure who she was apologizing to.

"We didn't connect the dots until just now—we were heading out to the store and saw the door standing open. That's when we realized what must have happened."

"We were just about to call you when you pulled up."

Janet turned away from them all, unable to control the emotions swirling up inside her. Shock, embarrassment, humiliation. For all three of them to be here with her at a time like this was terrible. There was nowhere to hide.

"So he—he took all of your stuff?" Kat shook her head. "I didn't see that coming from him."

Before Janet could answer, a van pulled up and rumbled to a stop, blocking the driveway. A worker from the gas company climbed out of the vehicle and hitched his pants up as he walked around to the sidewalk. He surveyed the crew gathered in the drive. "You folks heading out?"

"Why?" O'Dell asked, and Janet was grateful to have someone else ask the questions. Her brain was too overwhelmed to even get a single word out.

The gas employee took a pack of cigarettes out of his front shirt pocket and lit one before answering. "Starting in about thirty minutes, we'll have a crew out here rerouting the gas line for this property. The whole structure's gotta be evacuated for at least seventy-two hours."

Mel looked wordlessly between her house and her partner. It was Kat who spoke. "The entire structure?"

The gas worker dug a clipboard out of the passenger seat of his van and ran a finger down the paper, mouthing words silently. "Yup. Says right here the work begins at ten a.m., and the entire structure will need to be vacated for approximately seventy-two hours." He looked up and added, "You know, until the job is complete."

Janet finally came out of her stupor. "Who booked this project?"

He referenced his clipboard again. "The property owner." He sucked in a breath and the end of his cigarette glowed red. "Asked for a rush job. Said it had to get done now. Jason Brooks?" The employee looked up, a question in his eyes. "If we need to cancel now, it's going to cost you a cancelation fee. It's out of my hands so late in the project timeline."

Janet turned and apologized to her renters. "I'm sorry you two are getting wrapped up in this. I'll pay for your hotel until this is settled. Why don't you go pack bags and meet me up at the Spot for lunch, okay?"

After they hurried into their home, Janet climbed into O'Dell's car.

When he fired up the engine, his jaw was tight. "I never thought Jason would play you like this, Janet. I'm really sorry that this is happening."

But for the first time in twenty-four hours, hope kindled in Janet's gut. O'Dell looked at her expression and frowned. "Why are you smiling?"

"Jason is telling me it's not safe to be home." Her smile faded and her voice dropped until she was almost whispering. "He also doesn't want Mel and Kat caught up in whatever's about to go down...and that means he doesn't know what's going to happen. And that's why he made me leave, too. What's he so afraid of?" She stared out the window, hoping her brain might figure out what she was missing—what clue she'd overlooked or forgotten about.

O'Dell shook his head. "Don't give him so much credit. He's hiding something. You think he's trying to keep you safe—but that's clearly not his only priority, or else he'd be sitting here telling you and me what he's so worried about. What he thinks might happen." He sped up to make a light that turned yellow up ahead. When they were through the intersection, he glanced at Janet. "And he's not doing that. So you have to ask yourself, why? What's more important than keeping you safe?"

Janet's frown deepened. She wouldn't have put it that way, but now that O'Dell had, the question hung heavy in the air. Family. She knew that Jason must be trying to protect his father. But why? And what did William have against her? Was she in danger? She had a feeling whatever was about to go down would be over in seventy-two hours. Would Jason figure things out in time? Would she even make it through to find out?

CHAPTER THIRTY-SEVEN

Janet fired up the generator outside the food truck and even managed to turn on the grill, O'Dell offering helpful tips like, "You'll want it hot, but not too hot," and "Should you clean that before using it?"

Finally, when he said, "Should you defrost the burgers before you put them on the grill like that?" she shooed him out.

"Why don't you get drinks ready for everyone?" she said, then locked the door behind him. When she was alone in the food truck, she blew out a sigh and rolled her neck from side to side, stopping to stare up at the ceiling. Jason thought something bad was going to go down, and he wanted to keep her safe. But why was he protecting his father? Was William guilty of murdering Connie, and brainwashing Lola somehow? Family or not, would Jason protect a killer? She shivered, just as O'Dell tried to open the door.

"I smell burnt meat. Hey—is this door locked?" He jiggled the handle again. "Are you paying attention in there, Janet?"

She shook herself and slipped the patties off the grill, unlocked the door, and then turned the knobs on the control panel all the way to the right just as O'Dell pushed the door open and walked up into the truck. His nose wrinkled when he saw the black patties. "Well...I guess they're only burned on the one side?" He reached past Janet and, with a fork from the counter, flipped the top patty over and grimaced. "I'm sure it's not as raw as it looks." Then he added in an undertone, almost to himself, "We'll be fine."

Janet grabbed a bag of buns from the shelf and turned away from O'Dell to assemble the sandwiches. "Mel and Kat here yet?"

"Just arrived. They're sitting inside."

O'Dell picked up the plate of food and headed down the steps and out of the truck, leading the way into the bar. Mel was behind the bar. She looked up when Janet and O'Dell walked in. "I'm making Long Islands—you two want one?"

Janet nodded, but O'Dell shook his head. "I'll stick with soda, thanks."

"Where did you two end up?" Janet asked when Mel came back to the table with a tray full of drinks.

"Nowhere yet. We'll check in somewhere tonight. Figured we'd just kind of hang out today." Mel bit her lip as she studied her burger and grabbed the bottle of ketchup from the middle of the table.

"Maybe salt, too?" O'Dell said, shaking enough on his burger that it would float in water.

"Yes," Mel breathed, taking the shaker when he was done.

Kat pushed her plate aside and leaned over the table. "We're staying close. Something's not right, Janet, and we don't want to go too far until we figure out what, you know?"

Before Janet could object, O'Dell said, "I agree. None of you are safe—at least, that must be what Jason thinks. And until I know why, I want you all close."

Janet harrumphed and took a huge bite of her burger. The

patty was mushy on top and so crispy on the bottom that her teeth struggled to cut through the burnt side. She forced herself not to gag on the texture as she again attempted to bite through the meat.

O'Dell turned to face her. "Janet, what aren't you telling me?"

She twisted her mouth away from the burger and the bite tore off into her mouth. She forced the meat to her back molars and they managed to break up the burned food. She swallowed hard and then downed half her drink before her mouth was clear enough to answer. "What are you talking about?"

"Something happened when you and Quizz went to Memphis. She's on her way in, but I thought I'd give you the chance to tell me first."

She closed her eyes. It wasn't just her who was in danger now. Jason was worried enough that he and his parents had moved out of the house in the dead of the night, while also making plans to keep her, Mel, and Kat away. But there was no hiding the Spot. They were all like sitting ducks there at the bar. Jason knew it, and frankly, William did, too. She couldn't keep the information from them any longer. They might all be in danger.

While she was working over how to tell everyone what she'd known for weeks now, what she'd been keeping to herself—perhaps being criminally silent—the door opened and Quizz walked in.

"Something smelled kind of good in the parking lot, but now that I'm inside, I'm changing my mind. It's like bacon crossed with a fire alarm, you know? Just exactly that." Quizz squinted at the table and adjusted her glasses.

Mel bravely dipped one edge of her burger and bun into a pool of ketchup and cracked her neck before taking a bite.

O'Dell, the half-eaten burger in front of his face at eye-level, said, "It's not too bad, really. Considering."

Janet moved her chair over and pushed her plate away. Quizz took a chair from the next table over and squeezed it between Janet and O'Dell. She was glad for the added physical distance between them before she said what she was going to say.

"Where's Cindy Lou?" Mel looked around the bar after Quizz asked the question, as if the spunky bartender might appear suddenly from a dark corner.

"She's supposed to come in at three today."

"So, Janet?" O'Dell set his burger down on the plate and wiped his hands on a napkin. He fixed her with an unblinking stare and asked again, "What happened in Memphis?"

She fidgeted with her utensils. Her throat felt too thick to talk, and she swallowed a few times as too much saliva filled her mouth. "Quizz and I were looking for Lola's boyfriend, Matt. And we found...well, a house of horrors, really."

"That's an understatement." Quizz shifted Janet's burger farther away from her with a grimace.

"What else?"

Janet dropped her hands down into her lap and looked up at the people—her friends—gathered around the table with her. "I found a bill on the table as I was leaving. It was the light bill. The customer name—the person who paid the bills for that apartment? It's William Brooks. Jason's dad."

O'Dell's stare was unwavering, but Janet sensed a shift in his expression, too, as disappointment merged with anger. He shoved his plate aside and stood quickly, his phone pressed to his ear. "Yes, this is Detective Patrick O'Dell, calling in a BOLO for a possible murder suspect. Suspect's name is William Brooks."

CHAPTER THIRTY-EIGHT

O'Dell spent the better part of the next twenty minutes pacing in the parking lot. He swept back into the bar, rolling his neck, and asked Janet and Quizz several more clipped questions about their Memphis trip and the apartment.

Before Janet could answer any of them, Quizz stepped forward. "Here's the address of the apartment, along with the name of the cook who said he knew Matt." She took a packet of papers out of her bag and flipped past the first page. "This is the ID number for the MLGW employee who told me about the account information vanishing for the apartment in question, and this last page..." She held the packet out toward O'Dell. "This is a copy of the picture of Janet that we found in that apartment." Quizz turned toward Janet. "It's from your Facebook profile. I made a copy and blew it up to the same size that we found in the apartment."

"Thanks, Quizz. Glad someone is willing to be so forthcoming. Excuse me." O'Dell left the building without a backwards glance at Janet.

Janet gathered the plates from the table—including Mel's,

even though she was still gamely trying to eat the burger—and dumped the trash in the can behind the bar.

She must have been staring at the trash can for some time, because she didn't hear anyone walk up and flinched when a hand patted her shoulder.

Kat's face was full of concern when Janet whirled around. "It's going to be okay, but not if you keep operating like you're on your own. We're here. O'Dell is on your side. And Jason's not just abandoning you, even though that's what it might feel like."

"Hrmph," Janet muttered, hating how Kat's words lifted her spirit just a touch. "I know he'd never abandon me, especially now...but it sure does feel that way."

"It's happened before." Mel ran a toothpick gingerly across her gums and dug out a tiny bit of blackened burger. "Remember after Ike died? But that time he left us a pretty clear clue. I wonder why he's keeping us in the dark this time?"

Janet nodded, remembering the computer he'd set up in their kitchen, cued up to surveillance video that helped her figure out part of a murder that had happened at the bar several months ago. She wrinkled her nose. "Yeah, but that time he disappeared because he couldn't compromise a customer..." Her mouth froze open on the end of the word, and a lightbulb went off in her head.

Back then, he hadn't wanted to compromise a paying customer, but he'd left the information out so Janet could put it all together.

She gasped, and it was Kat's turn to flinch.

"Oh my God! The folder!"

"Huh?" Kat said.

But Janet blew past her without a word and barreled toward the office.

Just the other day, Jason's employee, Mike, had dropped off a folder of information supposedly for *Jason*. Janet had been so irritated by Mike's gorgeousness that she'd tossed it down in the office without a second thought.

She pushed the door open—and there it was. The yellow clasp envelope sat just where she'd left it on her desk. She carefully slid her finger under the flap, jiggled the seal loose, then sifted through the sheaf of papers that fell out onto the desk.

On top was the full bill from MLGW. It was only when Janet saw that it was three pages long that she realized she'd only seen the first page in the Memphis apartment.

The full bill included the payor's name, former addresses, and Social Security number. William Jefferson Brooks, 4444 Jones Parkway, Memphis, Tennessee.

But that couldn't be right. William had last lived with Faith, and their house wasn't on Jones Parkway. She flipped her computer on and did a reverse address search.

Quizz ambled into the room and came to a stop behind her. "What are you finding out?"

"I'm checking William's former addresses to see if anything stands out." Janet waited for the results page to load. "It looks like William Brooks's only other address was on Jones Parkway."

"I guess that makes sense, right?"

"Well, it would, but that's not the house Jason grew up in. It's not the home William moved out of when he and Faith got divorced."

"Oh. So that doesn't make sense...unless..." She waited until Janet met her eye. "Is it possible that he's kept a secret double life for years?"

Janet's vision went blurry as she considered the possibility. Would it be such a shock to find out that William had been living a lie for so many years? His former lover had been murdered. What else didn't they know about him?

Mel knocked on the doorframe but stopped just outside the office. "Hey, Janet? Your construction guy is here, asking about the parking lot project...I just don't know what you want me to tell him..." She looked apologetically at her employer. "I mean, I can send him on his way, but...You know it'd be nice if they would pave over the nonsense out there so everyone can park in the lot again..."

Janet blew out a sigh and pushed away from the computer. "It's fine. You're right."

She hurried out to the bar. Bruce waited by the door with his hat in his hands, an uncomfortable expression on his face.

"Hey, Janet, sorry for interrupting."

"No problem, Bruce. What's going on?"

"Well, Faith has us adding a thirty-foot pergola with full electric, plumbed for an outdoor kitchen, but I just wanted you to sign off on the project before we got started." His hand rested on the architecture roll, unfurled on the closest table. "Seems like she's not communicating with you as well as I'd have expected."

Janet attempted a smile for the first time in what felt like days. This was her chance—her opportunity to make the outside exactly how she'd imagined it from the beginning—just a small area offset from the main lot by some raised planter boxes with room for tables and umbrellas. But she looked down at the plans and bit her lip. It would be gorgeous. Faith had a good eye for this kind of thing, no doubt. Her shoulders drooped and she forced her lips up.

"Faith's paying?"

"She pre-paid for the whole project."

"All right, then. Let's do it." Janet peeked around Bruce out the front door and saw a full team of orange-vested workers milling around in her parking lot. "Let me send you out with some sweet teas for the crew. Sound good?"

"Sure. Thanks."

She led the way to the jug of tea on the bar. "How many?"

He held his hands up with his fingers spread wide. "I guess ten—nah, just make it an even dozen."

She nodded and pulled a stack of plastic cups down from the shelf.

"That's some great tea," Bruce said conversationally. "You usually don't find anyone who's not from Tennessee can make it so good. Where'd you learn?"

"Oh, this is all Cindy Lou! She's got a whole process and doesn't let me anywhere near it." Janet focused on the amber liquid streaming from the spout of the carafe as her brain made a connection she didn't realize she knew. Bruce certainly seemed to have known the Brooks family for some time. If he was in the mood to chat, she might as well take advantage of it. She looked up and smiled. "How's it going out there?"

Bruce picked up a stack of lids from the bar and started adding them to the cups as Janet handed them across. "No major surprises, that's the good news. But these jobs take time. We'd like to have the plumber and electrician out to lay the pipe work and lines today so we can get on with re-laying the asphalt and setting the posts on the same day. That'll save you some money." He grinned and started stacking the cups two high to transport outside. "Well, Faith, anyway."

"Here," Janet said, handing him a tray and then adding six cups to her own. "What's your connection to Faith and William? I never did remember to ask Faith how she knew you!"

He chuckled. "I did some work for the Brooks family when I was just starting out in Memphis. Years ago. Jason and William had been sharing a room, and apparently they were close to tearing the whole house apart. Faith wanted another bedroom added on so they could spread out."

Janet fumbled with the door as she looked back at Bruce. "Jason and William were sharing a room? Why? Were he and Faith having trouble even back then?"

A laugh rumbled out of Bruce. He stopped walking to balance his tray but continued to chuckle as they walked out of the dark bar into the waning afternoon winter sunshine outside. "Not William Senior! William Junior. Jason's brother."

"Jason's brother?" Janet felt like a parrot the way she was repeating everything Bruce said, but she'd known Jason for going on three years, and he'd never once mentioned a brother. Had gone so far, in fact, as to tell her he was an only child.

"What happened to him? William Junior, I mean?"

"Oh, he's still there in Memphis, last I heard." The twinkle in Bruce's eye faded, and his smile flattened into a thin line. "Those were happier times, that's for sure."

The construction crew gathered around her and Bruce, and soon she was walking back into the Spot with two empty trays and a looming migraine. Jason had a brother. But something bad had happened; that much was clear from Bruce's demeanor. Why hadn't Jason ever brought it up? Or his parents? What were they hiding?

CHAPTER THIRTY-NINE

"Did anyone hear from Cindy Lou today?" Janet looked at the clock again, and a knot of worry settled in the base of her stomach. Her assistant manager's shift was supposed to have started at three, but it was now quarter past four, and she hadn't called and wasn't there.

"Nope." Mel frowned. "It's not like her to just not show up. Did you call her house?" Janet looked down at the ground and Mel pressed her. "What?

"Well, I...I saw her this morning."

"Oh, good." Kat smiled and patted her on the shoulder. "I'm sure she's just running late." All three turned to look out the door at the cloudless clear blue sky. After a moment, Kat turned back to face Janet. "Did she look okay? Mel said she went home sick two days ago."

"She..." Janet gulped. She felt guilty just thinking about how she'd spoken to Cindy Lou that morning. "I saw her this morning, at a restaurant."

"What did you do?" Mel folded her arms across her chest and stared hard at Janet.

"Well...she was with a man—she didn't even know his last name, and I...I might have gotten a little...uh...judgmental with her."

Mel frowned. "She's a grown woman, Janet. Why do you feel the need to cut her down all the time?"

Quizz came out of the office before she could answer the unanswerable, holding the sheaf of papers from Jason's employee. "Hey. I think there are two William Brookses."

Janet nodded. "You're right." Through the lump in her throat, she filled in Quizz, Mel, and Kat on everything—from her investigation at the coffee shop to what she'd learned from Bruce about Jason having a brother. When she was done, Quizz's short purple hair stood straight up from the number of times she'd run her hands roughly through it.

"So let me get this straight. Your boyfriend has a brother that you didn't know about." Janet nodded. "It now seems likely that that brother was living in the apartment we visited in Memphis, which also means he could be dating—or doing something with—a minor named Lola *who we are charged with locating*, and likely is responsible for the illegal charges you investigated at the coffee shop earlier this month."

Quizz stopped to take a breath and Janet nodded slowly. How did the coffee shop fit in? It didn't make sense.

But before she could really consider the question, Quizz continued. "William Brooks *Senior's* last known girlfriend was killed and left for dead in your bar, and now," Quizz looked down to read something from the papers in her hand, "and now, we don't know where to find William Jefferson Brooks *Junior*? Am I missing anything?"

A clunk of noise echoed in Janet's brain as Quizz's last words thunked into place. William *Jefferson* Brooks Junior.

"This morning—Cindy Lou called the man she was with Jeff. I—I was angry with her because from across the restaurant, I thought she was sitting with Jason. So then I stormed across the restaurant, and O'Dell tried to stop me, but—but it's so clear now...so...terribly clear!"

Jeff's hair was the same color as Jason's, and he and Jason shared the same cowlick at the back of their head. And even though she'd dismissed Jeff's appearance as being different from Jason's, the resemblance was there. She knew it. "I think Cindy Lou was with Jason's brother this morning!"

Kat's face was pale when she spoke. "And now she's a no-show for her shift here? We need to find her. She could be in danger."

Janet already had her phone pressed to her ear. Someone picked up on the first ring, but it wasn't Cindy Lou.

"Hello?" Cindy Lou's son had moved home after almost failing out of UT Knoxville during fall semester.

"Chip, it's Janet. I'm looking for your mom. Is she there?"

"No. I—wait. I thought she was with you at the Spot?"

Janet felt that same pulsing worry in her chest from earlier. "She had the day off yesterday—how'd she seem then?"

"I didn't see her. I thought she was at work yesterday."

"I'm sure she's fine." The words sounded hollow to her own ears, and Chip didn't seem reassured, either.

"I have class tonight. Should I—" He cleared his throat. "I feel like I should stay here in case she needs me."

"Chip, you go on to class. I'll have your mom call you on your cell when she gets into work. I'm sure she's just running late."

He seemed relieved that Janet had taken charge of the situation and agreed to check in with her at the break time for his class. She gripped her phone tightly at her side and looked at her colleagues in the Spot. "We need to find her. If she's with Jason's brother, she's not safe."

"Where do we start?" Quizz asked uncertainly. "We know

about his apartment in Memphis, but we don't know where he's staying here in town."

"But I bet Jason does." She tapped Jason's name in her contact list with force.

"He's gone, Janet. He left in the middle of the night and he's not going to answer your call now." Quizz looked sadly at her apprentice, but it was Kat who answered.

"Jason left to keep Janet safe—and he kicked us out of our side of the house because he must have been worried about us, too. He'll answer."

Janet was glad Kat was so certain, because just then, she was doubting everyone and everything in her life.

After five rings, her call went to voicemail.

She hung up, refusing to leave a message. When she looked up at her friends, her colleagues, their expressions mirrored her own pain and confusion.

She squared her shoulders, but before she could come up with a plan, her phone rang in her hand.

She turned away from the prying eyes in front of her. "Jason Brooks, you have some major explaining to do."

"I know, but there's no time."

"No time? No time? I can't believe you have the gall to say—"

"Mom's missing. I think my brother took her. I wanted you to know that I called O'Dell and told him that Dad and I are coming downtown to talk."

CHAPTER FORTY

Janet nudged her way into the interview room slowly and held out a hand when Jason made to stand. "Don't—just...Don't." She waited for him to look at her. He didn't. "You could have told me," she finally said. "I could have helped you."

He shook his head. "No one can help with this. That's the problem. When he's off his meds, he's so unpredictable. So angry. I wanted to bring him to us—let him know that he was still our priority. But—" He looked up, his eyes imploring her to understand, "I had to keep living, you know? We've spent a lot of time and money on making sure he's okay. And I put my life on hold so many times—and was happy to do it. But at some point, you've got to live your life, and let him live his. I just never—I didn't think it would come to this."

Janet threw the manila folder on the table between them. "Your employee got some info. It might help."

Jason reached out to take the folder and opened it slowly, as if it might bite. He scanned the top sheet, then the second. His eyes widened and he flipped back to page one. "How did she find this?"

"She said she's the top security hacker in the state. And she's pissed that you didn't pay her last week."

He grimaced. "I was kind of busy."

"Apparently, so was she." Janet tilted her head to the side. "Why didn't you tell me Mike was a woman?"

He looked up at her, his eyes wide. "It never occurred to me that you didn't know."

She frowned. "Working with Mike at all hours of the day and night and you didn't think I should know?" His eyes squeezed together slightly—but it was enough to confirm to Janet that he'd purposefully kept the information to himself. "That's what I thought."

"It's not a big deal. I'm not worried that Cameron's your new hire."

"And I didn't tell you his name was Brenda!"

"I didn't make up her name! She goes by Mike!"

Tap, tap. They both leaned back at the knock on the door.

"Hello? Janet, Jason, are we on a tight deadline or not?" O'Dell crossed the threshold and set his laptop down across from Jason.

Janet felt heat rise in her cheeks; she'd forgotten that he was watching from the room next door. She squared her shoulders and faced Jason. "What do you know? And don't leave anything out."

Jason paled, and the determined expression slid off his face like melted wax, leaving behind a mess of emotions she'd never witnessed in him before.

"So William's younger than you, huh?" O'Dell's sad smile said it all.

Jason nodded slowly. "I was six when he was born."

Her heart hurt just listening to his broken voice. No matter how hard he tried, big brother couldn't stop this runaway train.

William Junior had done too much—made too many mistakes for Jason to help him now.

O'Dell must have felt it, too, because his voice was low, his tone softer when he spoke again. "You tried your best, Jason, but now it's our turn. So either you can tell us where to start, or we'll consider you a co-conspirator. Your choice for the next five minutes. My choice after that."

A somberness came over Jason. He folded his hands on his lap and looked down for a long moment before answering. Finally, he flinched, as if he'd come to some internal decision, some forgone conclusion that he could hardly face.

"He's been in trouble before, but nothing like this. Nothing so violent. But he—he's out of chances, you know? We were so lucky to get him into the facility—so, I mean, if this thing with Lola and Connie—I mean, if it *wasn't* him, if it was a terrible misunderstanding—it would have ruined things going forward, you know?"

"Why?"

"Huh?" Jason looked up, confused.

"Why was it lucky that you got him into the facility?"

"There were some... issues after high school. He...he couldn't really make the transition into life, and he had...problems."

"What kind of problems?" Janet asked.

"Legal problems." O'Dell turned his laptop around so the screen was facing Janet.

She squinted to make out the words. "Assault—"

"He hit a guy, but not on purpose. He just lost control for a moment." Jason's set face dared her to disagree.

"Battery—"

"Look, the guy was making fun of him. What kind of asshole makes fun of a kid with an illness?"

"*Felony* assault?" Janet waited for Jason's explanation. It didn't come.

"That was—that was when we got him into Liberty Mead-ows. It's a special facility, and they really know how to—how to handle Jeff. It's been a great place. I don't know why he wanted to leave."

"This is all from his adult record. Any juvie problems?"

Jason's lips clamped. He only shook his head—but not in a way that made Janet think he was answering "no." Just in a way that meant he didn't want to face the question.

"So what happened? Why is he doing this now?"

"Best I can piece together from talking to the staff at Liberty, my parents' divorce shook him. My dad leaving Memphis was another blow. Then, when Mom came here, too—I think he snapped." Jason pressed his lips together and looked at his folded hands again.

"Don't hold out on us now. There's no time. Tell us what you know." O'Dell turned his computer back around with his hands hovering over the keyboard, ready to take notes.

Jason blew out a breath and nodded slowly. "My dad got a call from Liberty Meadows that Jeff had become unpredictable. That he'd been caught trying to flush his meds—was causing trouble for other residents. Nothing serious, but enough that Dad was worried. Before he could get there, Jeff was gone."

"When was that?" Janet asked.

"It was right after you learned the Spot needed a kitchen. Dad got the call from Liberty Meadows, and I started working online to try and track him down. We hoped to keep it simple—find him, alert Liberty Meadows, and they'd get him back on track. We thought if I got involved right away, it might make him feel like we'd ganged up on him. We—we didn't know how far gone he already was."

"Did you know about Lola?" Janet heard the anger in her voice, but didn't apologize.

Jason didn't answer.

"Did you know about the secret app on her phone?"

He looked away.

"Jason!"

"When I saw the birthmark on that sexting photo, I knew that Jeff was involved. I copied Lola's phone onto my hard drive so I could investigate. That's when I left for Memphis to track him down. The apartment was empty by then. Jeff was gone. Then Connie was killed, and I—I didn't want to believe it. I figured there was another suspect. There had to be!" Jason's voice had gone brittle, and his pale face was tinged yellow, like he might get sick. "But I was wrong. It was him all along."

Jason ran his hands roughly down his face, then pulled some folded papers out of his back pocket. "This is what I know." He tossed the papers across the table.

O'Dell flipped it open. "What am I looking at?"

"It's a rental agreement. It's under my name, but I had nothing to do with it. It must be him. That's where you'll find my brother—and maybe my mom...Lola...Cindy Lou." He stared down at the floor again, his whole body bowed over as if he could no longer bear the weight of what was happening.

"When did you find out where he's staying?" Janet asked, one hand pressed against her chest. Was it possible all three women were still alive? What would the police find inside that apartment? She shuddered, images of duct tape and zip ties flashed across her brain. If his place here in Knoxville was anything like his place in Memphis, it would be a miracle to find anyone had survived.

Jason's head dropped down into his hands. "Just this morning. Mom said she was going out to get coffee, but Jeff must have gotten in touch, convinced her to meet him. When she didn't come back—didn't answer her phone—we got worried. Then I had a breakthrough with some malware I'd installed remotely on

Jeff's cell phone through an email." His eyes flicked up to Janet's, then sunk guiltily back down, and he fell silent.

Detective Rivera pushed his way into the room and stared down at Jason, his hands on his hips.

"We just need to approach him with caution—I don't know what he's capable of—"

"Well, unfortunately, we do," Rivera interjected. "One murder and now at least three missing women—that's just what we know of! Let's just pray they're all alive—because we know exactly what he's capable of."

Rivera snatched the papers out of O'Dell's hand and spoke into his radio. "SWAT call out. Gather and prep—wait to move out on my command."

Jason started. "The SWAT team? More people are going to die if you go in guns blazing. There has to be a better way. A smarter way!"

"This guy's dangerous, Jason. If we've got to take him out to rescue the women, then that's what we're going to do. There's no other way," Rivera said.

Janet steeled herself—she owed it to Faith, to Lola, and mostly to Cindy Lou to do her part to help bring them home. "What can I do?"

"Nothing," Jason and O'Dell spoke together, but Rivera's eyebrows raised as he appraised Janet.

"Come with me."

Without a backwards glance, she turned and followed him out the door.

CHAPTER FORTY-ONE

"The worst part of any SWAT situation is going into the house blind. We'd much rather have Junior come out to us. Safer for everyone that way." Rivera stood in a conference room in the heart of the police department downtown, surrounded by men and women in black SWAT gear. The men and women painted black and dark green paint on their faces as they listened to their commander.

As Rivera spoke, an enlarged map glowed behind him from a projector screen onto the white board at the back of the room. "Janet, that's where you come in—"

"I must state, again, that I completely object to this kind of use of a civilian. It makes much more sense to go in and get him than to put another person at risk." O'Dell stood glaring over the room from the corner; his lips barely moved when he spoke.

"Noted and dismissed. Again." Rivera hardly paused in his instructions. "You'll be standing by, Janet, using the phone to get William's attention. We suspect that he's desperate to talk to you —as he's not been able to take out anyone Jason cares about yet." He winced when O'Dell growled. "Poor choice of words, but you know what I mean. You are not to go into the house, but if the phone doesn't work, we'll put you on display outside."

Janet nodded. She was going to get the women out of there one way or another, but she didn't plan to share that with Rivera just yet. O'Dell seemed to know, though, and she pulled at her collar under his heavy stare.

As the team broke apart and headed for the parking lot O'Dell came up from behind her, breathing down her neck. "I'm staying with you, Janet. And I'll attach handcuffs to your wrists if that's what it takes to keep you safe, you hear me?"

"O'Dell, please. I'm not out to play hero tonight. Of course we'll stay together."

"Oh." He stepped back an inch but continued to look at her suspiciously. "I'm glad to hear you sounding so sensible." He pulled her arm and she turned to face him. They both stopped walking. "Cindy Lou, Faith—they might not even be alive, Janet. We're dealing with a sociopath. Nothing is certain except uncertainty."

She nodded, but didn't agree, at least not completely. Jason saw some redeeming quality in his brother, and that meant that somewhere inside, maybe *deep inside* when he wasn't taking his medicine, he had something worth saving—even if that was only so that he could spend the rest of his days in a facility. She was going to make sure that happened, if only for Jason. He'd helped her out of enough tight spots that she knew she owed him. Even if he didn't want her anywhere near his brother.

"What are you thinking?" O'Dell was close again, obviously not trusting her despite her words.

"I'm just worried about everyone," she answered truthfully. "Are Jason and his dad under arrest?"

"Jason just left. I told him to keep his distance, that we'll arrest anyone at the scene who's interfering with our operation."

"Why'd you let him go?"

O'Dell frowned. "We can't charge him, and we can't continue to hold him if he decided he wanted to go. Which he did. William Senior doesn't know that, but Jason did."

"So William's just...sitting there? Wondering if his ex-wife is alive?"

O'Dell's lips pressed flat. "At least he's safe there. Not everyone can say the same."

"She going with you?" Rivera called from his car.

"Yes!" O'Dell called back.

"We'll stage three blocks away. Then we'll move in to make the call."

Janet took in the information and her eyes swept the parking lot, looking for O'Dell's car. She spotted it alone at the end of the lot—the nearest car some dozen spots away. "You sure do worry about your car...which is great, but unusual, given its condition."

The blue Crown Vic was old and beaten up, with nicks and scratches that another car wouldn't have survived.

O'Dell patted the top with affection. "That's why I've got to be so careful with her. She won't survive much more." He glanced over at her and she swatted him.

"Don't look at me like you look at your car. I'm not that old and weathered, okay?"

O'Dell snickered and climbed behind the wheel. "Get in. Let's get this over with so I can make sure you're around tomorrow and the next day, too."

She grinned, glad for anything that lightened the mood, and walked around the front of the car. She saw Jason's truck out of the corner of her eye and it felt like her soul grinned. Of course Jason was going to watch over her. Whatever else was going on in his life, that hadn't changed.

"Are you ready?" O'Dell asked lightly, but his jaw was tight, his shoulders stiff.

She nodded, an uneasy feeling washing over her from the

inside out, and O'Dell pulled out of the lot, headed for William Junior, for Cindy Lou, for Faith, and maybe for Lola.

By the glow of the streetlamp, Janet read her watch. Just after six o'clock, but the sky was cloudy and the early winter sunset had already plunged the area into total darkness. A chill that had nothing to do with the cool winter air slid down the back of her neck and settled into the base of her spine. She shivered, and O'Dell looked over, concerned.

"You don't have to do this, you know that, right? This isn't your job."

"I know, O'Dell. But it's the quickest way to end this, and that's important."

He frowned, but nodded, too, and she tuned back into what Rivera was saying to the team.

"After Janet makes contact on the phone, she will glean as much information as possible from Suspect One on where he is in the unit." He pointed to a board behind him with a hastily drawn rendering of the apartment floor plan, taken from the owner of the unit, now standing alert next to the detective. "As soon as Janet gives us the signal—"

He waited, and only when O'Dell poked her in the ribs did she blurt out, "Do you need any food?"

Rivera glared at her before nodding. "That's when we know he's in the kitchen and it's safe for us to move in. If at any time we get word that victims are in pain, injured, or otherwise in bad shape, then we move in immediately on my command." He stopped and surveyed the team assembled in front of him. "Any questions?"

Janet half-raised her hand as if she was back in a classroom.

"I'm feeling a little underdressed. Do I need a bulletproof vest or anything?"

"You are not going anywhere near the scene, so there's no reason for you to have anything on other than your regular clothes," O'Dell growled loud enough for Rivera to nod approvingly.

"All right." Rivera's gaze swept the group one more time before he clapped his hands together. "Let's go get this guy."

A whoop of noise rose from the assembled men and women, and everyone broke apart and took up their posts around the perimeter of the building and up the back stairs under cover of darkness.

Rivera walked over and held a cell phone out toward her. "Are you ready, Janet?"

She quenched the sickening feeling in her stomach and squared her shoulders. "Let's do this."

CHAPTER FORTY-TWO

Her palm was sweaty, and the phone slipped down, just her fingertips catching it at the last minute.

"Got it?" Rivera glared and she gulped audibly.

"Yup. Sorry."

O'Dell opened his mouth but shut it before any words came out. His glare was enough to remind her and Rivera that he didn't like what they were doing. His grim attitude bolstered her own, and she wiped her palm off on her jeans and then gripped the phone tightly.

"Dialing," she said softly as she pressed the keypad, reading the numbers off a notepad Rivera held out. She held her breath. "It's ringing," she said, and Rivera pushed his fingers up to his lips. She nodded and pressed her own lips together. The call went straight to voicemail. She relayed the information to Rivera and he reached over to end the call.

"Try again."

She dialed the numbers a second time, and before she could whisper to Rivera that the call had rung through to the other end, a voice spoke.

"Who's this?"

Her eyes flew open, and when a bitter taste flooded the back of her mouth she realized exactly what she'd gotten herself into. There was no script, no help. Just her, a cell phone, and a madman. And several lives possibly hanging in the balance.

"This is...Janet. I—" She locked eyes with O'Dell. "I heard you've been looking for me."

A long pause met her declaration and Janet thought she might have lost him. But then he spoke.

"I've been watching you, that's true. Looking for you. Trying to meet you."

"Well, you should have stopped into the Spot to say hi."

"Jason has that place locked down. I could never get in unnoticed."

O'Dell raised his eyebrows and she shrugged. How could she explain what was being said without giving herself away? "Your dad is worried about your mom."

"I'll bet."

"Can I talk to her?"

"No."

"Is she okay?"

Rivera leaned in, as if certain he'd be able to hear Junior's answer through the line. But it wasn't going to be that easy. Of course it wasn't.

"What does Jason think?"

"Jason?" Janet was surprised by the change in topic. Was Junior worried about his older brother? Or did he want to impress him? "Of course he's worried, too."

"Where is he?"

"I don't know. He...he broke up with me. Did you know that?"

"Bullshit. He's just trying to keep you safe. Worked so far, didn't it?"

"Do you want to hurt me, William?"

No answer.

"Why? Why are you so angry?"

"You haven't seen angry yet." Another chilling statement, but Rivera was getting impatient. He glared at her and she bit her lip, then blurted out, "Do you have Cindy Lou?"

"You surprised me. At the restaurant this morning. I wasn't expecting to see you."

"You surprised me, too. From across the room, I thought you were Jason." She gulped; would the comparison make him angry? He didn't speak, so she asked him again, "Is Cindy Lou with you?"

"Not exactly."

Janet's breath caught. What did that mean? She didn't want to risk his wrath by asking, so she switched gears. "Is your mother alive?"

He snorted. "Of course. I wouldn't kill my own mother. She was just in the way, so I put her to sleep while I finish the job."

"Asleep? Not dead?"

He sighed "I'm bored with this call. Goodbye."

"Wait!" But only silence met her cry. She looked down at the screen—the numbers timing the call length ticked onward. Despite his silence, Junior was still on the other end of the line. She motioned O'Dell closer and held the phone between their heads. "Junior?"

"Don't call me that!"

"What should I call you?"

"Jeff! My name is Jeff."

"Right. Jeff, what are you going to do? You have to know this isn't going to end well, right?"

"I know." His voice was suddenly small, frightened.

"Then what are you going to do?"

"I guess I wanted to talk to you."

Relief flooded O'Dell's face. She felt it in her bones, too. Talk. They could do that. They *were doing* that. "I want to help you, Jun—Jeff. How can I help?"

"Where are you?" The mini blinds on the windows in the apartment above moved, a triangle of light now visible from the street below. "Are you out there with the police?"

O'Dell's face tightened. Janet felt the shift across the cell phone signal. What did Jason's brother know? She cleared her throat. "Um, yes. They thought I could help."

"Are you protected?"

"Well, that's a funny question, seeing as you know I'm with the cops. Of course I'm protected."

"I'm not stupid!" he roared. "Don't treat me like I'm stupid!" Heavy breathing shallowed out to a small cough. A deep sigh. "People always underestimate me. I hate that."

The streetlamp under which they stood suddenly went dark. Just coincidence. It had to be. But O'Dell must have felt the same uncertainty that roared up Janet's throat, because he clicked the safety off of his gun and held it stiffly at his side. She looked nervously around. There wasn't any movement from inside the apartment, but then the streetlights all down the block extinguished at once, plunging the team into complete and utter darkness.

She gripped the phone tightly in her fist, and when Junior spoke again, his voice was slick, slithery. "Oh, Janet. I've been waiting for you. Now I can see that it was worth it."

An explosion of sound and smoke fired from nearby, then another and another. O'Dell shoved her to the side and she stumbled down the ledge of the sidewalk onto the street and fell down onto the ground, dazed.

"Go!" Rivera roared the command, but it was too late. The chaos of the darkness and explosions rendered the SWAT team useless, their coordination completely destroyed.

O'Dell helped her up and pushed her down the street, away from the chaos, away from the dangerous madman who wanted to hurt her. The night was black, the smoke was chokingly thick, and O'Dell's gloved grip was painfully tight.

"Jesus H. Christ, O'Dell, I'm not going to run away from you! He's a lunatic!"

O'Dell turned to face her—only it wasn't O'Dell.

"What—"

"Move. Now." The man pushed her hard—shoved her—away from the SWAT team, away from safety, and she tried to plant her feet, but he was stronger, and he lifted her almost completely off the ground. She looked wildly around, but couldn't see through the thick smoke, could only tell they were getting farther away from her crew, from her team, because the sounds of battle were getting quieter. Her head finally swiveled away from the SWAT team behind them and she looked ahead to see where they were going.

"Junior?" she gasped, as his crushing grip on her shoulder blade threatened to break bones.

"Don't call me Junior!" he roared, and her legs shook at the raw anger in his voice. She stumbled and would have fallen if Jason's brother's grip on her collarbone hadn't tightened. She gasped at the fresh pain that shot through her shoulder and down her arm, and no matter how hard she tried, she couldn't stop moving forward, even though she saw where they were headed.

"No—no, no, no. I am not getting into a van without windows. Nothing good happens in a van without—"

But he opened the back door and before she could react, he lifted her effortlessly. She kicked, fought with everything she had, but he easily overpowered her. The fact would have been infuriating if she hadn't had other more pressing issues to deal with.

He tossed her into the back of the van like she was a snack

cooler. If only she could have absorbed the impact of the landing as easily.

The jolt of hitting the metal floorboards took her breath away, and before she could reconcile the pain in her head, elbow, and hip, Jeff slammed the back door, plunging her into darkness. She struggled to sit up, and as she writhed around the unforgiving metal floorboards, her elbow landed on something bumpy. She felt around with her hands and found herself situated between two lumpy rolls of carpet. Her fingers danced over the rough edges of the frayed material as the van began to move. Her hand shot out to steady herself, and then she flinched when her skin touched someone else's skin.

She wasn't alone in the van after all.

She tried to yell, but it came out more like a gasp. "What is happening?"

But it was no use.

The bodies lying next to her didn't seem able to answer.

CHAPTER FORTY-THREE

The van rumbled along, Janet increasingly uncomfortable by what she didn't know about her situation. Where was Jason's brother taking her? And who else was along for the ride?

"Are you okay?" she whispered to the dark rolls on either side of her. "Can you hear me?"

There was no answer.

Her hands skittered along the floorboards, searching for anything that she could use as a weapon. Passing over the lumpy carpet roll on her right, her fingers stretched to the cool metal side of the van without luck. To the left, her search was rewarded by something sharp slicing open her finger.

Janet gasped and raised the finger to her lips, sucking off the blood.

After a moment, though, she leaned over the carpet roll. Whatever had been sharp enough to cut her was sharp enough to cut someone else. She squinted, waiting for passing headlights to help her see.

Finally, a beam of light shot through the front of the car and lit up the interior enough for her to make out what had injured her. Her stomach dropped when she saw it—just a rusted out spot of the interior wall of the van. Not a weapon at all. Disappointment slid down the back of her throat like acid, and settled uncomfortably in her stomach.

Eventually the van slowed to a stop, and the driver's door opened with a click and then slammed shut. Footsteps crunched around the side of the van.

Janet climbed to her feet and balanced in a low crouch, her arms bent and ready to rocket out. She knew she'd have just one shot to overpower Junior, to escape; but when the door opened, he struck first, as if he knew she'd be waiting for him.

His fist connected with her right eye and the side of her nose. He might as well have used a stun gun on her; she fell back, immobile, both eyes watering and stinging, her breath gone.

After the ride in the back of the dark van, the light behind Junior felt as bright as fireworks. With her eyes still watering, she had trouble keeping them open at all. Before she could recover, Junior grabbed her ankles and pulled her roughly forward along the floor of the van, and jabbed her in the neck with something sharp.

"What was that?" she yelped.

He didn't answer, but she saw a flash of metal at his side, before it disappeared into his pocket. She reached up to touch her neck and wiped a drop of blood away from her skin. A panic, unlike any she'd ever felt, swept through her bloodstream and a shiver rocked her body.

"Was that a needle? What did you give me?"

When she kicked out, he jabbed her so hard in the kidney that she couldn't mask her gasp. He chuckled, then pulled her roughly out of the van and tied her wrists together behind her. She stood on shaky legs, unsure what he might do next.

Dammit. She tried to calm herself, to take in her surroundings. If she was going to have any chance of escaping, she needed to keep her wits about her; figure out where she was.

He shoved her forward. The contact helped snap her out of the growing sense of panic. But still, her legs felt unusually weak, her brain foggy. Gravel crunched underfoot, then the jangle of a keyring. She shook her head to clear it and recognized the brown metal door in front of her. The back entrance to Old Ben's restaurant. They were so close to the Spot if she turned, she could see it.

Her brain sparked with awareness. If she yelled, someone might hear her. But suddenly, her vision went sideways, then Jeff grabbed her under her arms. Had she fallen? Her joints felt loose, her mind out of focus.

She smelled day-old grease and burned hamburger, and an image of her food truck flashed across the back of her eyelids.

Why were they here?

Junior set her down on the floor, but her legs couldn't support her. Her knees felt weak and her vision—still blurry from the punch—went hazier yet.

"Why, Junior? Why...why are you... doing th..." But she couldn't finish her question. Instead, consciousness slipped away.

———

Sometime later, a pounding woke Janet from a very bad dream.

"Och." Keeping her eyes tightly shut, she gingerly reached up to touch her head. *Bam. Bam. Bam.* The pounding was slow, steady. "What is that?"

She blinked her eyes open and sucked in a sharp breath. Where was she?

The space was dark and smelled funny, like the inside of an old locker room. And it was hot. So hot that beads of sweat trickled down her arms; her shirt stuck to her skin.

"Fuuuuck."

"Cindy Lou?" Janet lurched forward, remembering everything that had led up to this moment in one horrible flash. "Cindy Lou, is that you?" She reached out toward the voice and held back a sob.

"I reckon so, but I feel like someone hit me with a sledgehammer. Where are we?"

"We're inside Old Ben's restaurant." Janet glanced around the dark space. "I think we're inside the walk-in cooler."

Janet ran her hands over the other woman's head. No bumps, no blood. "Do you know what happened to you?"

"I honestly don't." Her nose wrinkled and she looked up and searched Janet's face. "I saw you at breakfast—that happened, right?"

Janet nodded.

"Then we went back to Jeff's place and the last thing I remember is he gave me a cup of tea." She shook her head and winced. "But that doesn't make sense, does it?"

"He must have drugged you."

"But why?"

"It's a long story. Have you seen Jason's mother?"

Cindy Lou looked around the cramped room slowly. "No, hon, I sure don't see her."

"No—I meant—never mind." Janet stood and tried the door. "Locked."

Cindy Lou coughed. "Man, I would kill for some water right about now. My mouth is like the dang-Sahara."

Janet continued to search the room, her hands skimming the walls, they were almost too hot to touch.

"I'll tell you what, if we're in the cooler, the designer did something wrong. It's hotter than blue blazes in here!"

Janet blew out a slow breath, trying to force her brain to

work. Junior had tossed them inside, but when? How much time had elapsed?

"Hey!" Janet banged on the door with her fist. "Hey! Let us out!"

Cindy Lou joined in, but no amount of banging brought Jason's brother back to them.

Cindy Lou rubbed her knuckles and leaned against the door. "Is he gone, d'ya think?"

"I don't know." Janet wiped beads of sweat from her face and snapped her shirt away from her stomach.

"Do you smell that?" Cindy Lou asked, coughing again.

Janet nodded slowly.

"Smells like...a campfire or something. But with burning tire thrown on top. What is going on, Janet?"

"I think..." Janet swallowed, hardly able to utter the words. But with the heat, the smell, and what she'd mistaken for a fan earlier, it seemed the only explanation. "I think the restaurant is on fire."

"No." Cindy Lou shook her head. "No way. Maybe he's just makin' us a snack...or...oh, dear." Cindy Lou pointed to the ventilation slits at the top of the insulated walls. Smoke seeped into the room. They needed to find a way out of the building.

A sudden blast of noise knocked Janet off her feet. Cindy Lou screamed.

"Shh!" Though her ears were ringing, she thought she heard a scrabbling of noise at the door.

Janet leapt back up just as Junior stormed into the tiny space. He grabbed her arm. In a panic, she tried to shrug out of his grasp, but his grip was iron-like, so tight she felt a bruise blooming under his fingertips.

"Let go of me!" Panic rose up her throat, choking her, along with the heavy smoke now pouring into the small space. But he was stronger, and his grip didn't falter. When she tried kicking out at him, he slapped her across the face. Hard.

She hadn't been expecting it—which made it hurt all the more. But it also knocked some sense into her, and her panic disappeared along with the feeling in her jaw. This kidnapping had just ventured into bar brawl territory, and that knowledge hit her in the face almost as hard as Junior's open hand.

When he pulled his arm back again, she was ready. Just before his palm made contact with her face for a second time, she dodged to the right and used his momentum as a weapon, pulling against him with all her might, then shoving his body forward when he lost his balance. When he stumbled, he lost his grip on her arm. She brought her knee up with as much force as she could muster, and felt, rather than heard, his nose break against her kneecap. He gasped in pain, and she took the opportunity to strike. Her elbow swung down against his head with a crack that she felt all the way to the tip of her pinky finger. He dropped down to the ground, his face hitting the cement floor with a sickening smack. Cindy Lou crawled over to him and pried one eye open. It lolled like a pinball.

"You knocked him out cold!" She looked up in awe.

But instead of feeling galvanized, Janet dropped down onto her knees, suddenly hardly able to catch her breath. Hyperventilating when it was all over, how ridiculous! She raised her head in search of cooler, more oxygenated air.

Cindy Lou tottered to her feet, swaying with the effort. She poked her head out of the cooler and yelped. "We need to get out of here!"

Another blast of noise rocked the entire structure. Janet couldn't hear anything over the roar of the fire. *Think!* she admonished herself.

Though Junior was a killer, he was also Jason's brother. How could she live with herself if she left him here to burn to death?

Also, he was likely the only one who knew where Lola and Faith were—if they were dead or alive.

"This asshole is going to owe me so big," she growled. Light from the fire illuminated the inside of the cooler, and she made her way back to where Junior lay on the ground. "Help me, Cindy Lou!" she cried, and together, they managed to lift the upper half of his body up, but Janet couldn't find purchase to get his nearly 200 pounds of dead weight up over her shoulder.

"It's never gonna work, hon. Just leave him—you have to leave him!"

"But then we might never know what happened to Faith! To Lola!"

Cindy Lou grabbed Janet's arm and pulled. "I don't care right now! If we don't get out of here, we'll never get to wonder what happened to anyone. Janet, we're out of time!"

Another coughing spell grabbed hold of Janet, and when she caught her breath, she stumbled toward her friend. "Follow me!" she called over her shoulder, and stepped out into the main part of the kitchen. The heat was intense—but just from one side. Propane tanks lined up like soldiers from the wall of the walk-in cooler through the kitchen into the main dining area. Janet turned the other way and headed past the dishwasher station and toward a metal door. She hoped it led to safety.

She twisted the knob and pushed against the door, but it didn't budge.

"Come on, Janet! Together!" Cindy Lou joined her at the threshold, and they pushed, hit, and kicked at the door. Nothing happened.

Suddenly, the metal surface shuddered with a *thunk* of noise. The women looked at each other and leapt back.

"Someone's here! Someone's out there to help!" Cindy Lou cried.

The door shuddered again, but the lock held steady. A third

chop of noise and whatever had been holding the door locked broke loose, and the heavy metal slab swung open.

An axe-wielding fireman stood before them, and even in their precarious situation, with a fire raging behind them and choking smoke overhead, Cindy Lou ran a quick hand through her messy blond hair and smiled. "Boy, are you a sight for sore eyes, mister!"

Janet shoved Cindy Lou past the fireman. "There's a man back there. He's—uh, he's knocked out in the kitchen!"

She hurried out into the cool refreshing air and didn't look back.

CHAPTER FORTY-FOUR

Janet stumbled out of the burning building, gasping for air and squinting against the sudden bright flashing lights from the fire trucks. She doubled over and took huge gulps of air, never appreciating oxygen more than she did just then.

A medic led her and Cindy Lou forward, out of the way of emergency crews still trying to get a handle on the fire. As they walked past a truck, she caught sight of Jason and O'Dell, standing next to each other at the edge of the parking lot.

Jason's hand clutched his chest like he was trying to keep his heart inside of his body. His open mouth looked frozen in mid-scream, and the soot on his face had settled into the fine lines around his eyes.

O'Dell's rigid stance relaxed as soon as he caught sight of her, and his mouth moved, maybe saying her and Cindy Lou's names before he smacked Jason on the shoulder and jogged toward them.

Jason didn't move—he stood as far from her as the property would allow.

Her focus shifted to O'Dell. When he reached them, he

pulled them both into a hug, then stepped back and dropped his gaze, but not his hands, which squeezed her shoulder tighter. "I will never forgive myself, Janet. You were ripped away from right under my nose! I don't know how he did it!"

"It wasn't your fault, O'Dell." Janet reached out and lifted his chin. "I thought you were pushing me away to safety. I didn't realize it was Junior until we were halfway to his van." She shuddered. "It's all my fault." O'Dell didn't look convinced, but Janet had more pressing issues than his guilty conscience. "Faith? Lola?"

He shook his head. "Nothing yet. We thought they might be with you."

All three turned to face the building. And it might have been her imagination, but the flames looked smaller. Less intense.

"I don't know. They weren't in the cooler with us, but they might be somewhere else in there." Janet's stomach dropped again. Were Faith and Lola in there? Dead? Alive? Dying even as she took great gasping gulps of clean air into her own lungs?

A group of firefighters emerged from the restaurant, holding a gurney between them. Janet recognized the beanie covering the patient's head. "Junior."

"He was in there? That just doesn't make any sense." O'Dell's frown deepened. "What was his plan? To die in there with you?"

Janet couldn't even find the energy to lift her shoulders in a shrug. It *didn't* make sense, but then, nothing about Junior's actions in the last month had made sense. She looked back to where Jason had been—but he was gone.

"His mom's still missing. I'm sure he's worried." O'Dell squeezed her shoulder once more before dropping his hand. "We'll need to talk to you both—take official statements. But first," he held his phone out to Cindy Lou, "you should call Chip."

"Great balls of fire! Chip!" Cindy Lou grabbed the phone and turned away from O'Dell and Janet to dial the phone. While she laughed and cried into the phone with Chip, the scene commander gathered the firefighters near one of their trucks. The fire was winning, and O'Dell murmured in Janet's ear that they were going to probably change from attacking the fire to regrouping, finding a new strategy.

A third explosion rocked the building. Janet flinched against the noise, and O'Dell pulled her farther away from the restaurant. "It's propane tanks," she said. "They were stacked between the cooler and the restaurant. I think Junior's plan was to level the building and everyone who was in it."

"But why?" O'Dell scratched his head. "And why Cindy Lou?"

"What do you mean? Why any of us is the question!"

He turned to face Janet. "Jason told us that Junior was angry that the family had abandoned him in Memphis, that they'd chosen Jason, in a sense, by all moving to Knoxville. So in his anger, and more importantly, off his meds, he decided to target each family member. He killed Connie to get back at his dad. He took you to get back at Jason. But why Cindy Lou? You know?"

Janet chewed on her lip as she watched the firefighters break apart and surround the restaurant again. "Cindy Lou really admired Faith—" O'Dell snorted and Janet's shoulder slumped. "Okay, you're right. It was probably just another route to get to me." But her guilt over Cindy Lou's involvement in Junior's plan took a backseat when she looked at the burning building again. She sucked in a gasp loud enough that Cindy Lou looked over from her phone call.

"What?" O'Dell moved closer to Janet and grabbed her shoulders again, shaking her slightly when she didn't answer.

She shrugged him off and an animal-like sound came from

somewhere—maybe her own throat—as she ran toward the building. Toward Jason.

"What the hell is he doing?" O'Dell said when he caught sight of Jason, wrapping a bandana around his face, simultaneously cowering against the heat and stepping through a broken window into the inferno.

"Jason!" She tried to lunge past a fireman, but O'Dell held her back.

"Jesus, Janet—no. *No!*" He grabbed her from behind and locked down his grip. Her fingernails scratched at his neck, but O'Dell gently pulled her back, away from the building. The seconds passed like hours—everything moving in slow motion. Even the water was sluggish as it left the hoses, hardly making it to the building—to the fire—to Jason.

But just before she turned away, defeated, there it was—movement from within. Jason emerged from the orange glow of the center of the building, bent in half, lumbering toward the window, toward safety, the limp form of a person resting over his shoulder in a fireman's hold.

"Jesus," O'Dell breathed and dropped his hold on Janet to hurry forward and help, but a firefighter got there first and eased the body from Jason's shoulder.

Janet crept up behind O'Dell, drawn like a moth to the flame, even though she didn't want to know who Jason had found. Lola? Faith? Alive...or dead?

Jason stopped to cough, his face soot-blackened, his voice barely more than a croak. "Is she alive?"

Janet looked down at the ground. Faith lay crumpled—and it might have been her imagination, but she swore the older woman's chest rose up and down.

Before she could make sure her eyes weren't playing tricks on her, an EMT team pushed them all aside. The woman slipped an oxygen mask over Faith's face, then she and her partner lifted Faith onto a gurney and hurried away.

Only Jason's labored breathing punctured the relative silence.

Janet reached out to touch his shoulder, but when he flinched, she dropped her hand. "How did you know she was in there, Jason?"

"My brother," he said the word like a curse, "left a clue for me. I almost missed it. I almost didn't get to her in time." He choked back a sob.

"What clue?"

He didn't look up from the ground, but through barely moving lips he answered. "Her scarf. He left Cindy Lou's bandana, your jean jacket and Mom's scarf by the door. I didn't realize it was a clue until you and Cindy Lou came out. I almost missed it. This is my fault." His shoulders stiffened and he walked away into the night without a backwards glance.

O'Dell's radio crackled to life. He murmured something back to whomever was on the other end. Janet stood, staring into the darkness where Jason had disappeared.

She jumped when he tapped her on the arm. "What do you think?"

Janet wiped her eyes and turned to face her friend. "I'm sorry, O'Dell. What?"

"I said, Junior's regaining consciousness. Rivera's going to interview him in the hospital. Do you want to come?"

She wanted to curl up in bed in a dark room and never face anyone again. But that clearly wasn't an option, and she did have a job to finish. Find Lola. And that meant going with O'Dell to see the one person who might have some answers. She steeled her resolve. "Let's go."

"What about me?" Cindy Lou wailed.

"You'll take an ambulance," O'Dell said. "They'll want to make sure you're okay after everything that happened."

She nodded and followed an EMT toward a waiting ambulance.

O'Dell reached out for Janet's hand. "Ready?"

"Ready."

CHAPTER FORTY-FIVE

"What's going on?" Janet asked as they passed the hospital entrance and instead took a turn down an unlit path.

O'Dell smiled without taking his eyes off the road. "Rivera said the press is gathered at the emergency entrance. So we're taking the service road to a side entrance. A patrol officer will open the door for us."

He slowed the car as they drove past the hospital helipad. The chopper sat motionless on the pavement, waiting, no doubt, for the next car crash or shooting victim who'd need immediate evacuation to the hospital.

O'Dell eased the car into park but didn't turn off the engine. "I don't know if you should come into the room or not."

"What are you talking about? Then why did I come—why did you invite me along?"

"Honestly? Because I didn't want to leave you alone out there. You've been through a lot. I want to keep you close."

Her eyes filled unexpectedly and she turned away. Across the grassy yard, a pilot climbed up into the helicopter. The blades started to spin and soon, the rest of the flight crew spilled out of the hospital, gearing up for some kind of emergency.

"Life will never be the same," she said slowly. "Jason's family will never be the same. I don't know how we come back from this. But I do know that there's still a missing piece—Lola. And if I can help find her, if I can help shake Junior's tongue loose, then that might be the only thing I can do tonight. The only thing that might help me feel better about this whole lousy day."

O'Dell heaved out a sigh. "You're not allowed to actually shake his tongue loose. You know that, right?"

She smiled grimly. "Let's go."

Out on the pavement, O'Dell clicked the key fob to lock his car and motioned that Janet should follow him. He spoke into his radio and the side door opened just as they approached.

"Detective." The patrol officer nodded as they walked past, then resumed his guard duty by the exit. They took the elevator up to the third floor, and O'Dell led the way through the maze of hallways, past a nurses' station, and finally slowed at a room guarded by another cop.

That officer spoke into the radio clipped to the epaulette on his uniform, and less than a minute later, Rivera came down the hallway from the opposite direction.

"Any updates?" O'Dell asked.

"I just left Faith—she's fine," he was quick to add when a sound escaped Janet's mouth. "Some smoke inhalation, so they're keeping her overnight for observation, but the doctor said she shows no other signs of trauma."

"Impossible," Janet said, remembering her unconscious body sliding from Jason's grip after he'd rescued her from the fire.

"She says the last thing she remembers is that Junior called her, and said he was in trouble—that he needed her help, and only her help. So she gave William and Jason the slip and took an Uber to his apartment."

"The apartment where the SWAT team met?"

Rivera nodded. "When she got there, he offered her some tea. That's the last thing she remembers before waking up in the ambulance on the way here."

"Are there drugs in her system?"

Rivera shook his head. "No trace of anything. But if he used some kind of roofie on her early this morning, it would be out of her system already. He's smart."

O'Dell frowned. "That's probably what he did to Cindy Lou, too."

"And me." Janet reached up and rubbed the spot on her neck where Junior had jabbed her with a needle. "So what about Lola? She's been gone for weeks, but I swear I spotted her at breakfast yesterday—sitting right next to Junior and Cindy Lou. So how's he been keeping her, if he's not drugging her and he didn't kill her —what the hell is going on?"

"Time to find out." Rivera pushed open the door to the patient room.

William Jefferson Brooks Junior's bed was half-inclined, so that he wasn't flat but wasn't sitting up, either. Janet wondered if he'd turned away from the door when he heard it open, or if he'd been facing the window for a while.

Rivera cleared his throat, but Junior didn't move. The only acknowledgement that he knew they were there was the fluttering of his eyelids.

"You like to be called Jeff?" Rivera asked, his voice calm, pleasant, as if the man before them hadn't just tried to kill himself and three others.

"It is my name. So I guess so." His voice was soft but steely. Like his anger simmered just under the surface.

O'Dell edged slightly in front of Janet but didn't block her completely. The movement caught Junior's attention, and a spark of recognition kindled in his eye as he turned to face his visitor.

"You." He looked at Janet appreciatively, then said, "How's the identity-theft business going lately?"

"Huh?" The question was so unexpected that Janet was distracted from the much larger issues at hand. "What are you talking about?"

"Coffee, muffins...I wasn't sure how big I'd have to go to get your attention." When her brow furrowed, his lips pressed together into a bitter smile. "How disappointing. You didn't figure it out? Not as smart as they said, then. Hmm."

His expression jarred her brain loose, but she was still confused. "The credit card theft investigation? At the coffee shop? So that wasn't your father then, but...who cares?"

"I wanted to get your attention, but that firm you're working for is slow. I filed the theft complaint with Bexley and Associates weeks before you finally looked into it. I got tired of waiting for you."

"You? What do you mean *you* filed the complaint? We were investigating for some lady named Karla."

"There is no Karla. I made her up, opened a fake credit card account, and then hired you to investigate."

"But...why?"

"I'd heard a lot about you, Janet. I wanted to see you for myself. But Jason had your bar locked down. Your home was... inaccessible, though I continued to try. In the end, it only tipped my parents off that I was...interested."

Janet froze—remembering Jason's father randomly deciding to do a deep clean at her house just the other day. "The windows?" she asked.

Junior nodded. "Just a little love message to let you know I was coming."

"And they knew? They knew that you were out there and dangerous, and they didn't warn me?"

"It's like they don't trust you at all." Junior's somber face was worse than his chilling grin.

"All right, pal, we're not here to go over your greatest hits. We want Lola. And when we get her, no one's going to care about anything you do ever again, you got that?" O'Dell's hard smile would have made many people stand down. But Junior wasn't like many other people. His gaze never wavered from Janet.

"Where's Lola?" Janet's throat felt raw from the smoke, but she faced her kidnapper head on. His smile made her skin crawl. How she'd ever thought he resembled Jason was beyond her. There wasn't any kindness in those cold, calculating eyes.

"Where is Lola? That's a great question." He turned back toward the window, then murmured, "Tick tock."

Janet sucked in a loud breath and grabbed O'Dell's hand for support. "Tick tock? What does that mean?"

Junior blew out a slow steady breath and repeated himself.

"Is Lola in danger? Is she alive? Tell us where she is!" O'Dell barked.

Rivera held out his hand, a warning. "We can help you, Junior, but only if you help us, you understand?"

"It's Jeff, you asshole."

After a lengthy silence, Janet and the two cops headed to the door. At the sound of movement, Junior turned and caught Janet's eye. "Tick tock for Lola. And tick tock for Jason." Then he started laughing, and the crazed, joyless sound echoed around the small cold room.

Janet stumbled backward, away from Jason's brother, out into the safety of the hall.

Rivera gently closed the door on Junior, and he, O'Dell, and Janet gathered in the hallway.

"Chief's coming down to deal with the media. Turns out someone tipped them all off about this 'fire-revenge plan.' That's what they're calling it."

"What do you think? Does he know where Lola is?" Janet asked.

"She's not at the apartment. SWAT is still going over everything there, but there's no sign of struggle. No sign that Lola was ever there." Rivera rubbed a hand roughly over his forehead. "Plenty of other things—like a computer that had hacked into the city's electrical grid...but no sign of a missing teen."

Janet crossed her arms over her chest, trying to ward off the chill that bloomed deep in her core. "It's a game for him. A game he's still trying to win."

"The game's over, Janet. And I think we have to come to grips with the fact that Lola's dead." O'Dell gripped her shoulder and squeezed. "Maybe he gave her too much of the drug that he used on Cindy Lou and his mother. Maybe he dumped her body before we even got to his apartment tonight. It'll all make sense soon—someone will find the body. They'll call it in. There's nothing we can do until that happens."

She nodded, not believing anything O'Dell said. It wasn't over. Junior's words proved that he was still in the game, and he was still planning on taking Jason down.

O'Dell and Rivera had their heads together, talking about who was going to file which part of the report that would span several locations, multiple victims, and a recalcitrant suspect unwilling to confess.

She cleared her throat and held out her hand. "Can I have your keys, O'Dell? I need some air."

CHAPTER FORTY-SIX

If O'Dell thought she was only heading outside for some fresh air, he was more tired than he was letting on. Janet climbed into his car, cranked over the engine, then showed unusual restraint by easing slowly down the poorly lit path instead of laying rubber on the road.

Before she turned at the corner of the building, the lights on the helipad came up full. She rolled her window down and heard the *thwack-thwack-thwack* of the chopper's blades. Wind kicked up and pushed her car forward as the helicopter prepared to land. Had they saved someone, or were they too late?

She wondered the same thing about her own rescue mission.

Junior had given Janet a clue—a clue that Lola wasn't the only one in trouble. Janet wasn't going to sit by and wait for his twisted plan to come to an end.

She didn't think Lola was dead. She didn't think Lola was missing. She thought Lola had been a partner to Junior for weeks. It was the only thing that made sense in the completely senseless series of events of the last forty-eight hours. And that meant that Jason was in grave danger.

Out on the main road, she sped up, racing toward the Spot as if a life depended on it. Jason's just might.

Faith's restaurant—what was left of it—still smoldered next door.

The irony wasn't lost on her. The abandoned building next door was alive with activity—flashing lights from the fire trucks, emergency crews milling around, a fire line ringed by curious spectators. Meanwhile, her bar appeared dead and deserted.

She turned away from the circus and fumbled for her keys. She needn't have bothered. The front door was unlocked.

The sharp smell of gasoline greeted her when the door whooshed open unexpectedly.

"Freeze."

She flinched when the cool metal of a gun touched her temple. "Lola. I thought I'd find you here, I just didn't expect you to be preparing an arson."

"I'm just doing my part of the plan, just like Jeff asked. Besides, you don't fool me!" Her voice quaked. "You're the dangerous one! Jeff showed me pictures of how you've been stalking me at my school, my house. He said you were dangerous."

Janet knew it was critical to stay calm. Lola was terrified. Janet needed to show her she was not the enemy. But her heart beat so loudly in her head that she couldn't remember anything except the fact that a gun was inches from her forehead. She took a shaky breath and tried to make eye contact. Lola refused to look up. Janet spoke anyway. "Your mother hired me. She's worried about you. She wants you back home."

"Lies!" Lola pushed the tip of the gun against Janet's head, her hand trembling. "She didn't care about me when I lived in her house; she sure as shit doesn't care about me now that I'm gone."

"You're wrong, Lola. She's terrified for you. She misses you. She wants you to come home."

"She doesn't want anything other than her boyfriend. She's made that clear."

Janet's queasy stomach lurched, and she swallowed hard. "If you really felt that way, you would have told her you were going. By disappearing, you ensured that your mother would care. You know that's true. It's terrible that you felt abandoned. It's awful that you felt so alone. But you have a mother who loves you. What you're doing now—arson? It's a crime, Lola. Jeff knew it was wrong, and so do you. It's not okay, Lola."

The teen didn't answer, but the tip of the gun pushed against Janet's head with more force.

"When did you learn that his name was Jeff?" Janet tried to keep her tone conversational. As if she wasn't talking to a girl with a gun.

"Huh?" Lola's over-bright eyes blinked, and she refocused on Janet.

"It's just—well, I guess I was wondering..." Janet cleared her throat. "It seems like when you first met him, Jeff went by a different name. Matt. Why?"

Lola licked her lips and her eyes darted around the bar. "He's had to hide who he really is for ages. People—they just don't understand him. And that's made life really difficult for him."

Janet took a slow, quiet breath. "It's really awful when people don't understand you, isn't it?"

"Don't belittle me, please."

"I'm not. I know how you feel—how Jeff must have felt." Her mind raced—was it time to act? She'd never had a gun so close to ending her life. She might only get one chance. Was this it? The fact that she didn't know made her think it wasn't. She cleared her throat again. "Where's Jason?"

"Jeff said...he said Jason's a criminal, and that we can't be happy until he's...uh...out of the picture." Her voice caught; her hand trembled again and she swallowed hard. It sounded like a sob. "I—I—I don't know..."

"Then what? What are you going to do then?"

"We're going to go away. Live together. Love each other. Start —we're just going to start over."

"You could have done that anytime over the last month. Why did Jeff have to kill his family first? Burn down two buildings first? Think, Lola. Is that the plan of a good person?"

"Kill people? No. He didn't..." Her lips moved, but no more sound came out. Lola was lost, rudderless. Janet knew exactly how that felt.

"You're a minor, Lola. Police will take that into consideration. But Jeff—he's in real trouble. You should know that. Police are talking to him now, and it's not going to end well. He kidnapped me, my friend, and his own mother. He tried to kill us in the fire next door."

"No, that can't be. He was just going to burn down that deserted building. And I'm supposed to do the same thing here to prove my love to him. Then we get the insurance money and leave this crappy town. We can finally be together."

"Think, Lola! Neither of these buildings belong to him! The only way he'd get insurance money for them is if his entire family —and me—was gone."

The two women stared at each other. Lola was the first to look away.

"You're lying. Jeff said you were sneaky like that."

Janet shifted gears. "Who's idea was it for Jeff to sleep with Cindy Lou?"

Lola shook her head. "More lies! They didn't sleep together. He drugged her after he brought her back to his apartment. She only thought they hooked up."

"But why?"

"Because he..." she faltered, and the gun started to slip from her hand, so she brought her other up to support it. "He wanted more information on you and Jason."

"Why?"

"I don't know, okay?" she wailed. "I don't understand everything, I just know that we want to be together, and he had to take care of some things first."

Janet saw nothing but fear in the younger girl's face. Without Junior running the show, the girl had no idea what to do.

Janet chanced a quick glance around the room. Her office door was propped open, but the rest of the space was dark; she could barely make out where the back booths ended and the walls began. Jason wasn't here, but if Janet played her cards right, she just might keep Lola from burning down her business.

"Lola," she tried again. "Jeff is under arrest. There's not going to be a chance for the two of you to go away together. But you still have a get-out-of-jail ticket here; tell me what Jeff's plan is—for Jason. What is he going to do to his brother? We all know it wasn't your idea—" Her cell phone buzzed in her pocket and it might as well have been an actual buzzer in the room.

"Is this a trap?" Lola said, lowering the gun down to her side. "Are you going to arrest me?"

"I'm not a cop—I can't arrest anyone." She slipped her phone out from her back pocket and held it up for Lola to see. "But I'm friends with a cop, and I stole his car to get here. He probably just found out, and now he's worried about me. Should I answer the phone, Lola? Tell him that we're okay, but that we need help?"

The girl's face crumpled and she dropped her head into her hands, folding into herself. Her rounded shoulders started to shake with her tears. She nodded. "Yes, please."

"Okay, hon. Okay." She answered the call.

"Jason's here to check on his mom," O'Dell said mildly.

"Imagine my surprise when I went to bring you back inside and found you'd taken off with my car."

Relief flooded her veins and she blew out a loud breath. Jason was safe. With any luck, she could save her business, too. "I'm at the Spot with Lola. We need help."

"At the...Rivera! Keys!" O'Dell barked, his voice directed away from the phone. "I'm coming for you, Janet. Is everything okay?"

"It is now." Janet took the gun from Lola and tucked it into her back pocket. She saw a box of matches on the bar and grabbed them with her free hand, wanting to put them somewhere safe—somewhere far away from Lola.

"I'll be there in five minutes, ten at the most."

Janet set her phone down on the bar, the tension that gripped her chest loosened for what felt like the first time in hours. She blew out a slow breath and rolled her head from side to side. Jason was okay. She was okay. They were going to be okay.

But then, from behind her, a small snap of noise. When she looked over, a tiny orange-red flicker of flame lit Lola's face. The fire at the tip of the match danced and undulated, illuminating Lola's distress.

"It's over. There's nothing left for me now," Lola whimpered, and she dropped the match over the gasoline-soaked carpet.

CHAPTER FORTY-SEVEN

Besides a few bonfires in her younger years, Janet had never been one to seek out fires. She didn't light them in their fireplace at home; she didn't even use a charcoal grill, opting instead for the propane model off the back deck.

So, despite how she'd spent her night, locked inside a walk-in cooler surrounded by fire, she was unprepared for how quickly the fire from Lola's match spread.

It dropped from Lola's outstretched hand as if in slow motion, floating more than falling to the ground. The flames spread before it even hit the carpet—the fumes strong enough to ignite seconds before it would have hit the floor.

Lola stood rooted to the floor, watching the fire spread around her, transfixed. The heat and smoke quickly moved at lightning speed with the flames, and soon, Janet couldn't see anything except the red-orange fire as it snaked out along the carpet, lapping the bar.

Janet paused long enough to note the irony of a full team of firefighters being only hundreds of feet away—but not close enough to help her until it was undoubtedly too late.

"Lola! We've got to go." The girl didn't move. "Now!" Janet shouted.

The teenager stumbled backward—but not to make her escape. Instead, fire licked up the legs of her pants, greedily feeding on the gasoline that must have splashed onto her clothes as she prepared to burn the bar down.

"Dammit," Janet muttered. Her vision clouded, but she remembered the fire extinguisher Cindy Lou had bought. She jumped over the bar and felt along the shelves until her fingers hit the cool metal surface. That's when she saw them—four propane tanks, lined up between the Beerador and the entrance to the bartender area: the same kind of tanks that had been inside the abandoned restaurant next door. "Dammit!" she said louder, taking the extinguisher up to eye level, trying to figure out how to activate the life-saving foam.

She sprayed it at her feet to cover the path of the fire so she could find her way back to Lola. Screams of fear—maybe pain— led her around the bar back to Jeff's girlfriend. Janet flooded them both with the extinguisher and pulled Lola toward the door.

"Help!" She called across the parking lot as soon as they hit the fresh air. "We need help!"

The fire next door was burning itself out. Teams of emergency responders gathered on the outside of the building, waiting out the flames, but no one turned. They were too far away.

She deposited Lola on the pavement by the Dumpster and headed back toward her bar. She wasn't going to stand around and watch her business burn to the ground. The second fire extinguisher next to Mel's spot by the door could help. But she also needed to call 911.

Janet cursed her inability to think clearly—then charged back into the bar for the fire extinguisher.

The situation inside had deteriorated rapidly in her absence. Fire now raged in the front of the space. The Beerador gleamed an impressive silvery-red in the fire. She grabbed the extinguisher from the hook and ripped out the safety ring so she could press the handle down. The small amount of retardant that came out was no match for the gasoline that Lola had poured.

She doubled over with a coughing fit. By the time she caught her breath, she saw there was no hope. Flames jumped over a metal stool and caught the corner booth like it was made of kindling. The acrid smell of burnt plastic stung her eyes, and as the smoke grew thicker, she felt behind her, knowing she had to stay calm—not panic—if she was going to find her way back out of the building.

She thought she'd only taken one step inside, maybe two, but with the choking smoke and oppressive heat, she'd lost her bearings. Panic fluttered at the base of her stomach. Then, O'Dell crashed into the bar, a halo of light from the parking lot nearly blinding her. His strong, steady arms pulled her back—away from the fire, away from her bar.

"What were you thinking?" O'Dell screamed, ripping the fire extinguisher from her hands and pushing her toward the back of the parking lot. "You could have died in there! Are you crazy?"

"I just thought if I could get to the other extinguisher, I could stave off the flames until firefighters arrived."

"Did you call them?"

"N-no—" She doubled over when another coughing fit wracked her body, finally dropping to all fours when her shaky legs gave out.

O'Dell must have picked up his phone or two-way radio, because he spoke with his official-sounding cop voice, directing fire crews one address to the west of where they were gathered. "Need ambulances for two people. One with smoke inhalation, the other with burns."

Janet looked over at Lola, lying prone on the ground. She'd kicked her shoes off, but her pants still smoldered where they hadn't burned off completely. Janet was no doctor, but the girl looked to have some moderate burns on her calves and lower legs. But still, she was lucky.

They both were.

She tried to catch her breath, but a rush of emotion left her more breathless than the fire. She looked up at her bar and the tears spilled over, coursing down her cheeks, dripping uncomfortably off her chin. She rocked backward, sitting down hard on the pavement, and cried.

Once again, O'Dell's strong, steady hands reached out, this time gently, as he pulled her close. "I've seen you stoically face so many things. Murder, death, your boyfriend breaking up with you. But this breaks through, huh? It's going to be okay, Janet."

She rested her head against his chest and closed her eyes. It wasn't just a building—the Spot was more than that. It was her livelihood. A physical embodiment of her independence, her power. And it was gone.

CHAPTER FORTY-EIGHT

Never had Janet been in a room with so many people and had it be so quiet. The table in the conference room at the downtown police department was full. Two chairs at one end were empty, but the rest of the spots were filled with Janet, her employees, and Jason's family. Hardly anyone made eye contact as O'Dell and Rivera walked in, shuffling paperwork and taking their seats at the head of the table. It had been a week since the Spot, among other things, had burned to the ground.

"Thanks for coming in today. We wanted to go over the results of our investigation with you before we release it to the press at a two o'clock press conference." Rivera looked at his watch, as if counting down the minutes until he could head home for the day.

"Janet, as you know, firefighters were able to save the western shell of your building, but as I understand it, almost all of it will have to be rebuilt?" Rivera looked up, a question in his eyes.

She nodded. "Only the Beerador survived. Insurance will cover the cost of rebuilding completely, and we should be able to reopen by summer."

O'Dell leaned forward. "Mr. and Mrs. Brooks, you've met with prosecutors?"

"Yes." William's voice was clipped. He wasn't going to offer up any other pleasantries.

"They tell me they're moving forward with felony murder, kidnapping, attempted murder, and arson charges against your son, along with a number of lesser charges related to the events over the last month. He'll be arraigned tomorrow."

Faith bit her lip but nodded, not looking up from the table.

O'Dell cleared his throat. "Cameron? You wanted to say something?"

Janet turned in surprise to look at her cook. She hadn't been sure why O'Dell had invited all her staff. Looked like she was about to find out.

Cameron cleared his throat and fidgeted with the zipper on his jacket. "I..." He cleared his throat again. "I just wanted to clear something up. About the blond hair you found in my locker?" His cheeks flushed pink, but he straightened his shoulders and stared right at Janet. "My younger sister ran away a few months ago. She and my parents didn't see eye to eye on many things, and she hasn't been in touch since she left." He took a deep breath and hurried through the rest of what seemed to be a rehearsed speech. "I—I worry about her, and try to keep her close to me."

"A lock of her hair?" Mel said doubtfully.

"It's all I have. She left a note and her picture for me. She must have cut her hair before she left, because I got that out of the trash can—like she'd just chopped off her ponytail. It was still connected at the elastic band. Anyway. It's not as creepy as it looks. I guess I just wanted you to know that." He hunched back down into his chair and folded his hands in front of him.

"What about your parents?" Mel asked. "Are they looking for her?"

"No. And that's why I moved out and needed a job. If they don't want her, I don't want them, you know?"

A moment of silence as everyone at the table processed that. Janet had to wonder why families were so complicated.

O'Dell tapped the corners of his papers together and made to stand up, but Janet cleared her throat.

"What about Lola?"

"I'm afraid we can't release any information about any minors involved in the case." Rivera frowned. "But you'll find out more as we get into the legal proceedings. She's agreed to testify against Junior."

Both cops stood to leave. "Thanks for coming in, everyone. We'll be in touch if we need anything else." O'Dell raised his eyebrows at Janet, and she gave him a small smile. He nodded and left the room.

"Janet?" She turned to find Jason at her side. He winced when she stiffened, as if she'd punched him in the gut. "Can we talk?"

She nodded, and he led the way out of the building to a quiet alcove overlooking the parking lot. "So...good news about the insurance. The Beerador survived?"

Janet stared at a particularly ugly SUV as she answered. "Yup. The fire actually left it shinier than ever. Everything else, though—destroyed."

"And you're going to rebuild?"

"Of course. The new building will have a full-service kitchen, too. Insurance should cover the whole thing."

"So no more food truck?"

"Oh, no, we'll get another one of those, too—but the new one will be drivable. We can take it to festivals and add beer taps. Listen, I don't have time to chat, actually. I've got to meet with the architect to finalize the rebuild plans." That was a lie, but she couldn't bear to stand there making small talk. "What do you want?"

"I, uh...I know that I owe you an explanation."

"You don't owe me anything, Jason." Her voice was wooden. She didn't care.

"That's where you're wrong. I owe you everything."

"Fine," she snapped. "You owe me everything, and you trusted me with *nothing!* But worse than that—you left *me* vulnerable, because you didn't tell me what was going on."

"I thought I was protecting you! I thought if I could just figure out what Jeff was up to, I'd keep you out of it, and get him back into his home, and we'd all be okay. I thought I was doing the right thing! You have to know that I didn't know—"

"When did you know?" Janet interrupted him. "When did you know that Jeff was involved? What tipped you off?"

"The password to get into Lola's phone."

"What? How?"

"It's Jeff's birthday. Of course, I wasn't sure then, but when we saw the picture with the birthmark—that's when I knew without a doubt that he was involved. But I thought—I hoped— that I'd be able to track him down and no one would be the wiser."

She snorted. "Epic fail."

"I know." Jason shook his head. "He was one step ahead of me the whole time. I think he'd been planning it for months. The apartment in Memphis, meeting Lola. Did you know he's the one who suggested Quizz's agency to Lola's mom?"

"How?" Janet looked incredulously at Jason.

"He sent her a postcard he'd made up to look like an ad. Just to get her to call you guys. To get you involved."

"Wow. That's—that's...diabolical."

"I agree. I'd never seen that side of him before. I don't know, maybe I just didn't want to. But you have to know, I'd have never guessed he was capable of doing what he did. You have to understand —I was only trying to protect him. Protect my little brother." His voice was thick, his lips pressed into a thin line, and he stepped away from Janet. "So I just wanted to let you know that I'm going away."

"Away? What do you mean?" Janet wasn't ready to forgive him, but she wasn't ready to never see him again, either.

"I—I let a lot of people down, and I just need some space. Some space to figure it all out."

"You're leaving?" He nodded. "*You're* leaving. That's usually my move."

His short, choppy laugh held no trace of humor. "I'll miss you. But I get it if you don't feel the same. I wouldn't."

"Jason—" She stopped. She didn't know what to say, so she didn't say anything. Just watched him walk away.

Alone with her thoughts on the landing was a terrible place to be, so Janet drove to the Spot. She didn't know why—there wasn't anything there anymore. Even the Beerador was gone. She'd had a storage company pick it up for safekeeping until her new building was ready.

To her surprise, another car was waiting for her in the parking lot. Janet's forehead wrinkled when a woman stepped out onto the pavement. She had a familiar look to her, but it wasn't until she shrugged out of her puffy jacket and Janet saw her lumpy business suit underneath that a name came to the tip of her tongue.

"Amelia Turner?"

"Janet Black." The other woman fumbled with her clipboard. "Today is the day of your inspection with the Alcohol, Tobacco, and Firearms Bureau...but...Well, I've had people go to extreme measures to avoid a fine, but this seems over the top." She frowned and turned her kind eyes back to the burned-out shell in front of them.

"What happens now? Do we get some kind of deferment?"

"Are you rebuilding?"

Janet nodded.

"Then of course. We'll coordinate with the city on your necessary permits and codes. When you're ready to open, call for a final walkthrough." She handed her card to Janet. "Glad you're okay. Take care."

Janet watched her drive away, and an incredulous grin forced its way onto her face when a sleek black convertible slid into the lot and parked in the handicap spot by what used to be the front door.

Nell climbed sprightly out of her car. "I'm gone for a few weeks and the world ends?" Nell's silvery-white hair was tucked into a chignon, and her overcoat was open, revealing a black velour sweat-suit underneath.

"Nell! We've missed you."

"I think I'm glad I was gone!" the older woman said, assessing the ashes and blackened remnants of the building. "Is everyone okay?"

"They are now. And we're going to rebuild."

"Good," Nell said with a decisive nod. "But where do I get my vodka soda until then?"

Janet chuckled. "How was the cruise?"

"It was something else, Janet. You could be as alone or together as you wanted to be, you know? Just depending on where you went on the ship. Kind of great."

"Hmm." A buzz started to build at the back of her brain.

"What's Jason think about this?" Nell asked.

"I don't know. Well—I mean, we're kind of...taking a break right now. I'm staying with a friend while I figure out what's next." O'Dell had been kind enough to offer her his guest room permanently.

Nell launched into a series of questions but didn't give her time to answer any of them before the next one rolled forth. Janet finally held a hand up.

"Nell? What did you say the name of the cruise ship was?"

"Why?"

"I have no home to go back to, my business is totaled, and I won't be able to work for months. Now might be the perfect time to get away." *From everything,* she added in her head.

Nell narrowed her eyes and dug into her coat pocket, eventually holding out a crushed and folded brochure. "Great time to go, Janet. They're having a buy-one-get-one-free deal for the next month." Nell slung her purse back into her car, then stopped and turned to look Janet full in the face again. "You got someone in mind to join you?"

The buzz in Janet's brain turned into a fully formed idea. "I have just the right person, Nell. Thanks."

The older woman clucked her tongue with one final look at the missing building, then climbed back into her car and drove away.

It wasn't often that you could manage to run away from everything that was causing you trouble in your life and call it a vacation, not complete avoidance.

Janet picked up her phone and called an old friend. "This is going to sound crazy, but hear me out..."

Thanks so much for reading Last Chance! Help get the word out about the series by leaving a review. Reviews help other readers and the authors, too.

ALSO BY LIBBY KIRSCH

For updates on new releases or to connect with the author, go to
www.LibbyKirschBooks.com

ABOUT THE AUTHOR

Libby Kirsch is an Emmy award winning journalist with over ten years of experience working in television newsrooms of all sizes. She draws on her rich history of making embarrassing mistakes on live TV, and is happy to finally indulge her creative writing side, instead of always having to stick to the facts.
Libby lives in Michigan with her husband, three young children, and Sam the dog.

Connect with Libby
www.LibbyKirschBooks.com
Libby@LibbyKirschBooks.com

f facebook.com/LibbyKirschBooks

🐦 twitter.com/LibbyKirsch

a amazon.com/author/libbykirsch

BB bookbub.com/authors/libby-kirsch

g goodreads.com/libbykirsch

Made in the USA
Coppell, TX
14 July 2020